Protect The Flock

David Powers

PROTECT THE FLOCK
Copyright ©2019 by David Powers.
First Edition - November 2019

All rights reserved. No part of this book may be used or reproduced in any manner whatsoever without written permission except in the case of brief quotations embodied in critical articles and reviews, and short excerpts for educational purposes.

This book is a work of fiction. Names, characters, places, and incidents are either a product of the author's imagination, or are used fictitiously. Any resemblance to actual persons, living or dead, business establishments, events, or locales is entirely coincidental.

Library of Congress Cataloging-in-Publication Data
Powers, David.
Protect The Flock/David Powers.
276 p. 22 cm.

978-0-9985447-2-4 (hardcover)
978-0-9985447-3-1 (paperback)
978-0-9985447-4-8 (ebook)

1. Murder--Fiction. 2. Murder--Investigation--Fiction. 3. Mystery fiction. 4. Arizona--Fiction. 5. California--Fiction. I. Title.

Library of Congress Control Number: 2019915599
Printed in the United States of America

Eerie Forest
www.eerieforest.com

For Jennifer

ALSO BY DAVID POWERS

UNBURIED MEMORIES
TIDINGS FROM THE ABYSS
THE MAN FROM BUZZARD ROOST
THE TANDOORI BOX

The Battlefield

A sheep farm outside of Galveston, Texas

THE HARDENED COMBAT MEDIC squatted beside the Confederate drummer boy. Hart Henderson pulled tourniquets from his first-aid kit to tie around the youth's thighs, then groaned in frustration. Too much blood had soaked into the dry earth, and the closest hospital tent was ten miles away through enemy lines. He stuffed the strips of cloth in the canvas pack, took out a notebook, and sharpened the pencil tip using a scalpel.

Henderson quickly recorded his patient's vitals: body temperature, respiration, and pulse. He wished he had a method to measure blood pressure. "What's your name, son?"

The terrified lad gripped his arm, attempting to sit up. "Georgie Butler. Same as my pa. Mister, I can't feel nothin' below my knees."

Hart pressed the youngster flat with a gentle hand so he couldn't see the stumps. "Your legs are just asleep. Where is the pain and how bad?"

"It hurts all over! Am I gonna die?"

Henderson wrote this detail in the dog-eared journal. He lowered his ear to the child's mouth. "Georgie, is God near? Do you sense His presence?"

"I'm scared," the fifteen-year-old whispered. "I want my ma."

"You'll be with your mother soon enough." The medic waved at a goliath of a man turning the pockets of the warm and the cold inside out—both Gray and Blue. "Over here, Sergeant Crow! I need your assistance!"

Charles Crow emerged through a cloud of black flies swarming about a cavalry horse's entrails. He bent down and slit Georgie's throat with a Bowie knife.

Hart flipped to a new page and peered upward. "Charles, how did taking that boy's life make you feel? Happy. . .sad? Tell me, sir, did you experience any sorrow or remorse?"

The Terry's Texas Ranger packed a corncob pipe with a plug of scrounged Kentucky tobacco. He lit a wooden match with his thumbnail, held the flame to the blackened bowl, and puffed. The acrid smoke kept some of the buzzing insects off their faces. "Doc, you question me every time I do the tasks you cannot stomach. How can I give you a proper answer if I have no idea of your meanin'?"

A blinded foot soldier, his uniform burned from his blasted back, crawled through a paddock of dead sheep. Whenever the Yankee bumped into a wooly carcass, he cried out in fear and changed direction.

Hart Henderson contemplated the path of the eternally lost soul. *Why was I born a healer and not a killer? Nothing makes a damned bit of sense out here.* "Sergeant, go ease that fellow's suffering."

Charles Crow slid out his long fighting knife and did the work God brought him into this world to do.

Chapter One

Tuesday—November 21, 2017

LEROY DAVIS BRACED HIS ELBOWS on the sharp edges of the aluminum windowsill. The torn and bent bug screen rested against the wall. His left hand clasped the forestock of a hunting rifle. His right index finger rubbed the front of the trigger guard. Roy pressed his right eyeball to the eyepiece of the high-powered telescopic sight. One hundred yards away, beyond the bleakness of a plowed cotton field, Mrs. O'Sullivan's dog snuffled a hedge of scorched chaparral. The strong-minded German shepherd smelled a rabbit.

    The fifty-one-year-old man had dark circles under his hazel eyes, these sagging bags of flesh the aftermath of an endless night of torment—not fever dreams this time, merely the purgatory of four hours of tossing and turning. Pancho, ninety pounds of furry muscle, began barking at two a.m. and hadn't quit until the sun scraped the peaks of the mile-high Mule Mountains. Today, two days before Thanksgiving, Roy resolved to silence the mutt for good.

    To shoot an animal so far away required a high level of proficiency. The layer of moisture blanketing the earth lowered visibility. Thanks to the calm air, Davis did not have to gauge the windage. He *would* need to compensate for the distance. Roy adjusted the scope's elevation up three clicks and steadied himself. It was a long shot; however, he had taken longer shots in the past. The sharpshooter always hit his targets.

Pancho and Roy were well acquainted. Whenever he ran into Amelia O'Sullivan on the street or in town, he kneeled to pat the dog and say hello.

Roy peeked at his watch: 6:45 a.m. *I'm running late,* he thought. Pancho, as if hearing a noise, perked his tall ears. Davis swung the rifle toward the one-story home. He didn't want the old gal to catch him plugging her cherished pet. The only thing moving in the O'Sullivan's backyard was a gently flapping American flag. *Great! The fog is dissipating.* Roy aimed the Remington Model 700 at the spot he had last seen Pancho. *Where is that dog?* To the left, and closer, the German shepherd trotted around a pile of rotten lumber, a stained mattress, and a prehistoric Kelvinator refrigerator with the door removed so curious kids couldn't lock themselves inside.

"Now," Roy mouthed, placing his fingertip on the trigger. The curve of machined steel comforted him as it unfailingly did. He centered the crosshairs on the dog's thrashing tail and gradually slid the dot down the raised hips to the powerful chest—the heart region. Davis, about to squeeze the lever of death, hesitated, then, readjusting his grip, lowered the reticle to the wedge-shaped head nosing underneath a cardboard carton.

The rifle boomed. Roy, unprepared for the recoil, nearly dropped the firearm, but not until he saw the German shepherd's left ear vaporize into a red mist. He blinked and looked again—Pancho scampering back to the house yelping. The lucky bunny hopped away in the opposite direction.

The weapon had fired without Roy pulling the trigger. "Time to get this piece of shit fixed," he grumbled, hauling the long gun indoors. The man slumped against the bedroom wall, apprehensive he had been seen. *6:55 a.m. I ought to get to work.*

He stood up and leaned the defective Remington beside the dresser.

Roy disrobed and stepped into the cramped fiberglass shower stall. He shampooed the gray fuzz holding tight to his gleaming dome with Head & Shoulders and scrubbed his armpits with a lump of Irish Spring. Davis hummed the chorus of a Johnny Cash song as he rinsed the previous day's grime and sweat down the drain with lukewarm well water. On a bath mat, Roy dried his once muscular body with a ratty Arizona Cardinals towel.

Davis hurriedly dressed in the clothes he regularly wore. Standing in front of the fogged mirror, the six-foot-two man tamed the stray hairs sticking from the rear of his scalp and adjusted the brown necktie. Finally, Roy pinned the tin star onto the left chest pocket of his Cochise County Sheriff's Office uniform.

Thomas Hayden had one thing in common with Roy Davis. He had no qualms eliminating anything standing in his way. That is where their similarities in personality and lifestyle diverged. While Roy bunked in a mobile home on a half-acre of dirt landscaped with ornery weeds, Tom roosted in a luxury apartment looking down upon the lush trees in New York City's Central Park. As Davis collected paltry government paychecks, Hayden made millions trading stocks and bonds.

To fuel his capitalist gluttony, Tom worked for the Merriweather Financial Corporation on Wall Street in Lower Manhattan. He did not speculate, unlike amateur traders who buy and sell securities in the period of a single day. Shrewd and not easily ruffled, Tom invested long term. Akin to Roy, he too covered himself in a type of uniform: a business suit (sewn in Italy instead of Bangladesh) tailored to perfection.

On the hectic floor of the New York Stock Exchange, Tom stared at his iPhone. The market-movers graph showed blue-chip energy stocks dropping into the toilet—more like into the septic tank. The equity trader mulled over alerting his top investors, unable to resist the tidal pull of reading his email.

Among pages of junk, an urgent message from Tom's across-the-hall neighbor, Henry Ellington, stood apart. He opened the communication, surprised to see a URL in place of Henry's usual "Go Knicks!" or "What's up with those Jets?" sports blabber. Hayden, knowing Ellington sent the email, had no fears of infecting his iOS with a malicious virus. The black webpage he landed on in the Safari browser contained a solitary line of white text—a telephone number prefixed with an unfamiliar country and area code. Tom double-checked the sender's address: henryellington@gxops.com. *That's Henry's company. It appears legit.* Somebody touched his shoulder.

"Whatchu lookin' at Willis? Tinder?"

Tom swiveled to face another Merriweather employee.

"Yo, bro!" Troy Abington greeted. "At the closing bell, me and the fellas are heading to the Full Shilling for drinks. Are you up for it?"

No one ever asked Hayden to get together after work or even for lunch; being invited to a social function threw him for a loop. Tom knew he gave off bad vibes. His mother had told him so time and time again. He parted his lips to say no, then changed his mind. *You've got to play to win.* "Sure, Troy. I'll be there."

"Far out!" Abington flashed bogus gang signs and sauntered off to harpoon bigger whales.

On Main Street in Bisbee, Arizona, Roy walked between the four Ionic columns supporting the neoclassical building's flat roof and yanked the brass door handle. Nestled in a canyon, the sheriff's office served the tourist town's fifty-five hundred residents and those in the surrounding territory.

Margaret Connors saluted. "Good morning, Sheriff!" She pushed his favorite coffee cup (filled to the brim with black) across the countertop.

"Morning, Marge. Busy today?"

The lead 911 dispatcher wobbled her hand horizontally. "Slow. We did receive a call from Amelia O'Sullivan. Someone shot her dog."

Roy scrunched his face in disbelief. "Pancho's dead?"

"Poor thing's just missing an ear."

Davis pretended to be relieved. "I heard a loud noise last night. Thought a rig backfired on the 92."

Marge looked skeptical. "Sound carries that far?"

"When the moon is full and the windows are open."

"Though it isn't clear to me what the lunar phases have to do with sound waves, I will admit the weather has been unseasonably warm. Mrs. O'Sullivan wants us to check it out."

"I'll go." The sheriff wanted to contain the situation. "Amelia is my next-door neighbor."

The dispatcher glanced at the wall clock. "Not until ten. Mrs. O'Sullivan brought Pancho to the vet. She's praying Dr. Yut can sew his ear back on."

Roy strode into his office and shut the door with "Sheriff Leroy P. Davis" stenciled in black and gold on the frosted glass. He parked his butt in the oaken swivel chair behind the matching desk. The dinged-up furniture had done hard duty for generations of stalwart sheriffs since 1881. Roy cradled the "Leading The Way" mug in his lap and spun the spoked seat to the window. *Same old, same old. . . .* One more bright, cloudless, Arizonan day.

The thoroughfare droned with the morning commute, which wasn't much. This was Bisbee after all. Roy, in deep introspection, did not see or hear any of the traffic whishing by. Being Bisbee's Sheriff? *Boring.* A long-standing bachelor holed up in a thousand-square-foot double-wide on the outskirts of town? *Lonesome.* Except for trolling for single women at RJ's Roadhouse on Wednesday evenings, his love life left him unfulfilled. Roy had had two or three stable relationships (he missed Ruth Gordon, the owner of a local art gallery, most of all). The women invariably departed for greener pastures, this on the whole due to his ever-present, soul-sapping melancholy and cyclic binge drinking. And now, in middle age, the one-night stands were fewer and increasingly humiliating.

Sheriff Davis lit a Lucky Strike and blew the smoke into the blades of the ceiling fan hanging from the original pressed tin tiles. There had been hours before dawn when Roy contemplated taking his own life—more than once he had awoken with the aftertaste of sweet gun oil on his tongue—yet he had consistently talked himself out of this final act.

Roy's existence hadn't always been humdrum. He was reared in a loving household. This close family unit disintegrated the moment a public utility worker stumbled upon his older sister's body while digging a drainage ditch. At seventeen years of age, Roy moved in with a cousin leaving his younger brother, Timothy, to deal with the chaos. To get the heck out of Dodge, Roy enlisted with the Marines and fought the Iraqi Army in the Gulf War. Back in the States, as a civilian with posttraumatic stress disorder and lacking a high school degree, Roy applied for numerous entry-level jobs. Although he later obtained his GED, the paper diploma didn't earn him much more than a minimum wage.

For a time, Davis stacked planks at a lumberyard until he applied for a job at the Sheriff's Office. Hired, he wetted his feet in law enforcement as a traffic cop. Only three stoplights populated Bisbee. If the rookie prevented gridlock, the tourists were happy, and so was Mayor Dodd. Several years later, the deputy steered a patrol car through the county's rural streets. After the sun set, Davis studied at Cochise College. When Sam Worthington flew his Pontiac Trans Am into the nine-hundred-foot-deep Lavender Pit, a former open-pit copper mine, a post became available in the detective squad. Roy got the position and solved one case after another. Ultimately, in 2014, owing to subtle prodding from Mayor Dodd and holding a master's degree in criminal justice management, Davis ran for sheriff. To his own astonishment, he won a hands-down victory. Roy often wondered (others also questioned his motives) if he had sided with the law to avenge his sister's murder. If justice had indeed been the catalyst, so far, the sheriff had done a lousy job of finding her killer.

Roy raised the coffee cup to the silver frame placed on top of the file cabinet. The eyes, nose, and mouth of the girl in the color photograph bore a striking resemblance to his own. Sadly, the print had faded; nevertheless, his sister's wide grin prevailed as sunny as the last day he had seen her. "Here's to you, Helen. See you later."

The sheriff snagged his white cowboy hat from the rack, strapped on his Colt .45 automatic service pistol, notified Marge he'd be out, and plodded to the parking lot. He slid behind the wheel of a three-year-old, four-door SUV. The Chevy Tahoe's white body matched Roy's—both revealed the dents and dings of a life looking for trouble on the bumpy back roads of southern Arizona.

Davis planned to stop by Mrs. O'Sullivan's house, but for now, he needed some alone time. He drove along Main Street waving a hand at townsfolk he knew or tipping his head to sightseers navigating the confining lanes designed for horses and pedestrians, not automobiles.

Traveling south on Route 80, as the Lavender Pit passed by in a purple haze on Roy's right and the three rust-stained ore separating tanks zipped by on his left, the Chevy's dual exhausts rumbled melodic bass notes as he depressed the accelerator. In his element, the great outdoors, the sheriff felt better now. These were quiet moments when he ruminated on the issues of the day, free from subordinates driving him up the wall with frivolous requests.

On the opposite end of the Lowell traffic circle (now a ghost town), Roy exited onto Bisbee Road. He rolled through the bedroom community of Warren, turning right at the canopy-covered ballpark. Arizona Street, as straight as an arrow, aimed at the Mexican border, an eighteen-foot-high bollard fence bisecting the southern horizon as far as the human eye could see. Davis intended to circumnavigate the massive mine tailings ponds and return to base on the Naco Highway.

Roy shook his soft pack of Luckies, telling by the weight only a few cigarettes remained. Worried he'd run out of nickies before noon, he considered conservation. "Screw it!" Davis growled at the grizzled face in the rearview mirror. He pounded the coffin nail into the corner of his cracked lips and lit the tip using the plastic lighter that Burt the Ciggyman had thrown in at no extra charge. Blue smoke permeated the cab as the desert scenery flew by in a yellow blur.

The Remington 12-gauge pump-action shotgun and Colt .223-caliber patrol rifle locked in the metal rack behind Roy's shoulders rattled as the truck crossed the abandoned San Pedro & Southwestern Railroad tracks at Bisbee Junction. Now, he was deep in "The Bottoms" (as in The Bottom of the Country), an area truly "On the other side of the tracks." Here among the scrubby acacia, cacti, and ocotillo, impoverished whites, blacks, and browns put down roots. These hardy souls hoed the lettuce fields, wrangled cattle on ranches, stocked shelves at Walmart, grilled burgers at McDonald's, and partied like Dionysus on Friday nights. The great unwashed lived in trailers, old miners' shacks, or in the backseats of their cars. The Bottoms was also the tract of land where the sheriff pried off his cowboy boots every evening.

Born and bred in Bisbee, Roy Davis figured—short of divine intervention—he would be buried with everybody else in the town's cemetery. After the former Marine beheld the atrocities Homo sapiens inflicted upon one another, he believed God was a myth, or at least dead.

Whereas the sheriff resided in the low-income section of town, he wasn't penniless. Roy Davis had no kinship with the cold-hearted Ebenezer Scrooge; he simply did not take joy in spending money. Roy occupied a dilapidated 1970s mobile home. The Sheriff's Office furnished his uniform in addition to his vehicle. He only doled out the greenbacks from his ninety-thousand-dollar-a-year salary for TV dinners, cigarettes, and booze.

Roy Davis was alike Tom Hayden in one way—they were both keen investors. He had focused past the millennium's internet bubble and bought shares of Apple, Google, and eventually, Facebook. Recently, Roy gambled on bitcoins, cashing in the volatile cryptocurrency at a high point. Nobody could tell by looking at him, but the sheriff had accumulated three million dollars in the last decade. Though Roy audited his monthly totals for inaccuracies, he filed the financial reports away with no afterthought.

The Chevy's interior became stuffy as the shadows shortened. Already eighty degrees outside—*too hot for late November*—the sheriff cranked up the AC and steered west.

Up ahead on West Purdy Lane, a silver sedan with its hood raised had stopped on the side of the road. A tall, thin male leaned on the fender. Roy braked onto the shoulder. He decreased the air conditioner's fan velocity (the vents blew artic air into his face) and ran the license plates. The Mazda CX-5 was registered to the Save Big Rental Company based out of the Los Angeles International Airport.

The sheriff couldn't see the driver's eyes through the dark sunglasses. He guessed, by the spiked black hair and light-brown complexion, the man was of Asian ethnicity. Bisbee's demographics were largely Caucasian and Hispanic, relatively few Asians except for globetrotters wanting a taste of America's "Authentic Wild West." Roy found the cut of the fellow's jib conspicuous, even for these parts: long-sleeved plaid western shirt and stonewashed straight leg jeans. The starched outfit looked right out of a Cavender's catalog. He thought, *all the dude needs is a cowboy hat and a lasso.* Roy radioed the dispatchers to inform them he was assisting a stranded motorist.

Davis crammed his Stetson on his head and stepped into the billow of grit blowing southward to the Los Ajos Mountains. When the urban cowboy lifted his hands, he said, "It's okay, sir. We're not in Ferguson."

The man hoisted his palms higher.

Roy crossed the street. "Broke down? Did your car overheat?"

The motorist replied in Korean.

"Do you speak any English?"

The driver touched his mouth, and said in a thick accent, "No English."

Roy lowered his arms to signal the man to drop his. Reddish liquid pooled beneath the ticking engine. "Looks like your transmission sprung a leak. Shall I call a tow truck?" He pantomimed hooking a cable to the Mazda's front bumper.

The driver nodded. "Yes, yes!"

Davis led him behind a guardrail. "You don't wanna get creamed by the Border Patrol." He used the push-to-talk button on his two-way radio to transmit the mile marker to Marge. Roy informed the motorist, "A tow truck will arrive in roughly," he tapped his watch and raised five fingers three times, "fifteen minutes." The walkie crackled again. *Must be Connors with an update.*

"Sheriff, you still there?"

"Yeah, wrapping this up."

"A truck driver phoned in. Name is Hal Sanders. He's at the new dog park."

"The old little league field?"

"Roger. Mr. Sanders pulled over to use the restroom and saw a body by the bleachers—a biker."

"Motorcycle accident?"

"No, not a Harley. A bicycle. The fatality is wearing cycling clothing. But he's not near the main road, and there's no sign of what he was pedaling."

"On my way, Marge." Roy told the man, "Sir, I have to go. As I said, the wrecker should be here shortly."

The motorist bowed and mumbled, "Thank you."

Roy headed north on the Naco Highway, driving past two unsmiling men in a white contractor's van parked outside the entrance to the United States Border Patrol Station. He turned at the Safeway and zoomed toward the Bisbee Dog Park in Huachuca Terrace with his red and blue emergency lights whirling. Davis monitored the dashboard-mounted mobile computer for supplemental data. The dispatch software stated: Deceased white male approximately thirty years of age with a broken leg and head trauma.

The sheriff downshifted and swerved onto the public land. At the very end of a washboard road, an 18-wheeler was parked under a copse of shade trees. The driver saw the lawman and jumped down from his cab.

"Hey!" the trucker shouted. "How long is this gonna take? I gotta make a delivery or I ain't gettin' paid."

Roy twirled his forefinger. "Show me." They approached a baseball diamond delineated by chain-link fencing. The turf in the outfield had gone to seed. Urine spots polka-dotted the infield. "You're Hal Sanders?"

"Yes, sir." When Davis gestured for more, the driver added, "Came from Naco with a shipment of window blinds. On my way to Flagstaff. That's where I live."

Behind the concrete bleacher's bright blue steps, a young male encased in a vibrant magenta jersey and black cycling shorts lay on his back staring at the sun. Roy, heedful not to disturb evidence, cautioned Hal to stay away. For the sake of appearances, he checked the dead man's vitals. Red fluid leaked out of the cyclist's cranium and a white fibula protruded from a compact fracture located an inch above his green clip-in shoes. There were no blood traces on the ground or indications of a struggle.

Davis squinted along the hundred-yard driveway ending at the highway. No smashed bicycle in sight and no drag marks. *There's no way Mr. Tightpants crawled this far on that mangled leg. Somebody dumped the body.*

The sheriff checked for footprints in the sandy terrain. He imagined many of the tracks belonged to the trucker or the dog lovers who frequented the park. Roy took a hard look at Hal Sanders: chunky neck, big tattooed biceps, the bulk of him soft. He didn't appear guilty. Unless the person had a swastika inked on his or her forehead, the average criminal rarely did. Davis' mind rewound to an image of the man standing next to his stalled automobile.

Roy pressed the mic. "Marge, has the tow truck left for the 10-47 on Purdy?"

"10-4. Steve from Dick's Towing is en route. Should be on site in a jiffy."

"Put that on hold. I want you to send a patrol car out to detain the driver."

"Roger. I'll try to find someone nearby. Is this related to the bicyclist?"

"Too early to say. Just be sure he doesn't go anywhere." The sheriff did not recall any major dents in the Mazda CX-5—tired and remorseful for wanting to blow Pancho's head off, he hadn't been concentrating. "Call Tucson and get their crime scene investigators down here ASAP. I'll be tied up for a while. Have someone else talk to Mrs. O'Sullivan about her dog." Davis turned to Sanders. "Let's walk to your vehicle."

They circled the Peterbilt rig. The tractor unit and semitrailer were spotless. Chromed wheels mirrored the ground and sky.

Roy touched the undamaged front bumper. "Do you own this?"

"She's my baby." The proud trucker frowned at his watch. "But not paid for till March 2024 *if* I keep making the monthly payments."

Davis recorded the driver's contact information and got ahold of his trucking company to confirm employment. He instructed Sanders to drop by the Sheriff's Office to make castings of his shoes. As Hal sped off with his truckload of Levolor blinds, a line of law enforcement vehicles entered the rectangular lot. Roy grabbed rolls of police tape along with glove and bootie dispensers from his Tahoe. Deputies used the supplies to establish a perimeter encompassing the body.

An insistent notion niggled the sheriff. *I need to interrogate that motorist. Something's not right about him.* The Tucson CSI team had a two-hour commute. For now, there wasn't much to do except guard the crime scene. Davis advised the sergeant he'd return later.

As Roy drove back down the Naco Highway, he reflected on his time as a second lieutenant in northern Iraq. On a winter morning, his patrol had stopped at a remote village in the Hamrin Mountains to meet with the elders. Headquarters had briefed Davis on the situation. The townspeople were not al-Qaeda, yet he also understood the terrorists often coerced the locals into hiding weapons and food.

Roy had been sitting on a handwoven rug in a cinderblock domicile conversing with a tribal leader when he spotted a bulge under the bearded man's vest. The Peshmerga translator ordered the chief to put his hands up. Davis' squad provided cover as he inched forward. In alarm, the elder scuttled rearward into a corner. Below a framed portrait of Mahmud Hafid Zadeh, the man stretched his fingers into the folds of his baggy pants. A high-strung soldier's M4 carbine deafened everyone in the small room. The suspicious bulge turned out to be lunch—dolma wrapped in newspaper. Roy, his uniform splattered with the Kurdish chief's gray matter, never forgot the women and children's wails as his platoon mounted Humvees and hightailed it to the badlands.

Roy saw the Mazda in a mirage of heat waves. The motorist had long gone. He stooped to stroke the streaks of red paint adhering to the silver right front fender. Davis inspected the car's interior through the windows and jiggled the locked door handles. He gazed up and down the empty lane and into the barren land. *Maybe the driver hitchhiked to town.* After the sheriff gave Marge a description, he ordered the dispatcher to put out an all-points bulletin.

Tom Hayden arrived home at eleven that evening. As a result of the three craft beers he had imbibed to assimilate with his unrestrained coworkers, Tom's brain chemistry had transitioned from a decaying buzz to a full-fledged headache. Ordinarily, the stock trader didn't drink and spurned drugs. He even shied away from popping an aspirin unless one of his regular skull-splitters came a-knocking. Hayden, reserved in social gatherings, brooded. *Did I say anything out of line? Did I shine a spotlight on myself?*

In his minimalist-decorated apartment, Tom placed his MacBook on the glass dining room table, propped reading glasses on his straight nose, and combed the black waves from his brow. He wanted to review the overseas markets, specifically Japan. The TSE/TYO acted as his canary in the coal mine—hopefully chirping happily today and not lying feet up on the cage floor. Since the financial graphs exhibited no peaks or valleys, the share trader opened Outlook.

Tom scanned and deleted emails, once more coming upon the strange message from Henry Ellington. He selected the URL, using the mouse to copy the eleven numbers from the black webpage and paste them into the Google search engine. *Zilch. I thought all telephone numbers were listed somewhere.* Hayden replied to Ellington's email questioning the number's meaning. No immediate feedback, however, at this hour, Henry would be watching the day's sports roundup on ESPN. Tom looked up the country code finding 971 indexed for Dubai. He had multinational clients, many in the United Arab Emirates, still, he felt odd calling this number. Hayden closed the laptop, drank a glass of water, and slid into bed.

Chapter Two

Wednesday—November 22, 2017

TOM GOT UP AT FOUR A.M. TO DRAIN HIS BLADDER. Back in bed, the man stared at the time projected on the ceiling for thirteen long minutes before he flung aside the Millesimo Egyptian cotton sheets, pulled on Gucci slippers, and trudged to the dining area. The computer's glowing screen sharpened the angles of Tom's face and enhanced his piercing blue eyes. He picked up the phone, entered the United States exit code, and dialed the eleven digits. A woman answered.

"Good morning, Mr. Hayden." She sounded French. She sounded young. She sounded pretty. "We've been anticipating your call."

Tom pressed the phone to his ear. "Who are you?"

"Tanda," the woman purred.

"Tanda? Is that French?"

She didn't reply.

Hayden, about to hang up, wavered when the screen fluctuated. A moving image of a young female replaced the eleven-digit telephone number. Her face filled the frame—a decidedly elegant face. He attempted to pigeonhole her ethnic background: jet-black hair, pale skin, pert nose. The woman's eyes engaged him. Almond in shape, they sparkled as blue, *and as frigid,* as the depths of Lake Tahoe. Tom's fingertip hovered over the power button, prepared to pop the battery if necessary. *My computer must be infected with ransomware.*

"Mr. Hayden, I wouldn't do that. Not until you hear me out. Scheduling conflicts hampered us from providing you with a live feed. Our IT staff apologizes. Nonetheless, I think you'll find our presentation very riveting. This happened yesterday morning." High-definition video displaced Tanda's visage.

A vein pulsed in Tom's forehead. "What happened?"

"Stop talking and watch."

The media player framed the interior of a car. A dark-haired man sat behind the steering wheel. The video's perspective originated from the back seat. *A GoPro,* he thought, *mounted to the roof.* The field of vision switched to an outside view, low below the bumper. Blacktop streaked past the wide-angle lens. The geography was uninhabited—the land horizontal and desolate. A long and thin object coiled in the street. The automobile shimmied as the front tire flattened a rattling snake. Tom, hearing Tanda's snicker, boosted the volume. The scene shifted to a camera aimed out the rear. Except for the twitching reptile, the roadway was vacant.

"What is this?" Hayden murmured.

Tanda's tone was as soft as melted butter. "Shush, baby."

Back in the car, the driver inclined frontward trying to see something in the distance. The Lilliputian figure grew into a male or female pedaling a bicycle. This road featured a four-foot margin between the solid white line and the overgrown shoulder—a bike lane. The motorist, his brow practically touching the windshield, grasped the steering wheel at ten and two o'clock. Tom listened to the engine rev as the speedometer's needle climbed. Again, the aspect toggled to the front view. On a hill, the bicyclist—a man—pumped hard to ascend. The scene changed, initially to the operator wrenching the wheel to the right, then outside as the automobile veered into the bike lane.

In flickering slow motion, the vehicle's bumper careened—whether influenced by inferior driving skills or pure intent—into the man's spinning leg.

The cyclist vanished off-screen as Tanda reappeared. "Do you want more?"

Not realizing his breathing had stopped, Hayden slammed the lid to hibernate the laptop. His heart in overdrive, Tom questioned what he had just seen.

Tom inserted the black American Express Centurion credit card into his wallet. He had stopped by the Apple Store after work.

The salesgirl handed him the receipt to sign. "Sir, if any issues crop up, stop by our Genius Bar. Our tech staff will be happy to be of assistance."

Hayden jostled his way around a horde of yapping Appleites. On the congested avenue, he dropped the sales slip in the bag holding his new MacBook and iPhone. Near the World Trade Center, Tom descended a stairway into the crowded subway tunnels and boarded the E Train. He took stock of his fellow passengers. The dullards resembled cattle loaded in a car headed for the slaughterhouse. Raw energy coursing throughout his nerves, Tom shut his eyelids to block out superfluous stimuli.

This morning, after watching the morbid video, Tom had removed the lithium-ion battery pack out of his laptop, unplugged his wireless router, and utilized a paper clip to pry the SIM card from his iPhone. Paranoid, he hammered all the electronics to smithereens in the bathtub, and dropped the shattered pieces down the building's incinerator chute.

Hayden, frying an egg, saw the Amazon Echo sitting atop his refrigerator. *She's listening.* He stomped the guts out of Alexa too. Breakfast burned as Tom ransacked the apartment for bugs.

He only found colonies of dust bunnies and a missing button from his shirt.

Trading stocks and making deals were the routine tasks which grounded him. Today, the stock trader couldn't fixate on his greatest love—money. His mind played an endless loop of the bicyclist turning into roadkill. Even Troy, perceiving his coworker was out of sorts, asked Tom twice why he hadn't jettisoned General Electric stock.

As Tom unboxed the hardened Norton Core networking device, he mourned the premature death of his vast collection of pornography. The sexual deviant had spent years impregnating his hard drive with illicit abominations dredged from the dark web. When the router's LEDs glowed a healthy green, he tested the MacBook's internet connection, nodding in relief as the Tor Browser started.

Tom Hayden, much the same as Roy Davis, had endured a tough childhood. He hadn't lived through the murder of a sibling; however, as an only child, he bore the brunt of his parents' consuming narcissism and irrational, often violent behavior. Many a night, the prepubescent boy had cried himself to sleep nursing plum-colored bruises or, if things got out of hand, oozing wounds. Whenever Tom looked back at his teenage years, he hated the verbal abuse even more.

His father had likewise worked on Wall Street, but not as an equity trader. In the midst of the night, when the golden towers of the moneyed were silent (except for the roaches and rats), Carl Hayden mopped the floors and emptied the trash cans. His mother, Sharon, worked in the Garment District as a seamstress until the United States sold its very last sewing machine to China. His mom and dad's meager finances generated daily squabbles. Tom was trapped in the middle. He received greater affection from Fins (a pet goldfish hidden in his closet) than he did from either of his parents.

Tom, examining the overseas exchanges with no real enthusiasm, heard a knock. The dinner order had slipped his mind. He paid for a bag of takeout, let the deliveryman hang on to the change, and set the burglar alarm.

In no way could Tom be branded as a foodie. From a young age, he had been a picky eater. Getting meat to stick to his bones was always a challenge. Only highly seasoned foods kept him absorbed long enough to force nutrients into his digestive system. Tonight, the underweight share trader drowned the pad thai noodles with extra sriracha sauce.

Hayden pushed aside the Styrofoam box and accessed Google News. He found an article in the *Bisbee Observer* reporting on an event which happened the previous day. An unidentified dead man had turned up at the local dog park. The brief description listed: male, white, thirty, five-foot-eleven, one hundred and eighty pounds, short blond hair, green eyes, no tattoos, dressed in magenta and black bicycling gear. Sheriff Roy Davis urged the public to contact the Cochise County Sheriff's Office with any information.

Despite the fact that Tom had seen the "accident" take place by remote means, he couldn't name the victim or the perpetrator. *I am not calling the police.*

Hayden, reassured the event in the video he had viewed had actually transpired and wasn't a hoax, demolished the stir-fried noodles with gusto. In the bottom half of the white clamshell, beneath a goulash of tofu, tamarind pulp, fish sauce, and dried shrimp, somebody had inscribed the words "DO YOU WANT MORE?" in black ink. Enticing messages weren't something Thai Nation's short-order cooks wrote in their food containers. The restaurant staff never even took a second to doodle a smiley face on his bill.

A chill scurried up Tom's spine as he recollected Tanda's final words—not a tingle of dread, but a rush of excitement.

"Want more?" the stock trader asked out loud. "Fuck yeah, I want more!"

A man holding an airline ticket imprinted with the name "Kim Jin-ho" boarded the blue and white jetliner. He clutched a shiny leather briefcase and a small satchel. The female Korean Air flight attendant guided the first-class traveler to his assigned Kosmo Suite. He reclined his lengthy torso in the extra-wide seat, tucked the plush blanket under his clean-shaven chin, and positioned the eiderdown pillow below his head. Park Jin-ho, his real name, turned down the complimentary cocktail and snacks. Bone-weary from his vacation, he needed to recharge. Jin-ho awoke in darkness unable to see any other passengers beyond the top of the wood-grained shell. Not wanting to leave the warmth of his snug cocoon, Park quelled the dull ache to urinate using pure mental willpower.

The shirt and slacks Jin-ho had purchased on the way to the Los Angeles International Airport emitted the effluvium of fresh dye. In the Boeing's belly, his brand-new luggage swelled with brand-new clothes and brand-new toiletries. The sunglasses in Park's chest pocket had not been worn.

Now, halfway across the North Pacific Ocean, Jin-ho felt confident nothing on his person tied him to the crime. The things he carried were new, including the forged South Korean passport and driver's license stored in his briefcase. All Park had to do was get off the airplane and go home.

Jin-ho considered switching on the television, soon forming an opinion that reminiscing about yesterday's incident would be far more thrilling.

This was not the first time Park had claimed a man's life, or a woman's life for that matter. However, this had been the singular occasion he had killed anyone with an automobile. Stuck in Seoul's metropolitan traffic, Jin-ho often fantasized about using his Land Rover as a battering ram. Running someone over with a car may not be as invigorating or as daring as, say, using a knife to slice a jugular vein or one's own hands to choke a throat, but vehicular homicide could now be checked off his "things to do before you die" list.

Park stiffened with arousal summoning up the smack of humanoid meat hitting the Mazda's bumper and the bicyclist's agonized scream. Mission complete, he had been ready to continue on to Los Angeles and fly to Seoul when the orange dashboard light began to flash. The rental car shuddered, then lost power. Jin-ho manhandled the CX-5 onto the shoulder and popped the hood. Translucent fluid gushed from the motor's transmission. He dialed the memorized emergency number. As Park hung up, a black-and-green-striped law enforcement truck approached. Opportunely for the murderer, the sheriff had been called away. Within minutes, a white plumber's van pulled up to the Mazda's trunk. Two men in black ski masks ushered the vacationer into the vehicle and whisked him to LAX. This trip had not gone as smoothly as he had hoped. Jin-ho stuffed the bag containing the gifts for his wife and daughter underneath the seat and went back to sleep.

Roy Davis had a homicide on his hands. With added pep in his step, he entered the Sheriff's Office, saluted Marge, and shut himself inside his office. Roy rocked backward in the swivel chair, kicked his feet up on the desk, folded his fingers behind his head, and closed his eyes. *I need time to think.*

This wasn't the sheriff's first murder investigation. Bisbee had over and above its fair allotment of trouble. At a mere twelve miles from the border, his town received a constant flow of Mexican visitors. By and large, the seventy thousand legal workers and shoppers crossing the Naco Port of Entry each month into the United States were law-abiding. But there were always a few who got in fender benders, bar fights, or were caught shoplifting meat or cosmetics. Undocumented migrants weren't Davis' problem. The United States Border Patrol rounded up these smuggled groups of men, women, and children and bussed them to the Santa Cruz County Detention Center. Politically and personally, the sheriff couldn't give a tinker's damn where anybody came from, looked like, or what language they spoke. Hell, Roy heard tell his maternal great-grandfather (or paternal great-great-grandmother, he disremembered who exactly) came from the State of Chihuahua.

Sheriff Davis had been elected to keep the drug cartels' gangland barbarism south of the border. His department was the cream of the crop, yet Bisbee persisted as a city with high crime statistics. Just last month, in Brewery Gulch (the historic red-light district), a drug dealer shot an innocent bystander in a failed opioid transaction.

Outside on the main drag, a dump truck backfired. Roy cracked his eyelids and sat upright. *It has to be the Asian Urban Cowboy.*

Later that day, at the Arbors in the Sierra Vista Memory Care Center, Roy leaned over the gray-haired women sitting in a wheelchair. "Hello, Mom." He kissed her on the cheek.

She rubbed her tummy. "Is it supper time?"

"No, Mom." Janet had eaten her nightly meal ahead of his arrival. "It's a nice day. Let's go outdoors." He rolled her along the waxed black-and-white tiled hallway.

Nurse Flores stood in a resident's doorway. Maria nodded at Roy and laid her palm on Janet's wrist. "Mrs. Davis, how are you this evening?"

"Just peachy." Janet made a face. "When is supper? I could eat a horse."

"Would you like another peach cobbler?"

"I don't want to ruin my appetite before supper time."

The nurse turned to Roy. "Your mom has been resting easier since Dr. Carter modified her medications. She's making it through the night without pressing the call button."

"Terrific! Thanks for taking good care of her, Maria."

On several previous mornings, Roy had received messages from the memory ward's night staff informing him that Janet had awoken shrieking. Each time, the conscientious son drove the long road to Sierra Vista to hold his mother's hand until she dozed off.

At the end of the corridor, the sheriff elbowed the push button that automatically opened the east wing's exterior doors. He wheeled the chair down a short path to the walled-in courtyard. Roy set the brakes and sat beside his mom on an iron bench.

Janet's face twisted in anguish. "Where's Helen?"

"Helen's still at school. She'll be home later."

"With Philip? That man is always working late." Roy's father—a vodka aficionado in his twilight years—died a decade ago of cirrhosis of the liver.

"Yes. Dad will pick up Helen after her band practice."

"And you are?"

Her boy pasted on a make-believe smile. "You know me. I'm Roy."

Regardless of how many times he heard it, this childlike query always stung deep. The day a parent forgets their offspring's face is profoundly traumatic to the spirit.

"Leroy," Janet croaked. She slouched under the woolen afghan, the outline of her bony limbs adding dimension to the crocheted geometric pattern.

When Roy first detected his mother's absentmindedness and confusion, he became annoyed. At her condominium, he noticed yellow Post-it notes stuck all over the walls, doors, and appliances. Some stickies were ordinary reminders, for instance, "Doctor's appointment next Thursday" taped to the medicine cabinet or "Meet Martha for lunch tomorrow" clipped to a refrigerator magnet. Recent fire-red notes were more distressing, such as, "Feed the cat at midnight" glued to the microwave or "Take a bath!" slapped on the washing machine.

Janet explained to Roy how the hundreds of slips helped her stay organized. He should have recognized these fragmented bits of her intellect as a crucial warning. Children do not want to acknowledge their parents are helpless, and the son had dismissed these artifacts as the normal progression of aging. Then, five years ago, after Janet nearly burned down her condo by leaving the oven on, Roy understood the time had come to act. Still and all, he had been aghast when the neurologist diagnosed advanced dementia. The Arbors cost the sheriff an arm and both legs, but he had money saved, and the supervised care was well worth every dime. Of higher significance, the Arbors offered assurance for his peace of mind.

As Janet's health declined, and she started to wonder who he was, Roy had responded with exasperation. When his mom questioned his sister's whereabouts, he gave her unvarnished honesty. "Helen's dead. She was murdered thirty years ago." The son, seeing his mother's instant and utter grief, learned to sugarcoat the truth with white lies—no need for her to roast in everlasting flames reliving her daughter's death every time anew. Nor could Roy bear witness to Janet's pain. Now, psychically exhausted, he kept conversations simple and, above all, positive.

If feasible, the sheriff dropped by the Arbors each night to visit, unless the day was Wednesday (happy hour at the Roadhouse), or an important case kept him at work. Under good atmospheric conditions, the two sat outdoors in the cozy courtyard. Roy mentioned, "the nice weather we're having," or, being that Janet had been an avid baseball fan, relayed how the Arizona Diamondbacks were doing—always "great, they may make the playoffs this year." Mostly, mother and son sat speechless watching the chattering goldfinches flit between the fragrant acacia trees.

Roy relished these borrowed moments alone with his mom, far from the stresses of the Sheriff's Office, the horrors of the past, and the loneliness of his mobile home.

The sun sank beneath the east wing's tiled roof. Above the stucco wall, the sky turned a hue seen nowhere outside of Arizona.

Janet crossed her arms. "Leroy, I'm cold."

Roy, gladdened his mother recalled his name without prompting, rolled her into the main hallway's greenish fluorescence. "There. That's better."

They entered the "Activity Room," a common area shared by both memory care and assisted living patients. An ancient episode of *The Golden Girls* blasted out of the television. Betty White, as animated as ever, warned her wide-eyed pals she might have contracted HIV during a blood transfusion. Roy parked Janet in a front spot.

The majority of the aged residents, eight women to every man, stared into space or snoozed in their wheelchairs. One of these sought-after men yelled across the room, "Sheriff! Get on over here!"

"Hiya, Bill!" Roy moseyed over to a black gent wearing a white T-shirt and blue sweatpants.

William Hill, handsome for his age, resided in the assisted living west wing. Bill had retired from the Cochise County Sheriff's Office two months after Roy came aboard. Bill's wife, Sarah, had died suddenly. Marvin, his son in Savannah, Georgia, blamed his father for his mother's death, refusing to visit. The resident stood up on spindly legs and pushed the foldable walker forward. "Sheriff, I saw a segment on the evening news about a truck driver finding a body at the Bisbee Dog Park."

Davis often discussed police matters (procedural and gossip) with the ex-detective. Hill's mind was as sharp as a tack. As an outsider, he volunteered unbiased insights.

"Yep, it's mighty perplexing." Roy gave Bill the gist of what had occurred and how the department ferreted out the renter of the car, a Mr. Kim Jin-ho. The sheriff didn't have misgivings about the former detective divulging confidential information. In this place, there were few who registered interest and even fewer who'd remember.

Hill arched his bushy eyebrows. "You think it's a homicide?"

Davis had received a preliminary autopsy report from the Pima County Office of the Medical Examiner in Tucson. Dr. Jensen discovered a fractured hyoid bone and pressure marks on the victim's esophagus. The CSI team had sorted out the trucker's shoe prints and the canines' paw prints from the additional impressions near the corpse. Somebody, *or somebodies* (several of the imprints stood out as deeper and wider than the others), shod their feet with paper booties to hide their tracks.

"Lookin' that way, Bill. Definitely not a normal hit-and-run." Until he located the family of the deceased, Roy wasn't releasing any postmortem information.

"And you haven't found the bicycle?"

"Nope. We don't know where our John Doe got hit or how he wound up at the dog park."

Bill kicked the Day-Glo tennis balls attached to the walker's legs with the tip of his Velcro sneaker. "I'd search the roads with you if I wasn't gumped up. Sheriff, in my day, I had a nose for sniffing out clues."

"You sure did, Detective. One of these nights, I'll break you out of this dungeon, and we'll cruise around town. Maybe lift a few with the old crew at Pogo's."

"Sounds like a plan!" Hill tugged on the tufts of his salt-and-pepper goatee. "Sheriff, I still dwell on it."

"What's that?" Davis could foretell the man's next words.

"Your sister. A moment doesn't go by without that girl crossing my mind. I feel awful about how it got handled."

Detective Hill, as well as the rest of the Sheriff's Office, had devoted the summer of 1982 to apprehending Helen's murderer. A handful of suspects were interviewed, but not enough evidence was collected to bring any one of them to trial. When Davis joined the department, he had been given full access to the case files and was permitted to speak to all involved.

Roy patted Bill's arm. "I feel bad too. You're not responsible. We'll probably never catch whoever killed her."

"I know Luke Bell was up to his neck in it." Hill's wrinkles multiplied. "Too bad his parents gave him an alibi."

Roy also believed in the guilt of Helen's high school boyfriend. The sheriff didn't admit to the former detective how he had wasted an abundance of his youth camped across from Bell's apartment waiting for the asshole to make a mistake.

And there had been a time when William Hill alluded to frontier justice. "If my pins worked as they were meant to, and I wasn't pushin' eighty," he lowered his voice, "I'd drag that son-of-a-bitch behind the woodshed and finish him off myself." Cold case nightmares plagued the ex-detective like a recurring bout of shingles.

Davis clenched Hill's hand. "Behave yourself."

"I'll keep an eye on your mom." Bill raised his sippy cup. "I'd be indebted if you'd apprise me of any breakthroughs in your investigation."

"Will do." Roy took his leave.

Outside, upwind from the stench of dirty diapers and despair, the sheriff inhaled the bracing air. He struck a wooden match on his boot heel and lit a cigarette.

Tom's long fingers were trawling the darknet for tantalizing videos when Tanda's face appeared on the MacBook's screen.

"Mr. Hayden, why are you trying to block me? That hurts my feelings." The woman's eyes did not seem to blink. "I see you're up to your old habits."

Embarrassed, he shut the other open windows. "How were you able to get past my new firewall?"

"We've got the technical resources to do whatever we please. You've also kept up with the Arizona news."

"Did you have anything to do with the bicycle rider's death?"

"Me personally?" She shook her head. "Our organization arranged the encounter. Why? Did you get a kick out of watching that pork sausage fly through the air with the greatest of ease?"

Tom watched Tanda blow a dense brume from an electronic cigarette. "No."

"Let the truth set you free, Mr. Hayden. We know you enjoyed every minute."

"What is that supposed to mean?" Tom regarded the small camera lens embedded in the laptop screen. *She can see me.* He obstructed her view with a folded envelope. *I want her to see me.* He tore the blinder to shreds.

"For months now, we've recorded your expressions using advanced facial emotion analysis software. From your high scores, you obviously loved the show."

"Is your game extortion? I send you money or else you have me killed?"

"Don't be so melodramatic. This isn't blackmail, and it's not ransomware. You'll pay us for a service you'd gladly pay Lucifer the skin off your back to receive."

"Are you assassins?"

"No." She let out a throaty laugh. "On second thought, once in a blue moon, our clients find themselves in dire straits and need a helping hand. Can you meet me face to face? *Vis-à-vis?*"

Tanda was gorgeous, intelligent, and very sexy. Although Tom appreciated these three qualities, because of his reluctance to reveal his perversions to any non-virtual woman, the thirty-six-year-old man remained a virgin.

He moved closer to the webcam. "I'd like that."

"Tomorrow, be in Central Park by the Wollman Rink. Ten o'clock sharp. Have your new cell phone handy. I'll text you with additional instructions. Oh, I almost forgot—no food beforehand."

Chapter Three

Thursday–Thanksgiving—November 23, 2017

PARK JIN-HO LISTENED TO HIS WIFE, Sun-young, playing with their daughter, Yu-jin, in the living room. Locked in the den, he turned on the laptop and launched the Tor Browser. While Jin-ho waited for the anonymity network software to load (the circular throbber spun forever), he gazed out the bay windows. Glittering buildings in the city of Seoul lost their luster in the thickening haze.

At long last, the homepage popped into view. The no-frills website contained a column of four unlabeled numbers. "1" could be selected to commence secure communications between himself and his Handler. "2" listed available vacations. "3" posted the results of these vacations. "4" was strictly reserved for emergencies. He had used the fourth option once, two days ago in Arizona, when he saw the approaching sheriff's truck.

Jin-ho, sipping Imperial whiskey from a crystal glass, chose option 3. The report listed data for the five trips he had taken over the previous three years: four positives and *one negative!* He gasped reading the Korean characters. *I didn't kill the man on the bicycle.* Queasy, Park expanded the details of his latest vacation, this text highlighted in bright red.

Apparently, when the backup team arrived to verify the outcome, *"the cyclist was still breathing and had to be terminated."* He shut the laptop and yanked the network wire out of the wall.

Park, a tax lawyer and a Nexen Heroes baseball fan, respected the sport's infatuation with statistics. He felt the feverish shame of losing a championship game. *Now, I'm merely batting 800.*

Sun-young called from the kitchen, "Jin-ho! Dinner's ready!"

Bill Hill hobbled across the activity room and sat before a triangular desk wedged in an unused corner. The yellowed Compaq desktop computer, comparable to the bulk of the Arbors' residents, was slow and had little random-access memory. For a moment, he appraised the gaunt face mirrored in the CRT monitor's curved glass. "How the hell did I get this old?"

"You're only as young as you feel!"

Bill turned his head to hear an electric wheelchair humming down the hallway. *Who said that?* He pressed the power button. The fuzz-clogged fan whined as the unsupported Windows XP operating system booted. Hill entered his username and password, his advancing rheumatoid arthritis causing him to fat-finger these twice. Once the blue skies and green hills "Bliss" wallpaper appeared (he had time to blow his nose into a hankie and plug the police scanner's earbud into his ear), Bill opened the Internet Explorer browser.

After the ex-detective typed "Kim Jin-ho" (the name Roy had told him the marooned motorist had used at the LA Airport to rent the Mazda CX-5 from the Save Big Rental Company) in the search bar, thousands of results filled multiple pages. Hill, researching given names and surnames, realized Jin-ho happened to be an extremely popular first name, and twenty-two percent of all South Koreans used Kim for a family name.

"That ain't gonna work," Bill muttered, massaging the cramp in his neck. He switched off the PC and glowered at the blank screen.

The former detective ambled to a window and stared at the passing traffic. *Everybody has somewhere to be except for me.* He contemplated his next steps. William Hill might be along in years, but he wasn't pushing up daisies just yet.

On Thanksgiving morning, Tom accessed Central Park through Scholar's Gate and strolled around the Pond to Wollman Rink. He bought a hot chocolate from a sidewalk vendor and perched on tiered seating overlooking the ice skating rink. Exuberant children and amorous couples glided across the oval of frozen water. The sound of joyful Christmas music made him despondent.

Tom, scalding his tongue on the blistering cocoa, wondered what his parents were doing this holiday season. Both had remarried, his father to a young, horny kindergarten teacher, and his mother to an old, rich-as-fuck airline executive. He hadn't seen or spoken to either of them in a decade, a mutual agreement neither side had any intention of breaking.

A pint-sized boy swathed in a red hat and blue scarf did his best to keep from falling. His mom took his hand, provided a few words of encouragement, and pushed the tyke on the white ice. Tom didn't want kids. The concept of fatherhood nauseated him. Hayden pulled up his collar and stuffed his numb fingers in his jacket's fleece-lined pockets. He couldn't comprehend why people went out-of-doors in the winter. Tom put a palm above his brow and scanned the vicinity—*no Tanda.*

The iPhone buzzed. The text stated: *200 yds NE past chess & checkers, cross center dr, find the Indian hunter.* Tom hoofed it down the winding footpath.

By the volleyball courts, he confronted a bronze statue of a long-haired boy restraining a snarling dog. The phone reverberated again. *Tanda must be nearby.* Tom read the message and headed north. His anticipation intensified seeing a female seated on a bench feeding the pigeons.

She tossed the bread crumbs on the ground and stood. "Nice to meet you, Mr. Hayden."

Tom rejected the outstretched mitten. "Where is Tanda?"

"You're looking at her." The tall, coffee-colored woman smiled. "Am I not what you expected?"

Well proportioned and on the athletic side, she was as beautiful—*or more beautiful*—as the woman who had invaded his MacBook. And like that woman, Tom had trouble classifying her racial makeup: a bewitching mixture of all nationalities. Below the brim of her knitted hat, large, golden-brown eyes turned him inside out.

"Mr. Hayden, I understand your bewilderment. You've been interacting with my avatar. Today is the only time we will meet in person. If you are curious as to what I have to put forth, follow me. If not, no harm, no foul. Turn back and return to your boring life."

Tom cast his beverage cup in the recycle bin and stayed close.

Rachel Martin packed a suitcase on the bed. During the last week, she had meticulously laid out her vacation wardrobe. Every stitch of fabric had been purchased from a distant Goodwill store using cash.

In the duskiness of predawn, Rachel drove to downtown San Diego and parked her obsidian black Mercedes-Benz AMG G65 in the lot farthest from the international airport, a strip of asphalt crammed underneath Interstate 5. At five dollars a day, the owner—even if he cared who came and went—could not afford security cameras. A concern entered Martin's mind. *What if my expensive SUV is stolen or vandalized while I'm away?* She shook her head slightly. *Whatever. . .I'll lease a newer one.* In the courtesy shuttle, seated on a duct-taped bench (the interior reeked of a lethal dose of Febreze), Rachel watched the rising sun reflect off the ships in the bay. She allowed herself a moment to envision the future.

The driver yelled over his shoulder, "Hey, lady, what airline?"

"Delta," Rachel lied (her purse held Alaska Airlines round-trip tickets printed with the name "Linda Taylor"). She had scheduled a week in Anchorage. Most of that time would be spent laying the groundwork for the final day.

Martin, a longtime member of the surreptitious group, 57, had seen and done it all. Yet, for this holiday, the method she intended to use to achieve her goal was atypical, *and tricky.*

Listed on the 57 webpages under the "Vacations/Transfixion" category, the words "Pins and Needles" had captivated the thirty-five-year-old, for she experienced a certain level of repose while sewing miniature clothes for her Barbie fashion doll collection. The size of the pin or needle was up to Rachel. *Should I use a teeny straight pin or a larger size twelve sewing needle? What about a jumbo size fifty knitting needle?*

The huntress pondered if she might choose a male or a female, the young or the elderly. Once she saw a suitable subject, she'd know. Drowsy, Dr. Martin rested the side of her head on the window.

Tom trotted to stay in stride with Tanda's long legs. *Where's the fire?* To the fore, a scruffy man clothed in a forest green parka and camouflaged hunting cap emerged from behind a denuded sugar maple and stepped onto the pathway. Hayden looked back. An NYPD police officer trailed at their heels. "Is Tanda even your real name?"

"What do you think?"

"Nah."

"To you, I'm Tanda. It's Native American. Means the Seer of Life and Death. Do you approve?"

Tom shrugged inside his insulated jacket. "I guess." He peeped rearward repeatedly. The cop had closed the gap. "Are they your bodyguards?"

Tanda chortled. "I can take care of myself." She chopped the crisp air with a sideways palm. "Karate. Black belt. Those men are here to ensure you weren't followed."

"I wasn't. Nobody knows I'm here."

"We have no indications you told anyone. Even so, it's in our nature to be discreet."

The man running point unlocked a chain strung between two poles. A red and white sign cautioned "RESTRICTED AREA – EMPLOYEES ONLY."

On a leaf-strewn driveway, a short, bearded chap in a cashmere topcoat and a tweed flat cap stood by a rusted Quonset hut. He dipped his head to Tanda and opened the metal door.

Tom, unable to see into the shed's interior, stopped in his tracks. "What's inside?"

Tanda put on a frightful face and intoned in a campy Bela Lugosi imitation, "There are far worse things awaiting us than the afterlife." When he didn't budge, she shoved him. "Move it!"

The shed smelled of grass, gas, and *breakfast?* A lightbulb swung from the ceiling. Push and riding lawn mowers were parked against the arched walls. Rakes, shovels, leaf blowers, and weed whips hung on the end's vertical wall. Propane heaters worked overtime to warm the corrugated steel structure.

A dining table, incongruous in these surroundings, stood in the midpoint of the large space. Three formal place settings and two ivory candles in gold candleholders rested on the white tablecloth.

Tom narrowed down the source of the aroma of bacon and eggs: Sterno-heated stainless steel chafers on a foldup table. His stomach rumbled. *I hope they feed me before they dismember me with that chainsaw.*

The shabby man took their coats while the cop slipped outside and locked the door.

Tanda motioned to the chair with its back to the exit. "Please take a seat, Mr. Hayden."

She sat to his left. The chap with the Vandyke beard sat directly across from him. He heard the crinkle of tinfoil as the food was uncovered.

Tom spread his hands. "What is all this?"

Tanda unfolded a napkin. "Let's eat, and then we'll get down to business."

A female forearm sheathed in black (Tom established her gender by the pink fingernail polish and the strong perfume) materialized on his left side to deliver a Mexican omelet with a dollop of hash browns. She set a cup of Americano on the table and asked if he wanted cream or sugar.

"Cream. No sugar." Tom only drank coffee when pressured to be sociable. Doctors defined caffeine as a stimulant, and he said no to drugs.

The three ate without speaking, the lone noise in the hut the clinking of knives and forks. If the stock trader looked up, he'd catch one or the other of his breakfast companions watching him. Famished, Tom wolfed down the omelet and potatoes. His taste buds vibrated as they never had. *I did not think food could taste this great!* After the diners finished their meals—the guest of honor held his tongue requesting seconds—the server removed their plates and swept away any stray morsels with a table crumber.

Tanda patted her lips and laid the napkin to the side. "Well then, let's get down to brass tacks. Mr. Hayden, did you tell anyone about me or the Bisbee video?"

"Of course not. I informed you I didn't say anything."

"Our relationship has to be built on trust. You must be totally honest with me."

Tom reacted to her lowered eyelashes by stuttering, "I...I am telling you the truth." He kept in mind the email that had initiated this whole affair: Henry Ellington's message containing the URL address.

The server's fingers (Hayden distinguished the owner by her essence) pulled his head back by the hair. Her dominant hand jammed a cold, tubular object into his throat. From the rustles behind him, somebody was unrolling a sheet of plastic.

Tanda drew in air to scream, "Who did you talk to?"

"I replied to the...person...who sent your link. Had...no idea what...it...was. Came from a friend."

Tanda's laughter held no mirth. "Mr. Hayden, you have no real friends. Surely, you know that." When she lifted a finger, the server let him go and retracted the gun. "Thank you, Danica."

Shaken, he brushed his hair in place. "What do you want out of me?"

"It's not what we want from you. It is what you'll receive from us. Did you find Bisbee's live feed entertaining?"

"I asked if you were assassins. Is that it? Are you recruiting me to join your gang of international hit men?"

The beardy chap addressed Tom for the first time in a chesty baritone. "There is a difference between assassins and hit men. An assassin kills politicians for political ideology, or, if deranged, for fame. A hit man will kill anyone if the price is right. We are neither."

"And who might you be, sir?"

"Call me the Accountant. We separated you out of millions of people by virtue of your special qualities."

"Because I make a lot of money?"

"No." The Accountant pointed his forefinger at Tom. "Because you are a true psychopath."

The equity trader's guffaw deteriorated into a dry cough. *I may be antisocial, but I'm not psychotic.* "That's a ridiculous statement!"

The Accountant drummed the tabletop. "Do you recall the ILOVEYOU virus?"

Tom took a moment to answer. "Wasn't that malicious software released in the '90s?"

"Y2K, the millennium. This love letter arrived in your inbox with the subject: 'I love you.' Everyone obsessed with finding out if anybody gave a damn if they lived or died clicked on the VBScript. Two kids in the Philippines wrote the worm."

"What did the virus do? Install a stupid screen saver?"

The man's middle finger flipped up. "The Love Bug fucked up your computer for good. Our organization uses similar, yet less destructive, malware to implant our own code worldwide."

"Emotion recognition APIs." Tom turned to Tanda. "You used computational methodologies on me?"

"Yes. Diagnosticating facial expressions is a component of our process. We also compile all your financial information, emails, documents, texts, and social media feeds. Oh, and let's not neglect that dark web shit you are so hell-bent on stockpiling."

"I'm no psychopath! I happen to prefer—"

Tanda cut him short with an upraised hand. "Mr. Hayden, there are psychopaths, and *there are psychopaths.*"

The Accountant asked, "Do you eat Thai food?"

Tom recollected the provocative phrase scribbled on the bottom lid of the Thai Nation takeout container. "You know that I do."

The Accountant completed the analogy. "You're a six or seven on the chili pepper scale." He ticked off five items on his left fingers: "Antisocial, manipulative, callous, superficial charm, and lack of remorse." Beginning with the thumb of his right hand, he added, "Need for stimulation." The accountant extended the last four fingers and grinned. "On the other hand, you got above average grades in school—even earned your master's degree. You have long-range goals, you're holding on to a high-paying job, and best of all, you've never been arrested."

Tom plucked lint from his shirtsleeve. "The guy that ran down the bicyclist. Who was he?"

"One of our clients," Tanda said.

He checked his watch. "And what do you do for him?"

She gave him the evil eye. "Is there someplace else you need to be?"

"No. What's your racket?"

Tanda rested her elbows on the table. "We'll call the gentleman driving the automobile, Mr. Smith. For his entire adult life, Mr. Smith worked fourteen hours a day amassing what at that time seemed of paramount importance—power over subordinates and tremendous wealth. At home, a mansion in reality, he has a doting, model wife and a cute, straight-A daughter. Mr. Smith should be content. Still, he isn't. *Or wasn't, until he met us.* At the office, Mr. Smith surpassed his every goal. All the same, money has become a column of numbers on a balance sheet. His family's emotional demands drain him. Mother and child want a part of his soul he's unable to give."

"You're saying Mr. Smith is also a psychopath?"

The Accountant said, "Our software uses artificial intelligence to analyze the greatest common divisors in the populations we are monitoring. Mr. Smith *and you Mr. Hayden* are the types we set our algorithm to spot. Repressed people desperate for a bloodletting."

Tanda chuckled. "In the days before the internet, our researchers had to slog up to the New York Public Library to page through the national and international newspapers. I can't imagine the amount of eye fatigue and sore behinds it took to find individuals such as yourself."

The Accountant smirked. "Don't forget the legwork inside the military recruiting offices, prisons, courthouses, and capitol buildings."

"What precisely did you arrange for Mr. Smith?" Tom asked. "Anybody can get in a car and turn somebody into road hash."

Tanda placed both of her palms on the white linen. "We offer our customers various packages depending upon—"

"Mr. Hayden," the Accountant interjected, "based on your current income and savings, you barely qualify for our entry-level package."

Tom's jaw tightened. "I've got more money in offshore bank accounts."

The Accountant's nostrils flared. "We factored in those Cayman Islands funds. Do not question my thoroughness."

Tanda, eager to unruffle the men's feathers, leaned across the table and smiled. "Mr. Smith is a Gold Level member. You, Mr. Hayden, would start off as Bronze. Gold is equivalent to the Bronze; however, with a Gold membership, you are authorized for two one-week vacations per year instead of one. Mr. Smith, agreeing to our terms and conditions, was presented with our darknet address and a phone number for emergencies. Our portal is accessible for you to work with your Handler, reserve vacations, view status reports, and contact your backup unit if, for any reason, you cannot use the telephone."

Tom tilted his chair back on two legs. "Mr. Smith used his time off to run over a cyclist? Is that how he gets his jollies?"

"Mr. Smith elected vehicular homicide in Bisbee, Arizona. I don't care why. His 'jollies' are none of our beeswax." She forged ahead with her sales pitch. "You opt for a convenient week, a desirable locale—international or domestic—and, in particular, the dispatch."

"Dispatch?"

"Gun, knife, rope, rock, your bare hands. There are 57 varieties to pick from."

The front legs of Tom's seat thumped to the ground. "Fifty-seven? Like the ketchup?"

Tanda elevated her eyebrows.

"What do I need you for? Why should I pay you a wooden nickel?"

"We cater to your every whim." Her shoulders tensed. "You'll get a crack backup team, top-notch logistical support, forged documents including passports and driver's licenses. Mr. Hayden, you'll never be on your own again."

"How do I know this isn't a scam? This whole—"

The Accountant's chair flipped backward as the wiry man sprang to his feet. He pulled out a snub-nosed revolver, aimed the sight at Tom's head, and fired. As a puff of wind parted Hayden's hair, someone behind him dropped to the floor.

The female server, a slender thing in black, lay crumpled on the polyethylene sheeting. The male in the green parka prevented her blood from trickling onto the oil-spattered cement by raising a corner of the tarpaulin. "Pete!" he bellowed. "Lend me a hand!"

The policeman standing in the open doorway slid his palm off his service pistol. He scooped up a roll of sealing tape and lumbered over to bag the body.

"This is no sting, Mr. Hayden." The Accountant put the gun on the table. "So, are you with us?"

Tom inhaled the acrid scent of burnt gunpowder. He stared at the plastic-wrapped corpse loaded into a wheelbarrow. "Who was she? Why did you kill her?"

The Accountant motioned to the man topped with the camo cap. "Mike! Show Mr. Hayden what Danica planted in a sack of Weed & Feed."

Mike held a Ziploc bag containing a ballpoint pen in front of Tom's nose. "The rat fink recorded us."

The Accountant smacked his fist into his palm. "Have you seen *Fight Club*?"

"I may have played it when I was a kid." Tom had been hooked on the PlayStation version.

"Hmm. Wasn't aware that Hollywood made that outstanding motion picture into a video game." The Accountant rubbed his chafed knuckles. "The Fight Club had a set of rules."

Tanda chimed in. "Rules number one and two: *You do not talk about Fight Club.* Danica violated the code."

"Is that what you call yourselves?" Hayden asked. "Fight Club?"

She glanced at the Accountant, and said, "Our organization has existed in one form or the other since the Civil War. Management doesn't post a formal name for security reasons, but if your mind cries out for a tangible substance to wrap itself around, try '57.'"

The stock trader studied the bottle label of the popular condiment he had used to flavor his hash browns. "For the 57 varieties of mayhem?"

Tanda softly clapped her hands. "Mayhem is a noble noun. Variety is the spice of life! Referring to our association as '57' has been a bit of a running gag over the years. Historically, we've only had two members—a married couple—who hit Platinum Level. Plats are not obligated to pay for our services. These connoisseurs partook of every variety of ketchup we have at our disposal—quite a feat, believe you me. As high performers, Plats create their own objectives. We assist them when we can."

Tom did the math and gulped. "Any more regulations?"

Tanda nodded. "Your victim, or 'Pawn' as we designate them, must be a complete stranger. No vendettas. No family feuds. No one under eighteen."

"Why no minors?"

"Offing children or families draws unwanted scrutiny from both the religious right and the liberal left." She frowned. "If little kids are your fetish, or you wish to annihilate entire households, this isn't the place for you. Our additional stipulations? You may use each 'variety' of murder one time. For example, you can utilize a handgun only once, so take this restriction into mind while making plans. In other words, don't pick a rubber band to bring down a seven-hundred-pound sumo wrestler. Just one Pawn per one-week vacation, unless there are extenuating circumstances. Holidays aren't for lounging poolside sipping umbrella drinks—you need to consummate your task. *Always* follow our advice. Please take into account we have years of tried-and-true experience. We're here to help you. The final rule is critical and far-ranging. *You can't get caught.*"

"What if *I am* taken into custody?" Tom gestured at the cop. "Are your people working inside the police force? High-profile mouthpieces to represent me in court? Judges on the payroll?"

"Nobody shall lay a hand on you, but in that one in a million chance," the Accountant whiffed the barrel of his revolver, "you won't get anywhere near an interrogation room. Listen up. This is my personal caveat with no exceptions—I am paid on time and to the cent."

Tanda groaned. "I nearly forgot to add one more important thing. No killing outside of 57—*no matter how much you may want to.*" She scowled at her wristwatch. "I've got a mani-pedi appointment to run too." Her eyes leveled on the equity trader. "Mr. Hayden, what'll it be? Are you in, or are you out?"

"Do I have a choice? Can I think about it?"

Tanda extracted a purple vaporizer from her pocket and took a prolonged hit. A silver stream of tetrahydrocannabinol shot out of her mouth. "No, Mr. Hayden. You must decide today—*right now.*"

Tom's mouth opened and shut. He swallowed hard, then uttered with spurious resoluteness, "All the way in. How much will this cost me?"

The Accountant peered up from his cell phone and flashed a set of rather sharp incisors. "The proper tense is, 'How much *did* this cost me?' After our oral contract, I transferred two million of your hard-earned dollars from Cayman National to our treasury. This installment covers the initial twelve months, plus registration fees. Thenceforth, the dues remain at a million per year in perpetuity."

"I. . . ." Tom fell silent considering the price tag.

When Tanda touched his arm, he shrank away. "Mr. Hayden, you'll be okay. I know two mill is a substantial investment. Nevertheless, we're not about to bleed our clients dry." She shifted her attention to the whiskered man. "Perhaps a financial tip for our newest member?"

The Accountant flossed a bacon bit from between his teeth with a pinky fingernail left long for this purpose. "On January the fifteenth, at the New York Stock Exchange's opening bell, buy MGIX. Every penny you have or can beg, borrow, or steal."

Tanda escorted Tom outdoors. Beneath gathering thunderheads, the alluring woman buttoned her overcoat. "Mr. Hayden, I look forward to working with you as your Handler." She trapped his skittish wrist and used a black Sharpie to write an IP address and telephone number on his palm. "Here's how you'll get ahold of me." Tanda clung to Tom's hand for a moment before letting go. "Good luck and good hunting."

Roy stood on the slope of the Naco Highway swabbing his temples with a sleeve. His team still hadn't located the missing bicycle.

Marge Connors drawled from his radio, "Sheriff, I have a fella named"—a Desert Diamond Casino bus roared by taking her words with it—"wants to speak to you."

"Say again!" he shouted. "Repeat!"

"William Hill wants you to phone him back. Do you know him?"

"Marge, look at the wall behind you."

"Oh, ha! The detective in the picture? That old hawk watches me all the livelong day."

"He's a fine man. I'll call him from my truck."

The Arbors' receptionist answered and, two minutes later, Hill came on the line. "Happy Thanksgiving, Sheriff!" he huffed. "Had to walk a mile to get to the phone. Jeez, my ticker's rat-a-tat-tatting like a snare drum on steroids."

"Bill, what's up?" The sheriff's eyeballs hurt from examining the roadway for skid marks and the bushes for bent bicycles. So far, he had only stumbled upon a gym bag bursting with 1980s adult magazines and a budding migraine.

"The guy with the broken-down Mazda? You said he rented the car in Los Angeles under the name Kim Jin-ho?"

"That's him." Davis rooted around in the Chevy's center console for the Excedrin Extra Strength.

"We've got the World Wide Web here. Slow as a salted snail, but I managed to conduct a Google query."

Roy grimaced, dry swallowing the acetaminophen. "What did you find?"

"Ninety-nine bazillion Kim Jin-hos. I'm thinking," the ex-detective paused for dramatic effect, "your suspect used an alias!"

The sheriff had already come to this conclusion. The photocopy of the man's driver's license appeared hinky. "We'll look into it." He regretted reviewing the case with the geriatric.

"And one more thing, Sheriff. Did you find John Doe's bicycle?"

"Not yet."

"Where are you searching?"

"Naco Highway. South of the dog park."

"Kim Jin-ho, or whatever he now calls himself, was presumably heading to the airport he landed at, LAX. Did you check north on US 80? His rental car faced in that direction, right?"

Roy felt silly. He hadn't thought of exploring that area, and here was this old man telling him how to do his job. "One of my men gave the 80 a quick drive-by. We'll investigate further. Thanks for your input."

"Just want to help." Well pleased with his contribution, Bill hung up and went to eat a glazed donut.

The sheriff assembled his squad and reassigned half of the deputies to scour US 80.

That same day, in the Wild West town of Tombstone, an officer dragged a wrecked red road bicycle out of a laundromat's dumpster. The G&G Cycling sticker on the Schwinn's seat authenticated the renter. The Medical Examiner's Office changed John Doe's toe tag to Daniel Charles Barton, 29, from Kent, Ohio. Detectives turned his room at the Miracle Mountain

Inn upside down. Although Barton's wallet and cell phone were nowhere to be found, his luggage tags contained emergency contacts. Roy learned from telephoning Beth Barton her brother had been recovering from a recent divorce. Daniel traveled to Bisbee to get away from it all. The sheriff notified Beth she must come to Tucson to identify the remains.

    In his office, Roy tugged open the drawer in the antique desk and withdrew a quart of locally distilled whiskey. The sweet and spicy Desert Durum burned away a little of the bitter taste from the "Sorry, Ms. Barton, but I've got some bad news for you" phone call. He jogged out a Lucky Strike and tapped both ends on the ink-stained desk blotter. Davis touched the unfiltered tobacco to his lips, and griped, "Gotta quit these lung busters." He tucked the paper tube behind an ear, solaced by the nicotine's proximity to his brain's pleasure center.

    The sheriff poured himself another two fingers of "Novocain for the Insane" and toasted his sister's picture. "Helen, everyone needs at least one vice!"

Chapter Four

Friday—November 24, 2017

As Cochise County's sheriff, Roy had assigned his chief deputy to lead the Barton investigation. Nora Clarke was competent enough to take over his job if he got voted out, killed in the line of duty, dropped dead from a stroke, or on a more positive note—a difficult miracle for him to conjure up—retired. *Let Clarke handle it,* Davis thought. But, in the wee hours, as he listened to Pancho's plaintiff yowls, he felt connected to this specific case. Graphic images of his sister's black and bruised cadaver flashed across the water-stained bedroom ceiling. The sheriff wondered if the two investigations were linked. *Maybe, I'm thinking so much about Helen due to her death anniversary being so near.*

In the kitchen hallway, his naked feet squeaked on the linoleum floor. "Sis," Roy said to his imaginary companion, "that happened thirty-five years ago. Sometimes, it seems like just yesterday."

He opened the humming refrigerator and, aided by the tiny bulb's blinding light, used a bottle opener to pop a Budweiser. The foamy head ballooned his empty stomach. *Did I eat anything besides beef jerky for dinner?* Davis spilled the contents of a Circle K bag onto the Formica tabletop and sat. He set the Lucky Strike cigarettes out of the way and tore open a box of earplugs.

"Aaah-ooooooooooooooh!" the hairless wolf ululated, testing the spongy inserts. "I can't hear a damn thing. Not a damn thing at all."

Roy, promising himself he'd reassess Helen's case files in the morning, fell into bed, and. . . .

. . . .cowered on the cold cement floor in the basement of his childhood home, the bungalow clinging to the mountainside on Laundry Hill Road. Above the rafters, on the main level, Leroy's parents argued with passion. Their footsteps, louder or softer depending on the hardness of the flooring they tread upon, roamed in endless circles around the living room, dining room, hallway, and kitchen.

Although the small boy could not piece together full sentences, he picked out word chunks, such as, "our dear, dear Helen," "slaughtered little lamb," "it's all your fault," and "I wish you had died instead."

Is that my father? Liver disease took him ten years ago. Mom is. . . .

The shelves and cubbyholes in this dank cellar stored his sister's belongings: moldering stuffed animals, moth-eaten clothes, diaries crawling with booklice, and in a padlocked steamer trunk—her darkest secrets.

His heartbroken dad ached to throw every trace of these grievous memories away. "Janet, get over it. We have to move on."

His headstrong mom turned a deaf ear. "Philip, we must preserve these precious keepsakes in Helen's honor."

This gloomy crypt below this house of sorrows would be the married couple's last compromise.

Leroy's bottom became damp. *I'm wearing my old cowboys and Indians pajamas.* As he searched for the water's origin, a clinking noise—*chains?*—spooked him. The surface of the inky liquid rippled. *This is only a dream. Only a dream.*

His father's low-pitched voice boomed from the furnace ducts. "Leroy! Where are you, Son?"

Leroy grabbed the wooden banister. Something else was down here with him—a malignant spirit hungry for unaccompanied children. The boy ran up the staircase, two steps at a time. *Please, God, let me wake up before it eats me.* He strained to force his eyes open. *Wake up, wake up, wake up, wake up. . . .*

Roy sat perpendicular in bed, his bare back sticking to the warped headboard. He couldn't quite remember the nightmare, but it had left a bad taste in his mouth. *Sirens.* The flip clock on the nightstand informed him of the time: 6:02 a.m. Blue and red lights colored the slats in the blinds. Davis suited up and raced his SUV down the road to the next house. A police car, fire truck, and ambulance blocked the driveway. Paramedics loaded someone into the meat wagon.

A man in a light green top and dark green pants gave a sloppy salute. "Nothing like working on the day after Thanksgiving, huh, Sheriff?"

Roy had already forgotten the holiday. "What's going on? I live out yonder." The paramedic stood aside so he could see the individual on the gurney—Mrs. O'Sullivan. "Will she be all right?"

"If you're asking if your neighbor is no longer feeling any pain, then, yes, she's playing hopscotch with Marilyn Monroe and Elvis Presley." The paramedic flung his medical bag into the vehicle. "Heart attack from the looks of the purple splotches. Her crazy mutt just 'bout ripped my arm off."

Davis walked up to the house. On his hind legs, Pancho stared through the thin mesh of the screen door at his dead master.

The sarcastic paramedic hollered, "Sheriff, need a dog? Fido needs a home, or he's going to the glue factory!"

Roy, murmuring soothing words, slid around the agitated German shepherd into the front hall. Pancho nuzzled his hand, as if in recognition. This was an old lady's house filled with old lady things: faded family pictures, dusty knickknacks, unfinished crochet work. The bedroom reeked of death. A bejeweled leash hung on the mudroom wall. Davis fastened the clip to Pancho's collar and notified the men boarding their emergency vehicles he would bring the dog to the pound.

At the Bisbee Animal Shelter, as Roy surrendered his hold on Pancho's tether, the attendant asked, "What happened to his ear?"

Outside the Anchorage Walmart Supercenter, Rachel Martin pulled the beanie hat over her ears to remain indistinguishable from the other shoppers. She dodged the greeter's false-toothed grin by turning to read a sign advertising "BUSH MAIL SERVICE." The doctor navigated the rat's maze of women's clothing to the less-traveled rear of the store. Near the Auto Care Center and Sports & Leisure, she located the Crafts & Sewing section.

Rachel ignored the scrapbooking materials, paint bottles, and silk flowers, alternatively attracted to a rack stocked with multi-colored thread spools. She trod down the long aisle past fabric by the bolt and bags of polyester fiberfill, coming to a standstill at a large arrangement of scissors. Her metallic blue eyes inventoried the plastic packages hanging on hooks under bright yellow price tags. "Buttons. Soft stretch elastic, iron on patches, Velcro. . . . Bingo! *Sewing pins and needles!*"

Martin took in the multitude of diameters and lengths. "Dear Lord Jesus!" The knitting needles and crocheting hooks stopped her. "Purple, green, blue, gold. . .so exquisite." *You could impale a vampire with one of these spikes,* she thought. *But is a stake what I really want? Shall that be too easy?* The doctor evaluated the tinier needles: sewing machine, basting, yarn darners, and curved. Though these "European-Quality" hooks beguiled her, she dismissed each as being too hard to handle.

Rachel, unable to choose between smaller and larger needles, grabbed an assortment pack. Distinct from the Fine Jewelry or Health & Beauty departments, Crafts & Sewing, owing to its declining baby boomer clientele, drew few kleptomaniacs. Ergo, no security cameras recorded the female shopper slipping the disk of twenty-five household needles into her jacket pocket. About to abscond with her pilfered goods, she reconsidered, and returned to the knitting needles. The doctor snatched a golden spike and whispered to her new ally, "A Girl Scout must always be prepared."

Sheriff Davis put down the lunch menu. He scanned Dot's Diner, a converted Little Chef travel trailer at the Shady Dell vintage trailer court, for people he knew and for people he hadn't seen before. And since next year was an election year, Roy aimed a full set of teeth at anyone willing to make eye contact.

"What are you getting?" his chief deputy inquired. Nora Clarke, ever the comedienne, pinched her chin. "Oh, wait. Let me guess."

Roy met her twisted smile with a laugh. Nora, towering in height at six feet three (mean kids in elementary school had nicknamed her "Bigfoot" and the "Jolly Green Giant"), was not a beauty in the classical sense, yet folks found her bubbly personality very attractive. "I'll give you three guesses."

"Turkey?"

"Nope. Ate turkey and mashed potatoes with apple cranberry for dessert on Thanksgiving." Solo in his mobile home, Roy had nuked a four-hundred-and-ten-calorie Hungry-

Man frozen dinner for eight minutes on high. He had chased down the dry white meat with a twelve-pack of Bud.

"Biscuits and gravy?"

"Hell, no."

"Gee, are you having a patty melt?"

"Brilliant deduction, Shirley Holmes. And curly fries just to switch it up."

Rueful, Nora shook her short blond tresses. "Why oh why do you always order the same thing?"

"My dad used to say," Roy waved for the waitress, "'go with what you know.'"

Diane took their selections—Nora also requested the item she always did, the Cobb salad—and slid the guest check through the kitchen window to the cook.

The sheriff and his chief deputy lunched together regularly, sometimes to discuss ongoing investigations, but mainly to debate humankind's general state of de-evolution. Clarke only called Davis by his first name outside of work.

Nora tilted her ear toward the lunch counter. "Roy, Freddie's here."

Frederick Morales, a corporal in the Sierra Vista Police Department, rested his palm on Justin Drake's shoulder. Drake was one of Davis' newer deputy sheriffs, an information specialist. The rumor mill predicted Freddie would run against Roy next November for Cochise County Sheriff. Justin picked up his takeout from Diane, paid with cash, and departed. Although the sheriff believed in his staff's loyalty, like any human beings, their allegiance could sway with the prevailing winds. He worried that given the rising crime rate, Cochise County's good citizens might vote for change. *Screw the overtime. I'll schedule additional patrols.* "Such a jackass."

"Forget about the election, boss." Nora forked a chicken strip. "Everybody knows Freddie sucks at his job. That d-bag doesn't have a chance to win."

Roy pondered if Nora was being truthful or just kissing the ass that signed her paychecks. From the girth of Morales' biceps, the corporal evidently hit the gym daily, plus he still had a fine head of hair. Davis noticed his own decrepit self in the mirror hanging on the wall and lowered his eyes.

Saturday—November 25, 2017

In his darkened den, Park Jin-ho jabbed the number two button on the laptop keyboard. He examined the lengthy list of available 57-sanctioned vacations. One foray held his consideration—a defenestration in Munich, Germany. At work, a soaring glass skyscraper in downtown Seoul, the attorney habitually wanted to push his irritating coworkers out of an upper-story window and watch them splat on the sidewalk. And in Vancouver, Canada? Death by asphyxiation using a plastic shopping bag. These tempting trips needed to be delayed. For now, the only way Jin-ho could get any sleep would be to put his earlier mission to bed. This undertaking required flying to Bisbee, Arizona, stalking another bicycle rider, and finally, the emphasis on *finally*, turning him or her into fender-ketchup.

Park gargled the Imperial whiskey, swallowed, and groused to the empty glass, "What a waste of *my* money and *my* time."

Regardless of how mathematically impossible it was to jack his performance average back up to one hundred percent, at least he'd be able to drop vehicular homicide in the out-tray and move on.

Jin-ho exited to the main menu and chose "1" to contact his Handler. The Korean, adept in conversing and writing fluently in English (his dad, a diplomat, had brought the family with him to Great Britain), canceled the built-in language translator. He wrote the five words he never expected, or wanted, to type in the secure message field. *Can I redo a vacation?* Park trimmed his fingernails with his dead father's gold nail clipper while he awaited a response.

Six thousand miles away from Seoul, Korea, a cell phone buzzed. The amateur mechanic placed the oil filter wrench on the concrete floor and used both hands to scoot the creeper from underneath the V-8 engine. She stood and wiped her greasy fingers on a shop rag.

In the course of the previous dozen years, the tall female covered in pinstriped overalls had adopted numerous monikers. Ernaline, Dabria, Lorelei, and Tanda were but a few. This morning, in the privacy of her two-car garage, the woman identified herself by her "birth" name: Olivia Stewart. Olivia lived alone with Kasha, her Siamese cat, in the pocket-sized mountain community of Creede, Colorado. She stayed to herself. The next-door neighbors seldom saw or heard her come or go.

At the plywood workbench, Stewart unlocked the Google Pixel phone reserved for messaging with Park Jin-ho. She started the instant messaging service and read the encrypted proposal. *Can I redo a vacation?*

Olivia peered down at the purring feline. "Kasha, the Korean wants to return to Bisbee. Is that a smart move?"

The one-eyed stray transplanted cinnamon-colored fur to her pant leg and meowed.

She nudged the cat with her toe. "Yes, you and I both agree this boob will get us both euthanized if we don't mind our Ps and Qs. I better run this up the chain."

After Olivia retrieved the invoice number for her client's last trip, she took out a Blackberry device, tapped her manager's code name, and thumb-typed this message: *Redo 8765B?*

While Park Jin-ho's personal Handler, Ernaline (Old Norse for capable, serious, or battle to the death), stood by for a reply, she blew a speck of dust off the candy apple red 1969 Boss 429 Mustang's polished hood. Stewart rarely drove this muscle car for fear of being pulled over by the police. The Blackberry beeped. Her supervisor's terse communication said: *Approved.*

Olivia sat on the flaking fender of her current commuter automobile, a gray 1999 Toyota Camry. Irked, she palmed the Pixel and texted Jin-ho: *Affirmative. Good luck and good hunting.*

The refreshed 57 website listed a special vacation for Park Jin-ho: Bisbee, AZ/Vehicle Manslaughter – Bicycle. He switched off his computer and unhooked the ethernet cable from the wall. In spite of Jin-ho's disgust at his own inadequacies, this second chance to complete the kill improved his outlook. The lawyer left the den and found his spouse napping in the family room.

The husband, suppressing his revulsion, shook his wife's shoulder. "Sun-young, Sun-young!" When she moaned, yet did not awaken, he jounced her harder.

Sun-young's eyelids parted in alarm. "What's the matter?" She sat up on the couch. "Where is Yu-jin?"

"Our daughter is fine." Jin-ho swished his hands in the way he had learned to pacify her. "My boss phoned. I must leave on one more business trip."

"How soon?"

"Two days."

Sun-young pouted. "Jin-ho, you just got back home. You hardly spend any time with me or the little one."

"My dear butterfly, I'll be back before you know I'm gone. Then, we'll take Yu-jin to Lotte World. She had such fun at Magic Island."

Apart from his sobbing wife, Park drank another tall glass of twelve-year-old whiskey and gazed out of the window. Far below on the city streets, a cyclist weaving between slow-moving cars and trucks caught his eye. He leaned closer to the window pressing his warm forehead against the cool glass.

Chapter Five

Sunday—November 26, 2017

AT THE DINING ROOM TABLE, Tom Hayden explored the 57 website. He scrolled through the vacation catalog having no inkling there were so many ways to end a human life.

The headings listed these topics in alphabetical order: Arson, Asphyxiation, Blunt Objects, Electrocution, Explosives, Firearms, Knives or Cutting Instruments, Narcotics, Personal Weapons, Poison, Transfixion, Suicide, and Other Weapons. Tom, surprised to see Suicide indexed, wondered how anyone ever became a Platinum member if he or she were dead.

Blunt Objects and Knives or Cutting Instruments had the most subheadings. Blunt Objects classified: Ball-Peen Hammer, Baseball Bat, Book, Bowling Ball, Broom Handle, Cane, Chair, Fire Extinguisher, Golf Club, Shoe, Sledgehammer, Toilet Tank Lid, and Umbrella. Knives or Cutting Instruments was composed of: Ax/Hatchet, Car Keys, Chainsaw, Corkscrew, Dessert Spoon, Glass, Guillotine, Knife/Dagger, Letter Opener, Razor Blade, and Samurai Sword.

Hayden found these methods of mayhem appetizing, but he kept looking. Under Personal Weapons, he hit upon a technique termed the Russian Omelet. Google Images brought up (not counting the thousands of egg recipes) crude artwork of a brawler crossing his opponent's legs, pinning his shoulders to the ground, sitting on his upside-down ankles, consequently breaking his adversary's spine.

Below the header Other Weapons were the subheaders: Crucifixion, Defenestration, Drawn and Quartered, Immolation, Microwave Oven, Subway Train, and Vehicular Homicide.

On business, the stock trader had traveled around the world several times. Whereas Moscow, Tokyo, London, and Berlin were populous cities, they held no thrill for him. Rio de Janeiro, Bangkok, and Budapest? Exotic locations, yet. . . . Beneath his hometown, New York City, he saw three vacation titles: Subway Train, Microwave Oven, and Immolation. The first one, Subway Train, was obvious. Local news stations often reported these accidents. The second? *Put someone's head in a microwave? Do you knock them out beforehand? And how do you activate the magnetron with the door open?* Hayden had to research the third selection in an online dictionary. The definition for "immolation" stated: *"to kill a sacrificial victim by fire."*

Tom logged out and squeezed a ribbon of toothpaste onto his electric toothbrush. *That's a lot for me to think about.*

Later that afternoon, at the NY Stock Exchange, while Troy Abington bedeviled him with inane questions referencing the economy's rate of inflation, Hayden viewed his colleague in a fresh light. He envisioned Abington's plump melon splattering the insides of a modified commercial microwave oven. *Fight Club,* Tom thought, remembering the box office hit (he had watched Brad Pitt's compelling speech to the mob multiple times after speaking to the Accountant). *Tanda warned me I can only murder strangers. Sorry, but them's the rules, bub.*

Disappointed, Tom pushed past Troy. "Asian equities are still as cheap as a bag of ramen noodles. Buy!"

Rachel Martin bemoaned choosing Anchorage, Alaska, for this year's vacation. In freezing rain, she hunched on an icy bench at

Centennial Village waiting for the Route 31 bus to cart her to the hotel. Cold and wet, Martin wished she was home baking under the hot sun at Moonlight Beach.

The All-Around City Tour just ended. The bus Rachel had ridden in for the previous three hours had stopped first at Ship Creek to observe a school of doomed salmon swimming upstream. At Wild Alaska Park, as the predominantly "mature" passengers marveled at a twenty-foot-tall chocolate waterfall, she had asked herself, *Isn't this monstrosity a humongous flytrap?* The jaunt concluded—*somebody, please jam a fork in my eye*—at a viewpoint overlooking the city skyline and Mount Denali's glacier-capped summit.

This hunting trip had been unproductive. Nobody on the excursion, leaving out the prattling guide, piqued the doctor's homicidal tendencies.

The petite woman—unable to feel her fingers, toes, and, as the glacial gusts whipped up, nose—had never flown this far north. Although Rachel began life in Hartford, Connecticut (a city whose snowfall totaled fifty inches last season), ten years ago, she had moved to San Diego to start a new job. Southern California's Mediterranean climate had thinned her blood to water. At the University of Hartford, Martin had earned a degree in child psychology and was eager to put the Ph.D. to use. Children's parents, as well as her colleagues, had looked upon the rookie doctor as a miracle worker. As a self-diagnosed psychopath (she understood her shortage of empathy resulted from faulty neurons in her right brain's supramarginal gyrus), Rachel demonstrated the clinical ingenuity to relate with young patients evincing similar traits and thus develop efficient long-term remedies.

At the uncovered bus stop, Dr. Martin reminisced over one of her accomplishments—a Pakistani-American girl accused of torturing dogs and cats.

Little Carol Kashani had denied these allegations.

During Rachel's initial session with the eleven-year-old, she had pushed back her chair and walked to the front of the desk. "So, Carol, what were you doing with the box cutter? That wasn't your blood on the blade or your dress."

The dark-eyed lass, cool as a January icicle, did not blink. Her measured chest movements could con any polygraph machine.

The psychiatrist leaned closer to confide. "Carol, let me share a secret. We've all done bad things. I've done bad things, awful things. Ever use a magnifying glass to burn ants? It's okay if you did. Generations of youngsters have played that delightful game.

"When my brother, James, was born, I became jealous. Suddenly, I no longer commanded every moment of my parents' attention. While my mother watched the *Wheel of Fortune* downstairs, I'd sneak my father's magnifying glass from his desk drawer. The afternoon sun came in at a perfect angle through the nursery's windows. No one in the family suspected me as the cause of the red welts on James' arms and legs. I had tested the procedure by focusing the sunbeam on the skin of my own forearm, quickly learning how to prevent blisters—the first hint of smoke. To this day, James shuns sunlight. As a matter of fact, he's the night manager at a movie theater." This last part wasn't true. Her brother had stepped off a bridge years ago.

"I am asking you one more time. Are you the kid who's been butchering the neighbors' pets?"

Carol twirled her raven ringlets. "You're trying to trick me."

Rachel snagged a dagger letter opener from the pencil cup, snared the child's wrist, yanked up her shirtsleeve, and slashed a two-inch-long incision on her upper arm. Blood beaded on the waxed desktop. "Carol, let me in on what is going on, or, I swear to God, I'll gut you like a rainbow trout."

The patient confessed sundry sins to her doctor that day, including how she had attempted to smother her bestie with a pillow. Her fun had been interrupted when the schoolmate's mother opened the bedroom door to deliver glasses of milk and a plate of chocolate chip cookies. Carol smiled coyly at Rachel, and said, "I wanted to find out what would happen."

"Happen? You'd get caught." Rachel bandaged Carol's bicep with gauze. "A judge will commit you to a psych ward for the remainder of your adult life if you continue parading around acting like a little psychopath. Do you know what that is?"

The child said in a monotone, "I lack the ability to love."

"Some members of society believe extreme egocentricity is a mental disease. I don't." Martin washed off the letter opener with a wet tissue and put it in the cup. "Do clowns frighten you?"

"No." Carol registered the first signs of inquisitiveness. "Clowns are retarded."

"Well, clowns scare the bejesus out of most kids and even many adults. They see the bulbous red nose, the creepy white greasepaint, the freaky Ronald McDonald mop top, and are afraid to discover what lies underneath. That's how you and I appear to others. Vanilla people, the so-called 'normal' people, can detect our psychological anomalies by looking in our eyes and listening to the way we speak.

"You must learn to cope as I did. Each session, I shall train you to outwit everyone you come in contact with: your friends, your classmates, your parents, and of more usefulness, the police. Carol, you need to hide your real feelings behind a mask. Not a Freddy Krueger Halloween mask—the facade of a cheerful, outgoing, well-adjusted child."

Rachel met weekly with Carol Kashani who, with her mentoring, grew into a charming, intelligent sixteen-year-old with the aspiration to apply for a wetwork position in the CIA. Dr. Martin's unparalleled brand of "mental modifications" were amazing success stories.

As the salt-encrusted Route 31 bus glided to a halt, Rachel pulled on her "I'm just as normal as you" mask and turned to the pig-nosed businesswoman seated next to her. "Isn't the weather we're having just wonderful?"

"Chow time," Roy growled. He poured a generous portion out of the bag of kibble into a casserole dish.

Pancho, leery of his new, gruff master, stared from under the coffee table. Earlier in the morning, against his better judgment, Davis wrote out a fifty-five-dollar check to the Bisbee Animal Shelter. After Helen's murder, Roy's father gave away his beloved pug. Since the loss of Happy, he hadn't any desire to own another animal.

Roy slid the improvised dog bowl across the linoleum floor with his boot. "Eat. I made a space for you."

The German shepherd stayed where he was.

"Fine, be that way." The sheriff strode to the second bedroom.

Manila folders from Helen Davis' homicide investigation covered the bed. When Roy handled the oldest file, the elastic band holding the bundle of crimes scene photographs together snapped. A horror show of disturbing images fell like dead leaves upon the green comforter. In the top photo, a bloated corpse floated in a puddle of muddy water. Helen's lips stretched into a rictus sneer. She seemed to be enjoying the climax of a private joke.

Roy shut the folder. "I can't look at these damn things again."

He unclipped the next packet and squinted at the medical examiner's notes. Dr. Robert Jensen had estimated his sister's time of death as the same day she had gone missing. Dylan Cox, the ditchdigger, found her ten days later. The doctor extrapolated from the contours of the injuries that the murderer had used a blunt instrument, in all probability a 5-iron golf club.

Helen Davis' front and rear forensic body diagrams illustrated all eighteen points of impact, the fatal blow being to the back of her head.

Roy went over the suspects' statements. Each read-through elevated his blood pressure. He recalled Bill's strong leanings toward Luke Bell's involvement and his interest in extrajudicial punishment. Wrought up, Davis contemplated having a private chat with Helen's ex-boyfriend, now a trash collector. Coming to his senses, the sheriff dismissed the notion as harebrained. *Christ, I'm running for office.*

Pancho bounded onto the bed. The papers flew high in a dog-made whirlwind and fluttered to the carpet.

"Get down, goddammit!" Roy bellowed at the playful animal.

He crammed the disarray in a dresser drawer and stormed out to visit his mother.

Bill Hill loitered outside the Arbors' front doors. The headlights of a truck with black-and-green graphics pulled into the parking lot. He wrapped his stiff fingers around the walker's padded bar, stamped his numb feet, and called out, "Good evening to you, Sheriff!"

"Buenas noches!" Davis called back. He followed Hill inside the building. "Shouldn't you be watching *The Dating Game* with the other residents?"

"A classic! I still chased skirts when Jimmy Lange hosted that TV show. I've been thinking about your case. Anything new to report?"

"Not really." The sheriff wanted to change the subject, yet he needed to thank Bill for his guidance in locating Daniel Barton's means of conveyance. "We found the bike stashed under a rug in a dumpster behind The Missing Sock."

"That coin-operated laundromat in Tombstone?"

"Yep. Between the Family Dollar and Boothill. Used to be Smokin' Guns Tattoos during the day and a meth lab during the night before the landlord evicted them."

Bill rubbed his thumb and forefinger. "Fingerprints? Blood residue?"

"Someone wiped down the frame and handlebars. They got a partial off the gearshift knob—the victim's thumbprint. No blood on the road bike. The medical examiner says the rider separated from the bicycle on contact—not enough time for any fluids to transfer. The silver streaks on the rented Schwinn's rear fork matched the rented Mazda CX-5's paint job. And vice versa, the red paint on the bike matched the paint stuck on the car."

Hill touched below his eye. "Any video camera footage?"

"We obtained clips of Kim Jin-ho filling out paperwork at the Save Big Rental Company and riding the courtesy shuttle to pick up his car at the remote lot. The credit card and bank account? Same as the driver's license and passport. Our team is sorting it all out."

"Are you able to tag him to a departing flight at LAX?"

"Kim wore a Los Angeles Angels cap at the rental company and on the shuttle. The day after the bicyclist was hit, our team spotted a comparably built man wearing an Angels baseball cap going through TSA. He boarded a 5:30 a.m. Korean Air flight to Seoul. We're fairly confident of the match."

"Were cameras installed inside the jet's cabin?"

The sheriff frowned. "Except for one by the cockpit door, no in-cabin video. Incheon International Airport has a camera angled to view passengers deplaning at the gate. Unusable—spiderweb gunk on the lens. ICN airport security offered us access to their entire system, but a thousand cameras are spread across thirty-seven hundred acres. Multiply that times twenty-four hours. That's enough eyestrain to drive Saint Monica bonkers."

"Did you pinpoint where Kim stayed?"

"We contacted every hotel in Bisbee, Douglas, and Sierra Vista. Nothing. Today, we're checking the bed and breakfasts."

"They're currently known as Airbnbs." Bill held up his cell phone. "I downloaded their app."

Roy scowled. "Now, you can get a flippin' app for everything."

Monday—November 27, 2017

From her office, Chief Deputy Clarke (unaware her boss was a mere one hundred feet away) dialed his cell. "Sheriff, do you prefer the good news or the bad news first? Or should I say, the 'weird news'?"

Two stores down from where Nora held the landline receiver to her earlobe, Roy stood in line at Old Bisbee Roasters. He prayed the coffee's magical healing powers would reduce his nicotine withdrawal symptoms: hand tremors and growing irritability. "Good. Gimme something good."

"The ME plucked an arm hair from between Daniel Barton's front teeth. Dr. Jensen also swabbed foreign blood cells out of the victim's mouth. Guess our bicycle rider got in one nice bite before somebody sent him up the golden stairway."

Davis thought back to last Tuesday, trying to picture any open gashes. *The Mazda's driver wore a long sleeve western shirt.* "And the bad news? What's weird?"

"The doc says limb hair is not as easy to analyze as head or pubic, but—here's the wacky part—it's not Asian. It's *European.*"

"As in Caucasian?"

"A white male. The evidence suggests your motorist isn't the perp, or—"

Flustered, Roy interrupted. "Kim hit the bicyclist. That's a fact. The paint on his rental matches the sample from the bike. The footprints by the deceased were obscured with booties or another type of covering. He had assistance."

"After the accident, a different individual must have murdered Daniel Barton and transported Kim Jin-ho to the airport."

Outside the coffee shop, the sheriff circled the flaccid Arizona state flag. Insomuch as the steaming java helped with his emotional state, the psychoactive drug exacerbated his trembling fingers. "This is some nonsensical shit. Who the hell is Daniel Barton and who in the hell wanted him dead? Vehicular homicide doesn't match the cartel's usual mode of operation. Those fiends like to make big statements."

"Yeah, hanging informers from highway bridges or burying them alive is their trademark. I read up on the South Korean mafia. The Kkangpae, not sure if that's the correct pronunciation, are unorganized street gangs who immigrated to the States. A few members are affiliated with Japan's powerful Yakuza. Barton's teeth evulsed the killer's hair shaft at the root. Jensen can use the pulp's nuclear DNA to search for a match in the FBI and Interpol databases."

"Dig up Daniel Barton's past." Roy watched a coyote running across the highway narrowly evade getting hit. "His sister, I forget her name, is supposed to identify the body this afternoon."

"Beth. She's flying in to Tucson."

"Right, Beth from Ohio. Ask her what our boy was hiding."

Tom finished reviewing the vacation options on the 57 portal. He weighed the three choices under New York City. The share trader discarded Microwave Oven (too many variables), yet he had trouble deciding between Immolation and Subway Train.

Hayden told himself, "Burning someone alive might be a little excessive for a novice to begin with." He placed an "X" in the "Subway Train" box. The cursor lingered above the "Select Dates" button. "This is insane. There's no way I'm ready to push an unsuspecting stooge onto the third rail."

During periods in his lifetime, Tom entertained thoughts of murder. Only once had he acted upon these primal urges. In the fifth grade, the boy had received an F on his essay titled "American Democracy Versus Chinese Communism: Why Diplomacy is for Pussies." The ten-year-old had asked his social studies teacher why he earned a failing grade. Mr. Simmons, daunted by his student's queer disposition and radical political views, had hemmed and hawed before blurting, "Son, you just can't blow up the whole planet!"

After school, as his parents quibbled over financial issues, Tom rummaged through the cans and bottles on the garage shelves, specifically looking for items featuring a skull and crossbones symbol. On his tippy-toes to reach the upper boards, the lad's lips moved reading the red warnings on the weed killer and pesticide jugs. Behind the apothecary bottle of sulfuric acid, Tom lifted a jar labeled in his father's angular handwriting as "Liquid Mercury." The silvery-white element exhibited more cohesion than adhesion as the glob rolled inside the container.

The previous week, a substitute teacher made the science class watch a black-and-white film entitled *Minamata: The Victims and Their World*. For forty years, the inhabitants of the Japanese town Minamata had absorbed dangerous amounts of mercury from netting and ingesting fish swimming near the Chisso fertilizer factory's discharge pipes. Adults suffered nervous system damage. The children were born with hideous deformities.

Tom had poured an ounce of mercury into one of his mother's empty pill vials, wrapped it in a napkin, and hid it in his Marvel X-Men lunchbox. Providentially for Mr. Simmons (and the amateur poisoner), when the pupil doused his instructor's ham and swiss sandwich with the heavy metal, the silver balls had trundled off the slimy cheese and disappeared beneath his desk.

"Fuck it!" Hayden cried, slapping his palm on the glass table. "They already took my two million dollars. I might as well get my money's worth!" He clicked "Select Dates" and reserved the next available week: December 1st through December 7th. Decision made, Tom tapped the red "Submit Order" button and confirmed the "Acknowledgement" screen without bothering to read the fine print.

Satisfaction tugged the corners of the stock trader's mouth into a rare, if horrid, grin. He visualized the murky subway tunnel, the side platform packed with milling commuters, and then, the explosive shoulder shove. Mr. Simmons, airborne and illuminated by the glaring lights of an oncoming train, would land with a bone-shattering thud on the steel railway tracks. Tom (the fifth-grade version) convulsed in laughter as the desperate man floundered in heaps of human debris and puddles of rat piss. The schoolteacher pleaded for his student to help him get up, only to receive a set of crushed knuckles. *That ignoramus said my essay completely missed the point.* Hayden's daydream ended with Simmons' head flattened to a pancake.

Chapter Six

Tuesday—November 28, 2017

Rachel Martin lived heterogeneous lives on this vacation. Each morning, she checked in to two different hotels in separate sections of Anchorage, one as a woman and the other as a man. The sex of the Pawn, or locality, would determine which lodging she used.

Rachel's female disguises were simple fabrications: a few colored wigs, fashionable eyeglasses, and various shades of makeup. The process of transforming into a male was more complicated, yet easier than she thought in this age of gender neutrality—although lowering her inflection to a masculine timbre could be rough on her vocal cords. In advance of leaving for Alaska, Rachel had trimmed her long, brunette locks into a short, pixie haircut. A dark trench coat hung above pleated pants and shined wingtips. Coke bottle glasses and a beanie hat (regulation headgear at this northern latitude) completed the bland ensemble. None of the harried hotel clerks openly questioned the sexuality of the effeminate lad checking in.

Tonight, the woman squeezed into her sexiest outfit, a red dress.

A polite roughneck fitted out in a yellow hard hat and an orange thermal suit held the door wide for Rachel. The Lost Nickel Saloon smelled of stale beer combined with an underlying tang of man musk. Dozens of flickering televisions tuned to ESPN brightened the drab tavern. She pushed her way through a huddle of flabby men debating the physical prowess of their esteemed sports heroes. The doctor took a stool at the midpoint of the long bar constructed from reclaimed wood.

A voluptuous vixen encased in a leather halter and torn hot pants placed her arm on the counter. "What can I get ya, darlin'?"

Rachel eyed the unfamiliar emblems on the colorful tap handles. "What draft beers do you recommend?"

The young bartender grinned. "You cannot go wrong with Fallen Angel. Midnight Sun's Belgian-style ale is so sinfully delicious," she tilted her chin at a customer wearing a clerical collar, "management retains a man of the cloth on hand for instant absolutions." The barkeep slid a pilsner glass overflowing with hazy suds across the countertop.

Martin sipped the fruity hops while she scoped the jammed room. At a round table in the corner, a ring of boisterous women traded anecdotes concerning their mischievous children. *Mommies' night out,* she thought. The down in the mouth priest motioned for the bar temptress to pour another boilermaker. *Father, you'd crap your cassock if you took my confession.* A stocky, dark-skinned male stood by the jukebox pretend talking to a taller, redheaded female. During the week, Rachel had seen both 57 backup team members trailing her at a respectable distance. *Stay sharp guys! This is my last evening in Anchorage. Tomorrow morning, I pack my bags and fly back to San Diego. Be ready for what comes next!* On the stools to her left, bearded lumberjacks bellyached about their wives' exorbitant expenditures.

The barmaid rested her amble breasts upon the bar. "Primed for a fresh Fallen Angel, darlin'?"

Martin realized her glass had emptied. "Why not?" She noticed the string of three Chinese characters running down the girl's forearm. "Your ink is lovely." Rachel stroked the final black symbol positioned to hide the jagged lump of pink scar tissue. The doctor pictured blood jetting from the slit radial arteries—an out-of-control lawn sprinkler. "What's this one mean?"

"Hope. The other two are love and fai—"

"Excuse me," a deep voice said. "Is this seat taken?"

Rachel swiveled to regard a clean-cut man in a business suit. The male chauvinists had left an opening.

"No, go for it. They say this is a free country."

"I see you have a drink. Are you hungry?"

"Food might interfere with my poor man's buzz."

The thirtyish-year-old chuckled and stuck out his hand. "Hi, my name is Paul."

Martin kept a mental list of aliases, each reserved for the appropriate circumstance. "I'm Madeline." She squeezed his fingers. Paul's baby-smooth palm and manicured fingernails implied he worked indoors as a desk jockey. A white line encircling his left ring finger signified this evening's status as temporarily unmarried.

Her mark moved closer. "That's not a spray tan. You must live in the lower 48."

She tossed her head, allowing silken blond hair to cascade onto her bare shoulder and down the back of her strapless dress. "Florida. Tampa Bay, to be specific."

Paul shouted, "Go Buccaneers!" and punched the air with his fist.

Rachel put on a long face. "Don't make fun. Our quarterback is having a lousy year."

"And why are you up here in the Land of the Midnight Sun?"

"When I'm not touring the local watering holes," she made the correlation between her brand of beer and Alaska's nickname, "I'm attending the National Principal's Conference."

"As in, you're a school principal?"

"Middle school. I'll be the keynote speaker." Martin pulled a short stack of cue cards from her jacket and fanned them with her thumb. "Student Morality in the Age of Hypocrisy will be tomorrow's spellbinding topic of discussion."

"Wow, teaching is really—"

"Boring," Rachel said, truncating Paul's feigned acclamation. She patted the packet of assorted needles in her jacket pocket and smiled.

"I'm chief loan officer at—"

Out of time, Rachel subdued Paul's flapping lips with a hard press of her forefinger. "Hush now. It's getting late. How about we go to my room, and I'll show you my teaching credentials?"

Park Jin-ho affixed "I (heart-shaped American flag) Arizona" and "Guns Don't Kill People – Stupid Liberal Gun Laws Kill People" stickers to the black Ford Expedition's front and back bumpers. On this visit to the United States, the Korean national wanted to more effectively blend in with the locals. He shifted the full-size SUV into drive, drove from the Rent This Car garage, and exited Las Vegas McCarran International Airport. The traveler, reluctant to enter his destination into the navigation system, opted for written directions. Jin-ho followed road signs to the 593. The dashboard clock displayed: 3:52. *I'll be in Bisbee by midnight.* Park popped two NoDoz into his mouth, washed the caffeine tablets down with hot Starbucks, and settled in for the long journey south. *Redemption time.*

Paul stepped over a frozen puddle. "Madeline, is it much farther? These are my new Brooks Brothers. I forgot my galoshes."

Rachel walked down an ill-lighted sidewalk without looking back. "Just another block or so."

He tripped on a milk crate packed with rubbish. "Are you sure this is the right way?"

The tiger led her prey deeper into the forest. "It's around the corner."

Plan A, terminating Paul in a secluded alleyway, did not appear to be panning out. They were only steps from the hotel room—this public place being Plan B. Martin, apprehensive that no Plan C existed, tightened her grip on the sewing needle. On the fringes of a streetlamp's halogen gleam, she took his hand. "I cannot wait to be with you," Rachel breathed, stretching up to plant a hot kiss on his cold lips. With her left arm wrapped around his neck, her right hand, the one clenching the size four embroidery needle, crept to the thick vein pulsing on his throat.

Martin sensed the backup unit's presence—a footstep here, a shadow there—unable to distinguish if the male or female followed, or both. Rachel, expecting this encounter to get sticky, had hidden a garbage bag packed with latex gloves, a jug of water, a roll of paper towels, fresh clothes, and footwear in a dumpster. For weeks in her hometown, the doctor had practiced her perforating skills on a honeydew melon. If Paul still stood with a ruptured carotid artery—his neck a living pin cushion—the red matador would perform the final act using the knitting needle. *The estocada.*

Paul had his tongue past Rachel's tonsils when she heard the Star Wars theme song.

He broke her embrace and reached into his trousers. "Shit," he grumbled, staring at the glowing cell phone.

She clutched his forearm. "What is it?"

Paul disengaged her fingers and backpedaled. "I better answer this."

"Can't you ignore it?"

He flipped up a palm for quiet. Paul whispered into the minuscule microphone, "Hey, baby." A pause. "I'm okay, how are the kids?" Martin's trophy animal paced in a figure eight with the phone pressed to his ear. "Not much. You?" An even longer interval of leaden silence. "The financial meetings? Yes, the breakout sessions were interesting. Grueling day...tired. That's right, ordered room service. Watching TV, nothing on." This awkward conversation continued for sixty more seconds, ending with, "Uh-huh, uh-huh. Heather, I'll ring you before I turn in. Yes...you too."

Rachel spread her arms. "Forget her. This night is for us."

"Gotta go." Paul waved his cell phone. "Can I call you tomorrow at seven o'clock?"

"No, I won't be around. I'm here now. If you leave, you'll miss out on a good thing."

Her quarry—his overpriced dress shoes ruined—hurried off in the opposite direction.

Dr. Martin moaned with ecstasy as the educated tongue roving her sweet spot spelled out the word "O-R-G-A-S-M" once, twice, three times. After Paul bailed on her, she had returned to the Lost Nickel and commandeered the same stool at the bar.

Rachel had responded to the barmaid's uplifted eyebrows with, "My coworker is such a lightweight. He went to his room to rest. Now that I think it over, the perv is probably surfing the adult channels for amateur college girls."

The bartender laughed. "Very funny. I get off in ten minutes. Want to hang out?"

"That'll be fun. What's your name?"

"Megan. I go by Meg."

"Hi, Meg. You can just call me Audrey. No nickname. Audrey is adorable all by itself!" Rachel giggled to indicate she wasn't serious. "While I wait for you, may I buy another Fallen Angel?"

Meg dried a beer glass. "Tonight, the drinks are on the house, Adorable Audrey!"

Not much later, on a bed at the Falling Water Inn, Meg raised her mouth from Rachel's loins to ask, "Audrey, do you like—"

Rachel clinched the bartender by the scruff of the neck and dragged her wet face onto her stomach.

"Ow, you're being too—"

The sewing needle pricking Meg's throbbing jugular vein seemed exceedingly large in Rachel's fingers.

"Ouch! You're hurting me!"

Rachel clung to Meg as blood flooded upon her contracting abdomen. Her right hand, a muscle-powered tattoo machine, traced a red zigzag down the girl's throat.

"Let me go!" Meg screamed, elbowing Rachel in the kidney. The barkeep spiraled off the bed, hitting the floor with a wrist-breaking snap. She scrambled for the exit on three limbs.

"Not so fast, sweet cheeks," Martin panted, crawling over the sopping sheets to the foot of the bed. Her left side ached fiercely, but the zealous huntress had spent many hours at the gym exercising on every endurance and weight apparatus. *She will never touch that doorknob.*

The naked athlete, her thighs coiled springs, leapt off the mattress, sailed across the expanse of carpeting, and landed hard on the girl's shoulders. Air expelled from Meg's lungs as her jaw smacked the floor.

"Momma's little helper," Rachel grunted, skewering her victim's larynx with the knitting needle she'd kept in reserve. The deflating artery spouted high-pressure freshets of blood onto the TV cabinet. She retracted the golden spike and forced the tip into an untapped vein. Crankcase drained of vital liquids, the beating engine fibrillated and, with a shudder, conked out.

The doctor, wheezing noisily, slid off the barmaid's lubricated skin and flopped upon her back. Coated in gore, Rachel slipped her fingers between her legs. Fifteen minutes later, the killer dozed off.

Chapter Seven

Wednesday—November 29, 2017

The vibrant stars shooting across Rachel's retinas evanesced into distant galaxies as her eyelids shot open in consternation. To her immediate left, a stout male dropped the arm he had used to slap her. "She's awake!" He pocketed the electronic device he used to bypass the hotel door's keycard lock.

A rangy female kneeled on her right, red curls escaping from her hood. She implored Rachel to get up. "You must go. *Now!*"

Even though the two individuals wore black ski masks, Martin understood the couple were her backup team.

The short man complained, "I can't believe she fell asleep." He stooped before the prone bartender. "The itty-bitty thing sure created a big mess."

"Shut your yap, Jack," the tall woman cautioned. "The client's right here, for God's sake."

"Sorry, Jill." Jack bowed and mumbled, "No disrespect intended, ma'am."

Jill's orange-speckled irises studied Rachel's pupils for signs of a concussion. "Are you injured? Is any of this blood yours?"

Martin rose to a sitting position. "Not mine." The sanguine fluid running down her chest had partly dried. Its crackled texture triggered memories of the Dead Sea mud treatments she had received at a posh Italian spa. "The bitch punched me in the side. Somewhat sore, but I'll live."

Jill scanned the room. "Your vacation profile states you chose transfixion. Did you use any weapons besides that ginormous nail jammed in her neck?"

With a gloved forefinger, Jack probed the dotted flesh of Megan's throat. "This girl's a sieve. There're hundreds of tiny gushers."

"Needles," Rachel informed. "Small sewing needles." She pointed a red-tipped finger. "Check my jacket pocket. The big one's not a nail. It's a knitting needle."

Jill held high the "Dial-a-Needle" plastic package of sharps. "This them?"

Martin nodded.

Jill, ascertaining not all of the twenty-five needles were accounted for, joggled the circular container. "One is missing."

Rachel's fingertips clawed the sodden carpet. "I. . . ."

"No problem. Jack, search the room while I clean her up."

"Somethin' shiny in her neck," he said. "Can barely see it."

Jill crouched over the corpse. The nub of an embroidery needle protruded a millimeter from the cooling epidermis. "Step aside. My fingernails are longer." She groaned. "I pushed the little stinker in deeper."

"Use a hair," Rachel proposed.

"Great idea." Jill yanked a lengthy strand out of Meg's scalp. "This should do the trick." She threaded the filament through the eye of the needle, and, using both hands to manipulate the ends, freed the steel shaft. "Got ya."

Jack clasped the knob on the knitting needle. "May I?"

Jill steadied Meg's head. "Be my guest."

All the evidence, including the barmaid's cell phone and a small purse, went into a two-gallon Ziploc bag. Jack tucked the transparent parcel in a good-sized carryall. He hauled Rachel to her feet. "Upsy-daisy. Time for your bubble bath."

She deflected his helpful hands. "I can do it."

Jill extracted a pair of disposable gloves and booties from the canvas bag. "Put these on and take a shower. What did you touch? We'll wipe everything down."

"I wore gloves to open the door and turn on the lights. While the bartender used the bathroom, I drew the bedspread, then the blanket. When she came out, I was lying on the sheets. I might have moved the TV remote. Oh, never mind. It's on the night table."

"Jack, strip the bed down to the mattress," Jill directed. "Did you bring anything else to wear?"

Martin unpacked a set of men's clothes from her carry-on luggage. "I also left a bag of supplies in the alley. My original scheme didn't go as I had planned."

"They seldom do," Jill said. "I saw you hide something in the trash. If you don't want it, we'll burn it."

Jack stuffed the soiled bedclothes into the carryall. "We're cutting it close. The early birds will get up soon."

Jill passed Rachel a jug of Clorox and a scrub brush. "Go!"

The doctor tugged the purple gloves onto her fingers, taped the gaps in the booties to her ankles, and shuffled into the bathroom. Beneath a bank of heat lamps, she appraised her crimson physique in the mirror. Rachel had to admit her uncountable repetitions at the gym had paid off.

Jin-ho spun the combination dial to the lockbox and extracted the brass key. He unlocked the door, entered the living area, and flicked on the ceiling light. Just like the previous Airbnb he had checked in to only twelve days ago, this nine-hundred-square-foot Tintown house smelled musty and, to him, foreign. *The Americans cook their unhealthy foods in bacon grease and lather their bloated bodies with perfumed soaps,* he thought. In the bedroom, Park deposited his few possessions in the fiberboard dresser and stripped to his underwear. About to stuff his dirty laundry in a sack, he hesitated. The man cocked his arm and pitched his shirt and slacks into a corner.

In the shoebox living room, Jin-ho settled into the green rocker chair facing the small television set and rested his feet on the royal blue ottoman. The owner had decorated the coral-colored walls with orange and yellow southwestern art purchased at garage sales. Bamboo shelves held flea market Indian pottery and baskets. *Not one thing in this dump matches.* He rubbed his palms on the seat's worn-to-the-foam arms. *Cat scratching posts. You get what you pay for.*

The time on the countertop microwave flashed 00:14 a.m. Sun-young would be in the kitchen preparing supper for Yu-jin. Jin-ho knew his wife awaited his call, yet his mind experienced no provocation to pick up his Google Pixel and command the Assistant to dial her.

Earlier in the evening, Park had stopped to fill up the Ford's tank at a twenty-four-hour gas station in the old movie set town of Mescal, Arizona. Inside the annexed convenience store, he had plucked an eighteen-pack of cheap beer from the bottom shelf of the reach-in cooler and grabbed an armful of snacks out of the impulse display next to the pistol-strapped cashier.

Jin-ho ripped a twenty-five fluid ounce Natty Daddy from the cardboard carton and pulled the aluminum tab. A volcano of white suds erupted out of the red, black, and blue "THE BIG ONE" can. He chuckled as lava flows of pale lager stained the chair's frayed fabric. Still sporting his wide grin, Park sized up the dingy room—a far contrast from the opulent penthouse apartment he occupied in downtown Seoul.

"I could get used to this, Hoppy," the tax lawyer remarked to the ceramic jackrabbit seated on the fireplace mantel. "Here is a place where I may be myself."

Jin-ho cradled the surplus beers in the crook of his arm and padded to the small kitchen. As he opened the refrigerator door, a gray mouse darted across the tiled floor. The man exhibited catlike reflexes as his bare foot stomped the life out of the gravid rodent.

Nora leaned her shoulder on the doorframe to Roy's office. "Got a minute, boss?"

The sheriff glanced up from the financial spreadsheet. He threw his pen on the desk and beckoned. "Come on in and join my pity party. Reading these operational budget reports is worse than shoveling hippopotamus doo-doo in a monsoon."

The chief deputy sat on the hundred-year-old Spanish-style leather bench. To Clarke, Davis, analogous to the scarred furniture she rested upon, looked worn-out and, sad to say, disheartened. She attempted to buck him up. "Doo-doo. Haven't heard that term since my niece graduated preschool. How can I dig you out of this mountain of poo-poo?"

Roy handed her a sheet of paper, then two more. In conclusion, he passed over the entire stack. "Try to make heads or tails of these figures. The negative balances are giving me a cluster headache."

Nora lay the spreadsheets on her lap. "I'll break out my abacus. Want some ibuprofen?"

"Thanks, but I have a pill that works better than those orange placebos." The sheriff wrenched open the stubborn desk drawer (unbeknownst to him, a lead slug from a gunman's 1873 Peacemaker had lodged in the slider) and set a bottle of Excedrin on the desk protector. He shut his eyelids and massaged the bridge of his nose. "Time to see an eye doctor.

Perhaps 20/20 vision will increase my IQ to a number above 70."

"Anything's possible in this era of parallel universes." The chief deputy grew solemn. "Dr. Jensen didn't find DNA matches in any law enforcement database for the hair pulp stuck in Daniel Barton's teeth. At least the record is entered and can be cross-referenced if something else comes up."

"Yep."

"I also talked to Beth Barton. She couldn't believe anybody had it in for Daniel. I confided that we think two men worked in concert. Beth almost fainted. Her brother was the 'flight' not the 'fight' sort of animal. He worked at a mortgage company—his home life just as boring. She described Daniel as self-conscious, shy to the point of being introverted. He played video games, not the first-person shooter kind. Beth said if Daniel bought new bike shorts, he'd wear them indoors for a week before venturing out in public."

"Bicycling is an outdoor physical activity," Roy observed. "Was Barton in any cycling clubs?"

"None that I discovered. He'd go on long rides with his wife every weekend. Sometimes, his sister joined them. Daniel rode solo following the divorce."

The sheriff clicked his pen and aimed the tip in her direction. "What about the missus? Got a name?"

"Julie. Johnson is her maiden name. After a decade on cloud nine, the couple severed the matrimonial umbilical cord last July. Daniel took it hard—fell deep into a vat of blue funk. Beth says he continued to meet with their marriage counselor."

"You interviewed her?"

"The wife? Yes, we spoke. His ex sounded honestly upset. Julie claimed she still maintained affection for Daniel."

"Why did they split?"

"Julie admitted it was all her fault. Same old story. Her boss started texting her at home. The attention made her feel young and desirable. A month later, the flirting evolved into sexting, then a full-blown affair. Daniel caught Julie cheating and flew off the handle." Nora ran a fingertip over her notepad. "He slashed her tires and defecated in her favorite pair of Jimmy Choos."

Roy's jaw dropped. "The husband shat in her shoes?"

"Roger. His wedding band served as the cherry on top."

Davis snickered. "Squat and plop is hardcore revenge. Did Daniel file the divorce papers?"

"No. Julie ponied up for the legal eagle. Thought she was in love. The hanky-panky did not make it to the next payday. The boss man transferred to Ireland with his fiancée. Julie came to the realization she had screwed up, but when Daniel learned she was carrying the other man's child, he refused to even speak to her."

"The wife is pregnant?"

Nora's two fingers shot up. "With twins."

"Mamma Mia! Then, the hapless SOB gets shwacked by a fuckit bucket."

"This job taught me life ain't fair. I don't think Julie Johnson had any involvement with Daniel Barton's death."

The sheriff sighed. "That brings us back to square one. I can see how after a hit-and-run—especially a DUI—the driver might try to conceal evidence. Why would anybody ditch a body at a public park?"

"Maybe he or she was in a hurry. If the Korean in the rented Mazda didn't strangle Daniel Barton, who did, and for what motive?"

"The hairy European acted as an accomplice—a helper." Davis' recollection before stopping to assist the motorist included an image of men parked in a van. *Something was off about those two.* They averted their eyes as he passed by. *What were the words on the side of the vehicle? Pool Maintenance? Painter?* On that morning, hot and bothered, he had been twiddling the air conditioning controls.

The chief deputy frowned. "Are you implying Kim Jin-ho had an assistant? Out for a Sunday drive, he accidentally hits a bicyclist. Maybe, as you suggested, the guy drank too much. Then, our mystery man has his man Friday tidy up the mess by, get this subtle point, *choking Daniel Barton to death?*"

"They may have been following the Korean. I recall a van."

Nora took notice. "'They' as in plural?"

"A pair of suspicious men sat in. . . ." Roy, using a memory association technique he had picked up in the military, suddenly saw a vivid mental image. "A white plumber's van!"

"Well, this hit-and-run investigation has certainly become fascinating!"

The sheriff dry swallowed another painkiller. "Way, way too fascinating for an election year."

At the 110th Street/Lexington Avenue subway station, Tom ate a hotdog. Over the last several days, he had taken a liking, even an obsession, to street food.

Today, forty-eight hours until the official start of his inaugural 57 vacation, the share trader had conducted himself in a manner contrary to his core principles. He called in sick to work. Hayden had spent the morning and afternoon riding the New York City Subway readying himself for his upcoming mission. With eight hundred miles of track and five hundred stations, Tom hardly made a dent in exploring the whole rapid transit rail system.

The 6 express train roaring out of the tunnel mussed up Tom's hair with gusts of ozone. The graffiti-tagged doors slid open, and a stream of passengers thronged to opposite exits. He tailgated a mohawked teenager into the well-crammed car and hung on to a hand strap next to a runny-nosed postal clerk.

The long snake wriggled from side to side down the dark tunnel, diving beneath the Harlem and Bronx Rivers. At Whitlock Avenue, the serpent's metallic head burst out of a black hole and climbed an elevated track into sunshine.

Hayden peered through the scratched windows at the automobiles, trucks, and pedestrians swarming the streets below. At each Bronx station, riders boarded or disembarked. Cast in the theatrical drama playing inside Tom's mind, every new character came to the same lethal ending—a railway worker squeegeeing their guts off the operator's windshield. At the terminus of the IRT Pelham Line, only three other passengers remained: a safety-vested stevedore reading the sports section of a leftover newspaper, a hyper college girl fiddling with a fidget spinner, and a shoeless vagrant alternately babbling, "You can't handle the truth!" and "They're coming to get you, Barbara!"

Tom gazed fixedly at the dockworker, wanting to ask him how the Knicks faired. He couldn't care less if the basketball team made it to the NBA finals or relocated to Timbuktu, but he always needed current sports-themed material to bounce off Henry Ellington.

The burly man glared up from the newsprint and yelled, "What ya lookin' at dickwad?"

"Nothing, sir." Hayden turned to watch the mesmerized girl. *Any of these subjects should make a fine victim,* he thought. Squealing brakes ceased his woolgathering.

At the Pelham Bay Park station, Tom hid his face from security cameras as he walked under the tracks and ascended the stairs to the southbound platform. He stood at the heels of an elderly lady propped up by a four-footed cane. *No one will miss you, Grandma Walton.*

Tom had speculated whether it would be smarter to carry out his murderous deed on an unoccupied or crowded subway platform. On a floor devoid of people, he'd be exposed to video surveillance and passengers staring from approaching trains, as well as commuters making unannounced appearances into the tunnel. A packed station could give him additional cover for a quick getaway.

Hayden leaned close enough to inhale the Woolite fumes wafting from the woman's cable-knit sweater. He imagined how her frail ribcage might feel upon his firm palm's impact. Only when Grandma Walton sent a gummy smile his way did Tom realize both of his hands were upraised.

Bill switched off the groaning Compaq and flexed his wrists. Although the Arbors' resident had saved enough money to buy himself his own ergonomic keyboard or a workhorse computer for his room, he didn't open his wallet. Hill enjoyed the challenges this obsolete hunk of plastic and silicon provided. Moreover, whenever the former detective sat in this public area, he felt productive—not just lying in bed counting the hours until the next dinner bell, or his final breath.

Bill opened a spiral-bound notebook, one of the many he purchased on the facility's weekly "Recreational Outings" to Walgreens. He paged backward and forward, deciphering his cramped writing. Notebooks of every color in the rainbow were piled in Bill's closet, underneath his bed, and below his window. These journals embodied William Hill's paper database: a growing collection of unsolved murders. He had jumped into this daily routine the morning after he retired from the Sheriff's Office. Of late, Arbors' management worried the clutter was a potential fire hazard.

The green book Bill grasped contained his notes, observations, and theories on local violent crimes. A black writing tablet documented his notions pertinent to Helen Davis' horrendous end. The other journals corresponded with United States Census Bureau-designated regions: Northeast, Midwest, South, and West. He even kept binders on international homicides. The latest entry in the green book detailed all the information Hill had accumulated on Daniel Barton's hit-strangle-and-run. The ex-detective underlined the words "multiple assailants are involved in the Barton case" twice and tapped the eraser on his stubbled chin.

"What are you working on today, hon?" Maria Flores reached into the pocket of her bright pink scrub pants and snuck him a Mars Bar.

The nurse showed kindness to Bill and allowed him his personal space. He had become Maria's dearest resident, and she looked forward to their frequent dialogues. Her father likewise resided in a "Leisure Community," a human junkyard not half as nice as the Arbors. She regularly lost sleep agonizing over his well-being.

"Just waitin' on the Rapture, Nurse Flores." Bill slipped the candy bar into his sweatpants. "Thanks for the fifty-one grams of coronary thrombosis. Your Christmas gift is in the mail. You'll be amazed when you open the box."

"Is it a Lamborghini?"

"You guessed! A yellow Countach. How was your day and how's your pa?"

Maria sat on a bench and rested her chestnut-highlighted hair against the floral wallpaper. "My dad is hanging in there. The orthopedist wants to do another MRI."

Bill exhaled. "Broken hips and broken hearts take forever to mend." He always wondered why this good-looker remained unmarried. She reminded him of his wife, Sarah, before misfortune drove a hearse up the steps and through their front door. Hill read the numerals on his digital watch. *Hope Roy Davis comes tonight to visit his mom.* He had something to show the sheriff.

The nurse twisted her shoulder to stretch her spine. Her lower vertebrae ached from moving invalids on and off of beds, wheelchairs, and toilets. "I want to bring Dad in for the test tomorrow morning. The problem is, I'm nervous about requesting the time off. We've been short-staffed since Rebecca got fired and Shawna quit."

Bill understood Maria had no siblings and how, as a child, the United States government deported her mother to Mexico, never to be seen again. Maria and her father, a former Lutheran minister, were born in Arizona. "Becky shouldn'ta 'borrowed' the vials of morphine. Hope they give Shawna a salary bump wherever she winds up. She was a hard worker. Can that man of yours take your dad?"

Her eyes, the color of deep sienna, shut as she snorted. "Peckerhead? You know I punted that degenerate to the curb two years ago."

Bill thought about Roy and thought about Maria and thought about the two of them together. "Have you considered asking Janet Davis' son out on a date? If 'dating' is what the kids still call stepping out." Roy and Maria seemed to be a couple of lonely souls. Bill, knowing both parties, reasoned they might be compatible.

"Your friend, the sheriff?" She laughed louder. "Please tell me you're kidding. He's a mite too long in the tooth for me, don't you think?"

Bill, a wise man, abstained from questioning Maria's age. He estimated the nurse to be in her early forties. Seven or eight winters in difference wasn't unorthodox for relationships nowadays. "Roy's only a few years your senior."

"My God! He lives by himself in a grody, little trailer down in the Bottoms. From the scuttlebutt I've heard at the hair salon, the man drinks like a fish and shags anything with at least one fin."

Hill, remembering conversations with detective squad alumni, had the impression Sheriff Davis squirreled away more acorns for winter than he let on. Bill also accepted the rationalization for Roy's isolation. The minor vices weren't anything Maria couldn't handle. "Nothin' a good woman can't fix."

"Look around you! I spend all day tending to *other* people's demands. Nothing personal, Bill, but when I go home at night, I need someone to pamper *me*."

Bill plinked away at the small chink in Maria's armor. "I've seen you and Roy chitchatting. Are you saying you're not interested?"

"We're reviewing his mother's medications, not the birds and the bees. And anyway, a real gentleman asks the lady."

"What if the sheriff takes your father to the doctor tomorrow? Then, as a kind of 'thank you,' will you invite him out to eat?"

"He'd do that for me?"

The matchmaker had no clue. "Sure, Maria. Roy's a swell guy."

"Fine." The nurse shook her head in doubt. "If your friend even touches a beer or looks at another woman, you'll never see another Mars Bar—not ever!"

Chapter Eight

Wednesday—November 29, 2017

As twilight dimmed to dusk, the greenish glow from the Expedition's dashboard lights extended up Jin-ho's neck to his chin and across his flushed cheeks. His amber eyes jerked left and right, scanning the street for bicycle riders.

Fifteen minutes ago at sunset, Park had departed the rental property bringing with him six cans of Natty Daddy and a family-size bag of Lay's. He slid a beer into the central console and threw the potato chips on the passenger seat. The Korean popped the can's top and tilted his head to slurp the malt liquor. The driver, savoring the effects of the supercharged alcohol coursing throughout his pickled ventral striatum and prefrontal cortex, swigged more chilly goodness.

Bottled up in the cottage, Jin-ho had frittered away the day consuming brewskis and daytime talk shows. He had mused over the steps needed to accomplish his 57 mission. Park, not wanting recognition, planned to hunt at night, knowing full well the number of bicyclists would diminish to a few migrant workers or tree huggers after sundown. Much of this time, he dwelled on his lot in life. *I no longer want to be an attorney. I feel nothing for my wife and child. I've got no ambition whatsoever to return to Korea. Am I too young to have a midlife crisis? Can psychopaths even get midlife crises?* When the unshaven, unwashed man clambered inside the Ford and cranked the 3.5-liter engine, he was already tipsy.

During breakfast, Jin-ho had texted his insignificant other: *arrived too busy to call.* Sun-young replied with a selfie of herself and Yu-jin sitting at the piano. His spouse of eight years wore a strained smile. *Is my wife happy, or is she displeased at my absence?* His daughter's blank face conveyed. . .what? *Emptiness?* Yu-jin rarely expressed her sentiments, and if she did, did he give credence to their authenticity? Sometimes, the father questioned if he had passed his psychosis on to his descendant.

Park became cognizant of his mental differences from other children in a middle school biology class. For the final project, he and his lab partner, Haneul, had to dissect a bullfrog.

Haneul was holding the tip of a scalpel to the lifeless amphibian's abdominal region when his pallor blanched to the pigmentation of whalebone. He clung to the lip of the granite table, and whispered, "Jin-ho, I'm feeling ill."

"Why is that?" Jin-ho had anticipated working on this assignment and didn't want Haneul's health problems to delay the necropsy.

His lab partner had dreaded this day and wished he had stayed home sick. "This frog is disgusting. It stinks. I can't do it."

The pungent, earthy odor intoxicated Jin-ho. "That's the formaldehyde." He desired to understand the root cause of Haneul's repulsion. "Are you scared of a dead frog? Mr. Froggy won't hop up and bite you on the nose."

Haneul's eyes and nostrils leaked water. "You're not grossed out? I'll have nightmares for a month." He squealed in horror when Jin-ho wiggled the dripping bullfrog in his face. "Get away from me, you psycho!"

"Give me the knife!" Jin-ho commanded. He snatched the blade out of his lab partner's quivering hand and divided Mr. Froggy into a hundred ragged segments.

Mr. Kwang scolded over Jin-ho's shoulder, "Why aren't you boys following the lab instructions?" The biology teacher took in the macabre study of anatomy. His facial muscles contorted from exasperation, to shock, and lastly, anger.

Haneul flaunted his clean palms. "I had nothing to do with it! Jin-ho is the psycho!"

Jin-ho talked his way out of the principal's office and dashed to the school library. He looked up "psycho" in the Encyclopædia Britannica. The child found a synopsis of an Alfred Hitchcock motion picture released in 1960. A male with major mommy issues slashed a female motel guest to pieces in the bathroom. The caption at the bottom of the black-and-white photograph read: "The shadowy figure from the famous shower scene." *I wonder if Mom will let me watch this film on videotape?*

A write-up on "Antisocial Personality Disorder" painted a portrait of the tween in fine detail. Jin-ho agreed with most of what he learned regarding psychopaths: wears a "mask" of normality that is both charismatic and amiable, confident, successful, the life of the party, has shallow emotional responses, devious, ruthless, and sexually promiscuous. The boy did not comprehend what "promiscuous" meant, but he often fantasized about kidnapping female classmates and binding them in suggestive positions with rope. *I am a confident and a successful human being. Everybody likes me.*

Jin-ho skimmed through the text: self-centered, impulsive, never acknowledges being at fault, lacks a conscience, a pathological liar. *There is nothing the matter with being self-centered or impulsive. That's how I get what I want. And what mistakes do I have to own up to? I am always right.*

The next paragraph declared: "In severe cases, afflicted males or females may loathe authority, resulting in higher rates of juvenile delinquency. Some subjects revel in animal cruelty or setting fires (Jin-ho had constructed a pipe bomb with chemicals filched from the science lab and had an electronic detonator under development). Twenty-five percent of criminals qualify in this category."

The concluding section stated: "Experts estimate psychopaths make up less than one percentage point of any population. These individuals don't care if they harm others, even family. Spiritually, their minds are devoid of guilt or remorse. Persons with this defect fake empathy by using mimicry." He reexamined this line: *"True psychopaths do not react rationally to injuries, deaths, or similar tragic events which cause deep negative reactions in others."* Jin-ho compared Haneul's hysterics to his own elation at viewing Mr. Froggy's ravaged internal organs. *This book is dead-on accurate. I am a psycho!*

A vehicle's headlights grew larger in his rearview mirror. Park lifted his foot off the gas—he'd been doing eighty in a fifty-five-miles-per-hour zone—and steered the SUV between the yellow and white lines. There wasn't much out here on Arizona State Route 90, only piles of rocks, widely spaced stunted trees, leaning telephone poles, and the occasional abandoned building. A long device topped the cab of the truck now filling his entire mirror. The impatient driver flashed his high beams. *The imbecile wants to pass.* Jin-ho kept his eyes on the road ahead, squinting behind to.... *Is that a roof rack or could it be—*

Brilliant blue and red emergency beacons flooded the Expedition's cabin with primary colors. *"Shibal!"* Park cursed, as the law enforcement vehicle's left headlight became visible in his side mirror. Beer saturated the cup holder as the all-weather tires encountered rumble strips. On a two-lane desert highway, fifteen miles from Bisbee and ten miles to his destination of Sierra Vista, Jin-ho's options were finite. *I can outrun him.* The lawyer pressed his toes to the go-pedal. *This American gas guzzler is a muscular beast.* Then, he realized the cop might drive a faster machine than his six-cylinder rental car and that the pursuer was assuredly armed.

Park saw a wide space surrounded by brush. *I have a weapon too—three tons of Detroit rolling steel.* He put on his right blinker. *I'll run the maggot over when he steps out of his truck.* As the Ford Expedition skidded to an uneven stop on the gravel turnout, the black-and-green-striped Sheriff Cochise County Chevy Tahoe blew past in a cloud of orange dust.

Jin-ho pushed open the car door and stumbled to the center of the thoroughfare. He sank to the pavement watching the red taillights vanish around a bend. "That's the same license plate number as the sheriff who offered to get me a tow truck!" Sour beer and barbecued potato chips spewed from his mouth onto the double yellow lines.

The SUV's headlights lit up a roadside adobe shrine built under the shelter of a hearty mesquite tree. Jin-ho placed the unopened Natty Daddies below a row of flickering novena candles. He kneeled before the weatherworn Virgin Mary statue and prayed. "Blessed Mother, I will not touch one more drop of alcohol until I rack up a confirmed win."

"Doofus!" Roy shouted through the windshield at the Ford Expedition. "Took you long enough to let me pass!" He jockeyed the Chevy Tahoe back into the right lane, turned off the emergency lights, and sucked in air. *I'd give my left nut for a Lucky Strike right now.* In a rush to complete his nightly trek to Sierra Vista, Davis pulled into the Arbors, killed the motor, and ran in to sit with his mother.

As Roy drank from a hallway drinking fountain, Bill hollered, "Sheriff, did you hear about that gal up in Alaska?" The retiree clutched a green notebook to his chest.

Davis blotted his lips on his shirtsleeve. "Why? Did a polar bear maul the fair maiden?" Preoccupied at work, he hadn't kept up with the news feeds.

"Anchorage is too far south for nanook." Hill laughed. "Though dollars to doughnuts, the city zoo probably has some on exhibit." He opened his journal and removed a computer printout. "Here, feast your eyes on this tidbit in the *Anchorage Daily News*."

Troopers Seek Killers

> ANCHORAGE, Nov. 29 – Alaska State Troopers are searching for two males and one female who might have participated in the stabbing of a North Star woman. Megan Guthrie, age 27, was found dead this morning by housekeeping staff at the Falling Water Inn on West Tudor Road.

At this hour on the clock, Roy had trouble focusing on crimes beyond his jurisdiction. "So?"

Bill, impatient, wagged his index finger. "Go on."

> The popular bartender at the Lost Nickel Saloon in East Anchorage was discovered by a maid servicing the room. Surveillance video shows Ms. Guthrie entering the building in the company of a blond woman approximately 5 feet 1 inch tall wearing a red dress. Inn staff identified this person of interest as Natalie Bailey, the guest who paid for the stay. There is no recorded evidence of Bailey leaving the premises; however, subsequent images reveal a heavyset, bald male and a taller, red-haired female arriving at 2:07 a.m. The same man and woman,

both in black tracksuits, left forty-five minutes later with a short, dark-haired male in a gray trench coat. The medical examiner has withheld from the public the exact manner of death. Alaska State Troopers ask for any information on this matter.

Bill fed Roy another piece of paper. "I enlarged screenshots of the suspects."

The sheriff pored over the grainy color photos of the three individuals exiting the hotel. He found the small, spectacled brunette walking between the short, bag-carrying man and the tall woman particularly curious. *Natalie Bailey?* Davis read the news item twice. "You think this incident is connected to—?"

The ex-detective raised an eyebrow.

"Anchorage is four thousand miles from here. What did the well-liked barkeep and our loner bicyclist have in common?"

Hill sat his scrawny keister on a stool. "It's strange that after the Korean fella winged Daniel Barton with his rental car, a pair of gentlemen emerged out of thin air to finish him off. Megan Guthrie's killer, Natalie Bailey—obviously disguised as a man to avoid arrest—also benefitted from outside help."

Roy pondered how Bill learned about the "pair of gentlemen emerging out of thin air" or how Barton had been "finished off." The sheriff did not remember telling the former detective the inside scoop. "And you happened upon this article reading *Alaskan* newspapers?"

"I might be physically unfit to compete in a marathon; nonetheless, I try to forestall my mind from molding into a lump of Play-Doh with a daily regimen of cerebral pushups." Bill's face buckled in embarrassment. "I meant no disregard for your mother."

"None taken. I'll contact Anchorage tomorrow." Roy folded the news item into a rectangle and put it in his jacket. "Thanks, Detective."

As Davis headed down the corridor, Hill's raspy farewell echoed off the walls, "Sheriff, I've been delving into similar homicides implicating numerous people after the fact."

Roy bumped into his mom's nurse in the lobby. She buttoned her coat with one arm slung through the handle of a lunch bag. "Putting in some overtime, Maria?" He held the exterior door open.

"I don't mind the extra cash, but my feet sure do. Although these black clogs resemble the clodhoppers my grandma wore to church on Sundays, the thick soles provide good arch support. Even so, at the end of a shift walking these tile floors, I want to either marinate my toes in Epsom salts or saw the damn things off."

Roy inspected her ankles. They posolutely didn't appear swollen to him. On the spur-of-the-moment, he asked, "What are you up to now?"

"Me?" She shrugged. "I'm on my way home to reheat leftover chicken and sip Merlot while watching the Kardashians make us mere mortals look like rocket scientists."

He chuckled. "May I take you out for a bite?"

"Did you talk to Mr. Hill?"

"Bill? Why?"

"You don't need to bring me anywhere. He was just attempting to—"

Roy grinned. "I want to thank you for being so nice to my mother. Dinner is the least I can do to demonstrate my gratitude."

On the Arbors' loading dock, Bill found a box of the correct size. In his room, he filled the carton with the color-coded notebooks arranged in numerical order. The ex-detective sat at his desk and wrote a letter.

Dr. Martin parked the rain-spotted Mercedes-Benz in the four-car garage of her La Jolla home. At a counter in the ultramodern kitchen, she uncorked a bottle of premium Zinfandel and poured the wine into a tapered glass. On a balcony commanding a bird's-eye view of the ocean, Rachel watched the blood-red sun reflect off the turquoise waters. As whales migrated south and pelicans flew north, she thought of ice-cold Anchorage. *I'll never go back to that hellhole.*

By the swimming pool, Martin reclined on a chaise lounge, reminiscing about the barmaid's long tongue. *What was her first name? Regan? No, Megan...wanted me to call her Meg.* She didn't appreciate how the male member of the backup team had slapped her. *Jack will receive one star when I fill out the vacation survey. Jill? Such seductive eyes—definitely five stars.*

Loud buzzing ruined the psychiatrist's reverie. "Crisis Hotline" flashed on the cell phone's screen—another patient threatening suicide. Rachel turned off the device and shut her eyes. "Oy vey, I'm still on holiday!"

Roy catapulted the tactical penlight over the edge. The gyrating cylinder, accepting the inevitable pull of gravity, cast sweeping golden rays along the gouged sides of the Copper Queen Mine's two-hundred-fifty-foot-deep Southwest Shaft. Halfway down the eight-foot-wide hole, the light hit an outcropping of chalcocite. The metal flashlight bouncing between the walls of stone sounded like a spring-launched pinball caught between thumper bumpers. The bulb shattered, but the racket sustained for another five seconds until the torch's journey ended with a resounding splash. In darkness, the sheriff yanked Luke Bell up by his jacket collar and whammed his shoulder blades against a wooden post. He lit a road flare and waved the hot end in the man's doughy face.

In the sputtering red glare, Davis bellowed, "Tell me you did it, and I'll let you live!" He had no idea if a full confession would indeed grant the garbageman permission to leave this horizontal tunnel vertically.

Luke blubbered, "I swear, I never touched her!"

Roy sent a clump of muck aloft with the heel of his boot. Pulverized basaltic lava—single-jacked by hand or blasted with dynamite one hundred years earlier by miners toiling by the glimmer of adamantine candles—rattled downward for an eternity. "The fuck you did!" Once more, the sheriff dragged the sanitation worker to the shaft. "Your filthy paws were all over Helen!"

Beneath the Mule Mountains, fifteen hundred feet into the Queen Tunnel, Davis and Bell hunkered inside an adit formerly utilized to haul oxide ores to the surface by donkey for smelting. Roy had gained entry through the mine's iron gate with keys the Sheriff's Office kept available for emergencies. Copper Queen Mine tour guides hosted thousands of visitors each year, and there was always a chance an adventurer might wander off and get lost.

The fifty-three-year-old garbage truck driver pleaded, "You know I was at home watching *T. J. Hooker* with my mom and dad."

"Piss-poor alibi," the sheriff growled. "Parents don't rat out their kids. The fools mortgaged their house to pay your legal fees. The last person to see my sister alive, the school bus driver, dropped her off near our house. Miriam Raft had an ironclad alibi—the thirty kids still onboard. Not you though. You weren't on that bus!"

"I walked home!"

"Eight miles? Students at Bisbee High saw you fighting with Helen on the day she disappeared."

Even though the temperature hovered at forty-seven degrees Fahrenheit, sweat ran in rivulets down Luke's creased brow. "We did argue. Adult relationships are tough. Teenage relationships are impossible."

Roy, envisaging the unmade bed in his empty double-wide, shared this truth. "What were you guys quarreling about?"

"She wanted to break up with me."

"Huh?" Roy didn't recall reading this assertion in any of the interrogation transcripts. "Why?"

"Helen filled out college applications to out-of-state schools. When I concluded that my high school sweetheart meant to leave me in the dust, I blew up—called her things I couldn't take back. She told me I had no future. Said I was a loser. That's why I walked all the way to my house."

"Helen got that right! Your life has been a waste, and from my perspective, your future is looking pretty bleak."

"I contacted the police the minute I learned your sister went missing. After the detectives brought me in, I told them what I knew, which wasn't much. The cops had zippo. The district attorney let me go."

Davis hooked his fingers under Bell's leather belt to improve his grip. The sheriff hoped his spinal column would withstand the torque of tossing the three-hundred-pound sack of offal over the brink.

How did these two Bisbee High School alumni wind up in this cold and dismal place, a mile closer to hell than to heaven? Only an hour earlier, Roy Davis had dined with Maria Flores. Manicotti for him, lasagna for her, and sparkling water for both (he refrained from ordering a fiasco of Chianti). Roy let Maria do most of the talking. He heard amusing anecdotes depicting the residents and staff at the memory care center.

As the waiter served dessert (a shared plate of cannoli), Maria questioned Roy about himself. He did not want to spoil the scrumptious last course by chronicling his own wretched story, so he gave her a boiled-down version of the official bio posted on the Cochise County website. The sheriff was incapable of determining from the nurse's expression if his job intrigued, bored, or even revolted her. Back at the Arbors' parking lot, Roy watched Maria hurry to her Subaru and speed off. He'd never felt so lonesome.

On the drive home, Davis had an urge to flick on the Tahoe's left turn indicator. Parked across from a shack in Huachuca Terrace, he visualized the candle flames shimmering in Maria's dark eyes.

At nine p.m., Luke Bell stepped onto the front stoop, cracked his knuckles, and itched his buttocks. The overweight man lit a joint and sat down on rickety steps hedged in by one pinyon pine that could use trimming and another pinyon pine that needed the swing of an ax. Roy drained the potent pint of revengicide and kicked open the car door.

Luke distinguished the hulking silhouette crossing the street. "Evening, Sheriff!" he stuttered, stubbing out the roach in a tin can.

Davis skipped the niceties. "Can you show me a medical marijuana ID card?"

Bell shook his shaggy head. "No, sir."

And now, on a night that began with good intentions, the sheriff had a big decision to make. The unmapped subterrestrial levels and miles of closed-off tunnels made the Copper Queen an ideal location to stash a body. Yet from his years in law enforcement, he knew there was no such thing as the perfect murder.

Roy peered into the depths of Luke's terrified eyes. *I want payback, but what if I'm wrong? He could be innocent. Someone may have seen me bring him here.* He held the sizzling fusee closer to his captive's face. "Helen said nothing about dumping you."

"Why would she?"

"It doesn't matter. You just plead guilty to the motive for killing her. My sister wanted to leave you."

Bell felled Davis with a rusty spike puller to the rear of his knee. As the sheriff stood, the garbageman bought him a first-class ticket to the land of Nod.

Roy opened his eyelids, initially only seeing blackness. As his nausea subsided, he saw a haloed light floating in the distance. *Am I dead?* The blood vessel pulsating in his skull synchronized to the rhythm of distant banging. Roy wiped the wetness from his hair and tasted—copper. *I bleed; therefore, I exist. This is the copper mine. Luke Bell is getting away.*

The sheriff grabbed for his handgun. *Shit!* He probed his front pockets for the phone and car keys. *Gone.* Davis felt a flat object in his back pocket and breathed easier. *Bell missed the gate key. He's trapped.*

The cool air drying the perspiration from Roy's temples drew him to the exit and away from the jumble of animal bones littering the lowest point of the Southwest Shaft. His knee struck a square of wood. Davis slid his palm along the railroad tie and touched a length of hot-rolled steel. His forehead thwacked the man-cart, a miniature train that once carried miners, and tourists in more recent times, in and out of the mine.

Roy used the squat engine's safety bar to pull himself upright and climb onto the little platform facing the control panel. He rotated the master switch to reverse and clicked the power lever to the last position. The lantern attached to the furthest car illuminated the curved walls of the carved-out tunnel as the whirring people mover surged rearward.

Until Luke Bell conked him on the coconut and stole his Colt, Roy Davis had leaned toward letting the man go. Now, as far as he was concerned—*there will be no mercy for the merciless.*

At four miles per hour, five minutes elapsed before the orange train neared the tunnel's mouth. Twenty-five yards from the gate, Davis stopped the motor and flipped off the lights. In the dirt on all fours, he whiffed the burnt sulfur from the extinguished road flare. Unable to see his own hands, the lawman distinctly perceived the bullet ricocheting over his head.

"Get away, Sheriff! Don't make me shoot you!"

"Luke, gimme my gun, and we'll call it even!"

"I didn't murder your sister. I loved her!"

Mine tailings crunched underfoot as Roy slinked to the rear of the man-cart.

Luke yelled, "Stay right where you are!"

When Davis hurled a rock in front of the disembodied vocalization, Bell fired two shots into the car's padded benches.

Roy responded to fists pounding on metal. "I'm holding the key—you can't break free. There's no cellular signal this far underground. Throw me my piece, and I'll toss you the key."

A female voice penetrated the solid door. "Sheriff, is that you?"

"Help!" Luke cried. "This maniac wants to kill me!"

Nora Clarke asked, "Who are you?"

"Luke Bell. Roy Davis kidnapped me!"

"Luke Bell from Huachuca Terrace?"

"Who else! Let me out of this deathtrap!"

The chief deputy increased her volume. "Sheriff, are you in there?"

Roy, unsure of his next move, or if he had any moves left, remained mute.

"Luke, I heard gunshots. Is anyone hurt?"

"Nah. I only let off a couple to keep him away. Drunken loon wants to fling me down the mine shaft."

Clarke grimaced. "You have a gun?"

"Not mine."

"You took the sheriff's service weapon?"

"Like I said, he was gonna kill me."

"Luke, where is the sheriff now?"

"He's. . .here someplace. Dark as a spider hole during an eclipse, but I can hear that tarantula crawling around."

"Is this about his sister?"

"It has everything to do with his sister. The whole town thinks I murdered that girl. Wasn't me. I worshipped her. We both need to come to grips with Helen being gone."

"Sheriff Davis!" Nora pressed her ear to the door. "You good?"

Roy winced. "Yeah. What are you doing here?"

"Picked up a 10-62 on the radio. I was nearby the Visitor Center, so I drove by to check on what set off the security alarm. Saw your truck parked at the mine entrance and a Bisbee Sanitation Division cap on the ground. I put two and two together."

"Are you by yourself?"

"I'm alone."

"Did you radio your status to the station?"

"Of course I did. Just the way you trained me."

Roy smiled. "The cavalry shall arrive before long."

Nora rapped on the barrier. "Luke, if I open the door a smidge, will you pass me the gun?"

"What do I get from this? Ten years in the state pen?"

"That's up to Sheriff Davis. You misappropriated a peace officer's firearm. Arizona law considers that felony assault." Nora tried a new tactic. "Sheriff, on this fine evening, did you take Mr. Bell on an exclusive Copper Queen Haunted Mine Tour?"

Roy, anxious to dig himself out of this airless tomb, projected his answer. "Yes, Chief Deputy Clarke. Mr. Bell and I had a terrific time learning how the past is mighty hard to scrape off your boot. We're both bushed and want to go home now."

"Is that true, Luke?" She hitched up her duty belt. "Did you come with the sheriff on your own volition?"

"For real, I can go?"

"You heard the man." Nora tugged on the weighty gate. "Hand me the pistol, Mr. Bell, and I'll give you a ride back to your house. My written report will state a stray cat set off the motion sensor."

Chapter Nine

Thursday—November 30, 2017

Jin-ho, hearing loud noises, woke up with a nasty taste in his mouth. *Nine o'clock.* He got out from under the covers, shambled to the rear window, and parted the curtains. A landscaper pushed a lawnmower around a tree trunk. In front, another worker used a string trimmer to whack the crabgrass bordering the flagstone pathway. Starved, Park searched the small house for the Lay's chips. *The bag is outside in the car.* Jin-ho flopped back into bed and dreamed of his childhood.

Three hours later, the vacationer arose from a restive sleep. In the kitchen, he pieced together paling dream-fragments. *Something about my father torching a blood-soaked mattress in the backyard...a woman's ethereal face. Mother?*

The Airbnb host had failed to clean the refrigerator. Jin-ho smell-tested the takeout pan of spaghetti and meatballs before he microwaved the week-old leftovers on a paper plate. The Korean squandered the remnants of the day on the couch watching American game shows.

Nora grilled Roy. "What in blue blazes were you thinking?"

At Goar Park, the sheriff and the chief deputy opened paper sacks of takeout.

"I wasn't." He squirted a ketchup packet between the griddled slices of rye bread. As the patty melt approached his lips, puréed tomatoes dribbled through the table's metal grid onto his uniform. "Crap! I just had these pants dry-cleaned." Roy looked Nora in the eyes. "Will you hold last night over me?"

Clarke spied a speck in her Cobb salad. She used the tip of a finger to remove the black dot and flick it away. "If Luke Bell presses charges, my neck shall be stretched out on the same rack."

Davis dabbed at the spreading stain with a wad of napkins. "He won't."

"Why are you so positive?"

He threw the napkins down. "Bell fired a gun at me, the sheriff."

"Umm, *your* gun. Hmm. Wonder how that happened?" She shooed a persistent fly. "How's your head?"

"Fine." Roy feared the goop oozing out of his nose was cerebrospinal fluid seeping from a fissure in his cranium.

"You should see a doctor. There's no hard proof Bell killed your sister. He's never even been stopped for speeding."

"Luke said he went berserk when Helen broke up with him."

"Remember the lesson our ethics instructor taught us in last month's training?"

He stared at her blankly. "Carry a second firearm to plant on the scene in case you shoot an unarmed citizen?"

"This isn't *Police Academy*. We learned self-control techniques. Were you really fixin' to drop Bell into that mine shaft?"

Davis, not sure of anything anymore, shrugged. "I agree I have a bunch of work to do in the self-improvement department. Life sans cigarettes makes me crabby. After work, I'll see about buying a nicotine patch."

Clarke scowled. "An understatement and a lame excuse." She lobbed the bowl of browning iceberg lettuce into the litter bin. "You asked if I'll hold something over you. Roy, you've got to get your act together. Quit drinking or else!"

"It's not an issue. After a brutal day on the job, I down a few cold ones to take the edge off."

"You think the staff can't tell? Each morning, you arrive at work reeking like a Budweiser brewery. Barley and hops bleed out of your pores. You're out of control." Nora held up a translucent bag containing two small objects.

Roy's intuition told him the lead mushrooms were slugs from his Colt. "What's that?"

"After driving Luke to his house, I circled back to the Copper Queen and pried these bullets out of the man-cart's seat cushion."

"Are you blackmailing me?"

"No, shithead. I'm helping you."

Davis was taken aback by his subordinate's sudden impertinence. "Doesn't seem so."

"You're boozing days are over. For the next election, our heroic sheriff must be bright-eyed and bushy-tailed. As an additional bonus, you'll lose that paunch and regain the ability to button your uniform." The chief deputy tucked the evidence in her pocket. "Don't you fret. I'll keep these little, bad boys safe."

Parked on a rust-colored bluff above Tintown, Olivia Stewart hung the binoculars from the neck strap and picked up the paper coffee cup. She drank the tepid grinds and chucked the empty container in the Toyota Camry's rear seat. A pile of trash had accumulated during the past three days, beginning with Tuesday's twelve-hour drive from Creede, Colorado, to Bisbee, Arizona.

Yesterday evening, while Olivia followed Park Jin-ho, a sheriff appeared to be pulling him over. The Handler, observing this risky interaction, had nearly terminated her client's vacation. After she saw the inebriate tossing cookies in the middle of the roadway, she photographed his every movement as evidence in the event preventative actions needed to be initiated. For all of today, and hitherto tonight, the Korean hadn't poked his head out of the rental unit. Stewart unplugged the vaporizer from the charger and loaded a fresh cartridge of cannabis oil. *What is Park doing in there?*

57 management held their Handlers to high standards. The organization hadn't endured for one hundred and fifty years without its leaders maintaining tight reins on paid underlings and paying members.

Not built to be a house of cards, the league used a clandestine system of individual cells. Olivia stayed in contact with her direct supervisor, the Curator; the men and women who handled finances, the Accountants; her backup teams, the Sentinels (these two-person units varied depending on availability and locality); and her seventeen affluent clients, the Patrons. Behind the scenes, a decentralized network of IT techs, medical professionals, legal advisors, law enforcement, politicians, and intelligence analysts kept the multifarious machine running smoothly. Personnel used Hive, a suite of encrypted helpdesk chat software, to collaborate.

If outside forces ever infiltrated any cell, every linked associate would be obliged to "drink the hemlock."

The second time Olivia met with her manager had been at a warehouse adjoining the Ohana Funeral Home in Garfield, New Jersey. Only the gray smokestacks protruding from the facility's tin roof hinted at what business went on within. The Curator, a steely-eyed woman who looked as if she'd sooner be sniping coeds from a clock tower, stood beside a long cardboard box resting on a metal conveyor.

Morrigan (her code name) had made her point perfectly clear. "Naturally, we never want to lose a Patron. Our company's mission is to ensure our clientele have an excellent time on each trip, returning home relaxed and thoroughly convinced the yearly membership fee is worth every cent. However, and we leave this up to your own discretion, if you judge a Patron is posing or will pose any peril to 57, you shall act quickly and definitively."

The Curator depressed a green push button on a computerized panel mounted to the closest of the five ultra high-tech cremation chambers. A coal black door raised mechanically. As the pasteboard casket automatically rolled into the fiery retort, hidden speakers played a wordless version of The Smiths *Asleep*. Stewart swore she heard kicks and screams until the iron hatch clanked shut.

Someday, the Handler aspired to be a Curator; yet for now, her job was to keep her Patron from screwing the pooch. And that is why Olivia dismissed the pair of assigned Sentinels to watch over Jin-ho herself.

Saturday—December 2, 2017

At the Georgia Institute of Technology, Alex Hill rubbed his brown eyes and yawned. In the dim, two-person cell of a dorm room at Caldwell Hall, the student set his elbows on the modular desk underneath his bunk bed and propped his chin on his palms. A month into the semester, Alex's roommate, Kevin, was out keg-standing with the other freshmen at a progression of wild and wilder pledge parties on Fraternity Row.

Hill withdrew another spiral-bound notebook from the cardboard carton. Yesterday, for the second time this week, he had discovered a United States Postal Service Priority Mail Express overnight delivery slip in his mailbox. Both Tuesday's and Friday's packages had nonexistent return addresses.

Inside the initial red, white, and blue envelope, a letter in his grandfather's neat longhand asked: "Grandson, how is college? Are you fitting in with all the other geeks and nerds?"

Alex had laughed seeing Grandpa Bill's slang, what jocks and gearheads deemed (prior to Steve Jobs and Bill Gates) as derogatory. The computer science major preferred the up-to-date and more respectful terms of "Techie" or "Guru."

"As you are aware, I haven't spoken to your father since your grandma died. This alienation grieves me to no end. I'm glad you and I stay in touch."

Alex thought about the feud between his dad and granddad. Although he had attempted to fill the rift—this chasm deeper and darker than the Mariana Trench—nothing he said had any effect. His father had made up his mind long ago.

Alex, still an unfertilized egg clinging for dear life to his mother's ovary, had no memories of the day his grandmother injured herself. That sunless, autumn morning, Sarah Hill had been up on the roof cleaning leaves out of clogged gutters and downspouts (a fall chore her husband usually took care of), when her rubber-soled shoes slipped on a patch of wet moss. The fifty-eight-year-old woman plummeted fifteen feet to the herb garden, landing hard on her tailbone. After a period of intense suffering, she crawled across the lawn, up the front steps, and into the living room. Late from an extra shift, William Hill came home to find his wife lying on the sofa in too much pain to sit up. He dialed 911 for an ambulance.

Three days later, Sarah Hill succumbed to her internal injuries on the same threadbare couch.

Sarah and Bill's son, Marvin, believed two things led to his mom's death. First, that his father had allowed his mother to climb onto the roof, and, second, he had brought her home from the hospital before the doctors signed the discharge papers.

There are two sides to every coin, and Alex only heard his parents' ireful version. He yearned to question his grandfather on what had truly occurred, but no time seemed the right time to rip open this festering wound.

Alex read further. "I've got a big favor to ask of you. I know handwritten letters have passed into the annals of history along with coin and stamp collecting, yet I couldn't risk somebody intercepting a clear text communication over the internet. Here's the thing I need you to do. Please hack into the Cochise County Sheriff's Office and find out what you can on Daniel Barton. He was killed in a hit-and-run. Thanks for your assistance! Study hard, stay out of trouble, and don't forget to brush your teeth!"

Alex had entered high school black hat/white hat hacking competitions. His team had placed fourth at the 2017 CyberOlympics. The computer jock hurdled over all barriers breaking through the Cochise County datacenter's eggshell firewall. Six hours later, the grandson notified his granddad that someone other than the driver had strangled the bicyclist.

Yesterday's delivery, twenty pounds of colored notebooks, also included an envelope. The body of this letter held another unconventional request.

"Alex, this box contains the project I've worked on since retiring. Unresolved crimes always captivate me—primarily, cold case murders. Now, being put out to pasture, I have all the time in the world for hobbies! At first, I listed the top-level details of unsolved investigations by geographic location and date. Later on, I got into the weeds, then into the dirt. I looked at the victims, the suspects, the witnesses, and especially the forensic evidence. It was easy to become obsessed with the 'whodunit' and why he or she chose bloodshed as a viable option. Writing everything down was busywork, but at least the days went by swiftly. At this ripe old age, is that a good or a bad thing??? Sometimes, the research was fun. Many times, it saddened me."

Alex, paging through the notebooks, muttered, "What is all this shit?"

"Hopefully, you are still with me and not off playing *Flappy Bird* on your iPhone. You mentioned that working with large amounts of data is your calling. Maybe you'll be able to codify my compilations to make more sense. I numbered each journal in the proper order. In the interest of time, it is prohibitive for me to disclose the secrets you will uncover as you turn every page. I can say this much. My latest endeavor has been to review worldwide homicides using these limited parameters: there were no apparent grounds for anyone to harm the victim, several people were connected (before, during, or after), and in ninety percent of the deaths, the foul play transpired employing 'bizarre' methods. The cyclical timings of the executions were odd and continued over numerous years. Bank heists, commercial robberies, and other organized crime ventures are excluded."

Bill had inked out a line and Alex only made out the inquiry, "Murder for fun – a club?" by holding the thin paper up to his desk lamp.

"In these ostensibly isolated occurrences, it did not take me long to detect frightening patterns. A prepaid phone is in this carton. Use this device to contact me. I may already be compromised."

His grandpa penned his name next to a telephone number and added this postscript: "Be inconspicuous. Tell no one, not even your parents. If something happens to me, Sheriff Leroy Davis is a man you can trust."

Alex adored his Data Analytics and Methodologies class. For extra credit, he tested custom library tools used for abstract data visualization. The student used humane society regional statistics (he hacked into ASPCA servers) to build a United States map graphically illustrating centers of dog breed aggregations. Alex recognized he could use this same interface to work with his grandfather's dataset. The task would go faster if he didn't have to manually enter every scribbled letter and numeral.

Sunday—December 3, 2017

At three a.m. on Sunday morning, what Alex gaped at (while Kevin and his new chums vomited gallons of Miller High Life and homemade sangria into the quad's water fountain) gave him goosebumps. Albeit the world globe filling the laptop screen measured little over nine inches in diameter, anybody with one eyeball and half a brain had the aptitude for interpreting the grim catch of William Hill's decades-long fishing expedition.

Alex jumped at the click of a key turning in the lock, certain he'd see the barrel of a hit man's silenced pistol poking through the door.

"Whassup, roomie?" Kevin snagged his toe on a wrinkle in the shag rug and nose-dived into the red beanbag chair. "You missed out on all the fun. These hotties from Emory. . . ." The political science major, walleyed and slack-jawed, focused on the slowly revolving globe. "What. . .is. . .that? It's—"

"A video game, K-Daddy." Hill shut off the computer. "Did you score us any good weed?"

On Sunday evening, southwest of Tintown, Park Jin-ho threaded the wide Ford through the narrow lanes of Huachuca Terrace on a quest for big game—in this case, a biped moronic enough to ride his or her eighteen-spoker after dark. Although he had finally whipped up enough motivation to tear himself off the couch and get behind the truck's steering wheel, the last two days had been fruitless. Park had driven the ponderous SUV up and down every hill and gully in Bisbee and its satellite communities without finding relief.

Yesterday, Jin-ho came the closest to fulfilling his goal. En route to Vista Park, he had glimpsed a young woman rolling a purple and pink beach cruiser through an opening in the elementary school's fence. The huntsman, hungered by the scent of fresh meat and encouraged that nobody else was present, pressed harder on the gas. The third-grade teacher grasped the bike's tasseled handlebars and set her left foot on the nearest pedal. She pushed the pavement with the sole of her right sneaker and, when the wheels whirled, swung her leg over the padded saddle. With no advanced notice, shrieking students raced across the crosswalk on bicycles, kick scooters, skateboards, or their own feet—swallowing her up. The Expedition's locked tires left black marks on the asphalt. The Korean's clenched hands made deep imprints in the leather-covered steering wheel.

In Huachuca Terrace, Roy parked crosswise from Luke Bell's shanty. He could not differentiate if he wanted to ring the doorbell and offer compensation for his former actions or kick the jambs in and wring the man's throat. Davis was on his way home from the dog park when, as had happened four days earlier, he made another unscheduled side trip.

The sheriff turned, and asked his passenger, "What should we do?"

Pancho licked his chops and resumed drooling onto the seat.

He stroked the dog's surviving ear. "Yup, Panch, you're right. We've had enough excitement for one night."

Roy reached for the flask in the glove compartment, reminded how he had poured its contents into the toilet bowl with the alcohol stocked in his kitchen cupboard. He slid his fingers in his cigarette pocket and dug out a lint ball. "Sheesh."

Davis' mind rotated through a litany of subjects, each more funereal than the previous. *Mom.* His mother had become a shell of her old self. He hardly recalled what she had been like. *Maria.* Whenever he caught sight of her at the Arbors, she was always unavailable to talk. The woman overtly sidestepped him.

A large SUV whizzed by rocking the Chevy's suspension. Whereas civilians universally braked upon seeing a cop, the male driving the black Ford Expedition sped up. This renegade act captured the sheriff's scrutiny.

Park Jin-ho had blown the afternoon drinking—he'd completely forgotten his roadside oath to the Blessed Mother—and didn't spot the idling law enforcement vehicle. For hours, he had driven endless loops around Bisbee's scattered neighborhoods. Ready to drop, Park yenned to claim his kill and return to Korea.

Roy shifted the transmission into gear and followed. *That's weird. His license plate matches the dumbass who blocked me on the way to visit my mother last night.* He lowered the passenger window for Pancho's olfactory enrichment. "Let's see what the doofus is up to, boy." The Ford clipped a post-mounted mailbox turning south on Cochise Lane. "This skunk is drunker than Pepé Le Pew at Club Hedo."

The sheriff, preparing to pull the driver over for a DUI, noticed a gray sedan on his tail. He stuck his hand from the window and signaled the leadfoot to let up. The Toyota Camry backed off. Roy concentrated on the lead vehicle now drifting toward a cement wall. Ahead, a long-haired teenager rode a yellow BMX bike on the sidewalk. The SUV swerved in his direction.

Davis hissed to Pancho, "This knucklehead will hit that kid!" On instinct, he opened the throttle and eased the Tahoe up to the Expedition. As his right front bumper contacted the leading vehicle's left rear fender, Roy steered hard right. Fortuitously, the PIT maneuver worked as calculated—the Ford spun one hundred eighty degrees and halted a car length from the bicyclist. The unscathed teen stopped and took out a cell phone.

Davis exited his Chevy, and bellowed, "Cochise County Sheriff's Office! Sir, shut off the engine and put your hands out the window!" The man stared blankly at the headlights making no movement to comply. As Roy edged closer to the Ford, the Toyota kept pace. *Witless leadfoot wants to get by.*

The sheriff repeated his command without response. A case of beer occupied the passenger seat. *This guy looks awfully familiar. Did I see his face on a wanted poster?* Roy rapped on the glass and ordered the motorist to lower the window. *Something shiny is in his hand!* He placed a palm on his TASER stun gun and yanked the driver's side door handle. When the drunkard sprang from the bucket seat, Pancho clamped onto his forearm. A nine-inch steak knife fell to the blacktop. Davis kicked the stainless steel blade under the Expedition and pinioned his attacker against the back door. Roy, swinging the man around to slap on the handcuffs, realized—*he's the Korean in the broke-down Mazda. This guy is Kim Jin-ho.*

The Expedition's side mirror exploded as a projectile slammed into Park Jin-ho's shoulder. Roy scanned the distant hills and the nearer rooftops. He zeroed in on a shape bent over the Camry's hood. A muzzle flashed three times. One bullet holed the Ford's windshield. Two sheared off the top of Jin-ho's head at the hairline.

Roy, his vision clouded by blood and brains, dragged Pancho behind the liftgate and squeezed the mic button. "Code 999! Urgent! Officer needs help!"

The sheriff returned fire over Park's body, his .45 no match for the shooter's more accurate weapon. He ducked as a barrage of hollow-points turned the Expedition's grill into Swiss cheese. Roy sniffed smoke and saw gas puddling beneath the oil pan. *I've got to get the rifle from my truck.*

Sirens howled in the distance as the man and dog ran across the kill zone.

Chapter Ten

Monday—December 4, 2017

Nora sat on the leather bench in the sheriff's office. "You weren't able to determine the sex of the gunman?"

Roy shook his head. "By the time I grabbed the patrol rifle out of my truck, the Ford Expedition was in flames, and the Toyota Camry was gone. *And*, if *you* recollect from *our* diversity training, to be gender-neutral, the Sheriff's Office now uses the term 'gunperson.'"

"'Assassin' has the word 'ass' in it twice. Is your 'triggerperson' a contract killer?"

"The *ass*assin sure as hell knew how to handle an *ass*ault rifle."

"Oh, you're so witty. Ex-military?"

"Plausibly. The United States Marine Corps were our tickets to these illustrious careers in law enforcement."

"*Semper fidelis!*" Clarke fist bumped Davis and walked to the Cochise County map thumbtacked to the wall. "Do you presume the shooter left town?"

The sheriff joined his chief deputy at the large topographic map. His first finger traced the thicker lines. "Four highways connect Bisbee, each heading north, south, east, and west—all blockaded. Then, we have the unpaved roads crossing the mountains. They'd need four-wheel drive to get through the passes. If it were me, knowing the time it takes for the police to set up roadblocks, I'd haul ass to Sierra Vista, swap cars, then putt-putt up to Tucson. Buh-bye. See ya later, alligator."

"There's that 'ass' word again. What about Mexico?"

"*Sí, claro.* If the person, or persons, had help, they might be anywhere."

"Are they the same people who smothered Daniel Barton and shuttled Kim Jin-ho to LAX? Those men you saw in the plumber's van?"

"My gut tells me someone different drove the Toyota—a female."

"A woman? You said you couldn't identify the perp."

Davis itched the short hairs on his neck. "Dunno. It's only a feeling."

"A female hired gun? Unique even in these days of breaking the glass ceiling. Why didn't La Femme Nikita put a bullet between your eyes, the sole eyewitness?"

He heightened his shoulder blades. "I assume whoever followed Kim Jin-ho had a problem with me taking him into custody. Once Kim's lips were sealed and his Ford in flames, the hatchet man punched the time clock and scrammed. Plus, he *or she* heard Arizona's finest coming to the rescue."

"Hatchet *person*. This sounds more and more like a conspiracy." She frowned. "Wish we'd been faster to the scene. You were nearly killed."

"Then, you'd be a sheriff."

Her mouth hinged open. "That's not funny."

"Nora, have you considered running in the upcoming election?"

"Pah! Who, me?"

Davis gestured vigorously. "Why not?" He toyed with the six-point star pinned to his chest, and mumbled, "I don't have the constitution for dealing with this shit anymore."

"Nonsense. You're just recovering from a near-death experience." Uncomfortable with her boss' dejected stare, Clarke brought up a new topic. "How's your dog doing?"

"After Pancho saved me from getting jooked by the Korean, I bought him a giant bag of Snausages. Gobbled so many he puked on my bed. I wonder how my hound learned that neat trick?"

"Biting the assaulter to defend you?" Nora looked surprised. "You don't know?"

"Panch is part wolf?"

"You adopted a retired police dog. A K-9. Mrs. O'Sullivan's husband worked South Central."

Roy stared in disbelief. "Los Angeles?"

"For thirty years. George O'Sullivan was Pancho's handler. When George died suddenly, Amelia moved to Bisbee."

"Did he buy it on the job?"

Clarke poked her forefinger to the roof of her mouth. "George kicked the bucket 'cleaning his service weapon.'"

"That's tough. I should have been friendlier to Mrs. O'Sullivan."

"Boss, you should be friendlier to everyone. You've got a reputation for being an—"

"Asshole? Prick? Douchebag?"

She smirked. "You're none of those."

"Gee, it's great to be so admired. Er, Nora, can you answer something for me?"

"That's why you pay me the big bucks."

Roy placed his elbows on his knees and clasped his hands. "Would you go out with me?"

Nora's face turned red. "I don't think Aron, *my fiancé*, would be cool with that." The sunlight refracting through her engagement ring shot colorful stars across the tin ceiling. "You realize I'm—"

"Taken. Not you. I—"

She gasped. "Roy, do you have a crush on somebody? Or, are you pulling my leg?"

"There is a woman who. . .I cannot stop thinking about her."

"I told you to lay off the liquor, not to fall in love."

The ringing telephone curtailed his boyish chortle. "Sheriff Davis."

"Roy?"

His pulse quickened. "Maria, I meant to contact you. I had a nice time the other evening."

"Uh, so did I. That's not the reason I called."

The timbre of her voice tore his heart. "Is my mother all right?"

"Don't worry, your mom's fine. It's Bill Hill. He passed away early this morning."

Thursday—December 7, 2017

On Fulton Street, Tom Hayden, clad in gray janitorial coveralls and a matching cap, entered the underground Lafayette Avenue Station. He used gloves to adhere the "Gentleman Mustache – *Made with Real Human Hair*" to his upper lip and to adjust the tinted eyeglasses. On the deserted mezzanine, Tom paid cash at a vending machine for a SingleRide MetroCard and pushed through the turnstile. He descended a stairway to the southbound tracks.

A female dressed in a puffy, pink jacket over a short, black miniskirt stood a high heel-length from the yellow warning line marking the boundary of the ten-foot-wide railway platform. A bulky handbag swung on her arm. Hayden, unsure if the young lady came from a holiday celebration or worked the streets as a prostitute, strolled closer, and leaned against the grimy tiles.

Beyond the sets of stairs, the unoccupied concrete slab ended at a wall posted with "DO NOT ENTER OR CROSS TRACKS" and "CAUTION THIS AREA HAS BEEN BAITED WITH RODENTICIDE" signs. The rumble of a subway train advancing from that direction compelled the woman to pivot toward the dark opening. On the second set of four parallel tracks, an empty southbound train rocketed out of the tunnel's center tube. In the leading car, the operator peered ahead as the silver bullet whooshed past them and hurtled into the opposite passageway. The A express didn't stop at this station.

The woman removed a phone from her purse and began texting.

Tom thought of Tanda's admonition. *Don't waste your vacation sipping margaritas by the pool. It is essential for you to finish the task at hand.* He had spent the previous six days hanging around countless subway stations and riding miles of subterranean and elevated railway tracks. Twice, Hayden came within a hairsbreadth of shoving a stranger into an oncoming train, yet both times he faltered at the final instant. The worst part? Tom couldn't fathom what held him back. *Am I a man of mettle or a spineless toad?* The prosperous stock trader crept forward, mouthing, "Now or never."

The partygoer or hooker looked his way.

He pressed two fingers to his mouth. "Pardon me. By chance, do you happen to have a cigarette? I left mine in my locker."

She offered a pack of Virginia Slims and smiled. "It's forbidden to smoke in the subways, but what the heck, nobody's here to snitch. I apologize for the chick sticks. Tobacco's tobacco, right?"

Hayden plucked a tall and slender out of the box, put the white filter between his lips, and stood motionless as she lit the tip with a blue New York Mets lighter. He puffed on the cigarette, trying not to cough. "My mother smoked this brand while washing dishes. She used to sing the little jingle."

"*You've come a long way, baby*?"

"That's the song. I still remember how good they smelled."

The late-night local A train to Far Rockaway arrived every twenty minutes. As a substitute for using his hands, Tom intended to use his feet. They stood less than an arm's length from the edge of the platform. *It won't take much effort—just a nudge.* To kill time, and to keep her nearby, his mind reeled, thinking up subject matter to continue the conversation.

The woman smoothed her mane of fuchsia hair. "Where do you work?"

Tom, inept at reading emotions, could not establish the genuineness of her curiosity. He recalled passing a block-sized building filled with stores. "Over at the mall. I meet all kinds of interesting people, and the company offers a competitive benefits plan."

"I bet they do." She flicked her butt at the tracks. "What's with our train?"

"Should be arriving any second now." The cement vibrated beneath his shoes. "How do *you* pay the bills?"

The woman unzipped her coat to reveal a skimpy French maid's costume. "Like it, hun? Does your mall sell anything this sexy?"

Metal against metal screaked from the horizontal shaft. Hayden stared at her bare midriff. *That belly button ring is my bull's-eye.* "What's your name?"

"Sharon! Cutie, are you interested in a date?"

"That's my mother's name." Headlights reflected off the masses of electrical wires strapped to the curved walls. Rodents scurried into holes as a roil of dust and debris preceded a blast of hot air. 57's latest member braced himself. Her backside to him, Tom knew his timing had to be spot-on. Brakes screeching, the subway train shot out of the sooty tunnel. *Get ready. Wait. . .wait for it. Almost. . . . Now!*

Tom screamed, "Sharon!" As the woman pirouetted on her stilettos, the man extended his arms to steady himself and kicked out his right foot. Concurrent to his heel striking nothingness, he saw the orange "NOT IN SERVICE" sign in the subway car's window. The train slowed but didn't stop.

The NYC Transit undercover officer shouted, "Police!" as she seized Tom's calf with both hands and twisted. He toppled sideways and hit the floor. "You're under arrest!" Sharon flipped him onto his stomach, wedged her knee into the small of his back, and yanked a handgun from her bag. "Don't even breathe, dickhead!" The cop used a cell phone to request backup.

The moment Tom heard the clink-clink of handcuffs, he tore his arms away, overturned Sharon, and pinned her shoulders. His superior weight and strength kept the muzzle aimed elsewhere, yet as he tried to pry the gun from her fingers, she flung the weapon aside. Sharon jammed a TASER in Tom's ribs, struggling to switch off the safety. On the tactile warning bumps, as he wrenched himself from her, they tumbled over the platform and onto the train tracks.

Sharon landed on Tom, knocking the wind out of him. Stripped of her service pistol and stun gun, the policewoman immobilized her aggressor using a rigid forearm and a backup set of handcuffs. When she glanced up, a pair of headlights bloomed from the depths of the tunnel. Sharon had to make a hasty decision. Even if the driver noticed them, the train would never stop in time. Room to dodge forty tons of rolling death did not exist on either side of the tracks. The woman didn't have the brawn to hoist the two-hundred-pound man over the four-foot-high wall, and, as a sworn police officer, she couldn't leave him here to die.

Sharon held a key. "Sir, a train is coming. We've got to get off the tracks. Remain still. I am uncuffing you." She freed her combatant and steadied herself on the platform. The handgun and TASER lay a yard out of her reach.

On a bed of greasy gravel, Hayden watched the barefooted charlatan lunge for her guns. Inches from his ears, the steel rails strummed a stereophonic song of destruction. He clearly saw the white "A-LOCAL" in the blue circle on the right window of the oncoming subway car. Framed in the left trapezoid of glass, the female operator's eyes and mouth opened wide in horror.

Tom clung to Sharon's ankle and heaved her into the two-foot-deep trough formed in the center of the tracks. He pulled her on top of himself, wrapped his arms around her waist, and exhaled. Her cries for help went unheard as the A roared into the station. As the train barreled overhead, Tom pushed her torso into the undercarriage, watching as the mechanical viper bit and dragged her away. When the brakes ceased whining, he crawled rearward and egressed from below the last subway car.

A short male and a tall female wearing matching black ski masks stood on the platform. The man yelled over the side, "The police are on their way! Give me your hand!"

Tom allowed the Sentinels to pull him up. "Who are you?"

The woman with reddish hair used the code names Olivia had appointed for this mission. "I'm Cher. This is Sonny. We thought you were a goner! Follow us!" She tugged his sleeve and led him underneath a safety chain and down a ramp.

In the tunnel, Sonny turned on his phone's light and shined the weak beam across the railbed. "Take care stepping over the third rail." Past the electrical conductor, he guided them onto a ledge. "Emergency exits are installed between stations."

After they trotted single file for a mile along the narrow walkway, Cher saw an "EXIT" sign.

A claustrophobic staircase dead-ended at an iron plate. Cher gripped a revolver while her partner pressed on the locking bar.

"Come here," Sonny huffed. "Damn thing's rusted shut."

Tom hopped across a half-eaten rat, put his shoulders against the rod, and thrust with his legs. The hatch sprung upward on hinged counterweights.

On the wet pavement, the three followed separate paths into the city.

Outside Saint Patrick's, Roy settled on the low wall abutting the county courthouse. As a practice, he went outdoors to fill his lungs with smoke. Today, the sheriff needed unpolluted air to clear his mind. The old Roman Catholic church had been packed to the rafters. An assemblage of friends, family, and members of the Sheriff's Office came from near and far to honor William Hill.

Maria walked under the cross' elongated shadow, and said to Roy, "My father was a pastor." She chewed over how, only a week ago, Bill assured her Roy would bring her father to the hospital for the MRI test. The man standing before her hadn't lifted a finger. *My supervisor is still ticked I took the day off.*

Davis loosened his brown tie and hooked his forefinger over the khaki shirt's top button. His uniform felt snug around his throat—a hangman's noose. The sight of the former detective lying in the mahogany casket had distressed him greatly. *Why didn't I give Bill more of my time? I never took him seriously. Now he's gone.* "What did you just say?"

Flores, miffed he wasn't listening, restated. "I said my dad was a minister."

"Oh? When did he die?"

"My father is alive. He's in a nursing home."

"Not the Arbors?"

Maria's harsh laughter echoed off the church's brick walls. "No way we can afford that place. I got him a shared room in

Silverton Terrace." She questioned if Bill had even mentioned her predicament to Roy.

Davis had toured Silverton Terrace Elder Care while evaluating assisted living residences. He had generously rated the oppressive facility one star out of five. "And your mom?"

"Haven't seen her since I was six." She turned up her nose. "My mother is dead for all I know."

"Sorry. Any brothers or sisters?"

"None that I've met. You?"

"I had a sister."

"Is she the one your mom keeps referring to?"

"Helen died in her teens. Dad hit the bottle. Mom got electroshock therapy. I signed up with the Marines. My brother, he— Sometimes, I think the treatments and me leaving home accelerated her dementia."

"Janet is such a nice lady." The nurse inspected the crusty lump on his scalp. "What happened to your head?"

The sheriff stroked the butterfly tape his chief deputy had used to seal his injury outside the Copper Queen Mine. "I clocked my noggin on a kitchen cabinet."

"Sloshed?"

Roy, abashed by Maria's forwardness, stammered, "Yes, but today makes seven days sober. And Thanksgiving was the last time I smoked a cigarette."

"You stopped drinking on the night of our dinner? The day before you were supposed to bring—"

"This gal is much too good for you, boss." Deputy Clarke extended her right hand. "Hi! I'm Nora. May I have a word with you in private?"

Maria and Nora wandered off to find some shade. Roy hankered to hear what they could be discussing.

"Sheriff Davis?"

A red-eyed man with features mirroring the corpse now being loaded into the hearse, a clear-eyed woman who must be his wife, and a lad who took after them both, emerged from the narthex into the sunshine.

Roy gave Bill's son a curt nod. Over the years, Bill repeatedly spoke of how deeply the father-son estrangement dismayed him. The sheriff spoiled to break Marvin Hill's nose.

Marvin approached Roy. "Thank you for your eloquent eulogy." He looked to his wife and son. "We live in Savannah and haven't seen Dad in a while. Growing up, I never understood what he did for a living or why his job was so important. I knew as a detective my—"

"Your father talked fondly about you. It's a pity you waited until his death to come out for a visit."

Marvin recoiled from Roy's hard words.

Mrs. Hill's eyes shot poison darts. "Sheriff Davis, you have no right to speak to my husband that way. You don't know the whole story!"

"Marjorie, he's not wrong. I'm a rotten son. Please, excuse us." Marvin steered his wife to the stairs.

Alex lingered as his mom and dad climbed inside the black limousine. After the youngest Hill squeezed Davis' hand, he hurried down the steps to join his parents.

The sheriff watched the long Cadillac turn south onto Tombstone Canyon Road. He flattened the small paper slip and read the block letters: "MIDNIGHT ALONE – MY GRANDFATHER'S GRAVE."

Maria and Nora returned from their palaver. Flores seemed less tense and giggled when Clarke asked, "Whatcha holdin' there, boss? A coupon for fifty percent off your funeral?"

Roy stuffed the mysterious message in his pocket. "Let's hope not."

Friday—December 8, 2017

A bone's throw from the Shady Dell travel trailer park, Roy motored under the green cast-iron "Evergreen Cemetery" arch and through the open gate. In 1914, following a rash of typhoid outbreaks, the Common Council of Bisbee carted all the remains from the old Brewery Gulch graveyard (imprudently built upslope from the town's drinking water wells) to this new out-of-town locale. Fourteen thousand townspeople were buried here, including a number of Cochise County sheriffs. He rolled along the juniper-flanked lane and stopped in the Veteran's section by a World War I era field gun.

The sheriff used a penlight to detour around the sorrowful little plot of hardpan designated as "Baby Land." He read the chiseled epitaphs of the dead, coming upon what he searched for: William Hill's fresh mound of dirt. Roy confirmed the time on his cell phone, five minutes to the witching hour, and squatted on the raised curb of a concrete grave. The swinging shaft of light spawned restless shadows on the monumental Kosok mausoleum's Doric columns. *Everything sure is spooky in the dark.*

Davis hailed, "Anybody above ground in this boneyard except for me?" The hairs on his neck stood on end when a bush rustled.

Alex Hill corporealized from behind a headless cherub statue. A pack hung on his back.

Roy stood on wooden legs. "Why the cloak-and-dagger meeting? Do your parents know you're here?"

"Nope. Snuck out of the hotel and hired an Uber to bring me over." Alex gazed at the buildings skirting the property. "Will the caretaker see us?"

"The maintenance crew calls it a day at five. How's your father doing? I regret busting his balls about not coming to see his old man. Probably had something to do with my own daddy issues."

Marvin's son unzipped the backpack, withdrew a laptop, and balanced its flat bottom on the curved top of Sarah Hill's tombstone. "Dad's not taking it well. Feels guilty for never reconciling with his father over his mother's death. I've attempted to talk sense into him. He's as hardheaded as his dad, and I guess I'm destined to end up just as bullheaded. Pop's not a bad guy—more like his father than he'd care to think."

"Alex, your grandfather was a man of his word and a great detective. He assisted me on several investigations. So, why are we freezing our tokuses off with the ghosts and goblins?"

"My grandpa worked with you on the Daniel Barton murder?"

"Bill helped me with a couple of things. To be honest, he had a few suggestions I shoulda paid closer consideration to. How did you hear about Barton?"

"A week and a half ago, Grandpa Bill had me hack into your department's network and give him everything on that hit-and-run."

"Bullcrap! I realize you're enrolled in computer classes at school, but our datacenter is as secure as Fort Knox."

Alex extracted a green notebook from the bag and passed it over. "These are his most recent notes."

Roy clamped the flashlight between his teeth and turned the creased pages. Bill had circled, boxed, or underlined notable words, phrases, or sentences. Double-underlined text caused him unease. "Multiple assailants are involved in the Barton case." Davis hadn't given the ex-detective this bit of knowledge. *How could Bill know all this? That information is confidential.* "Are you aware that breaking into a government database is a federal offense?" The sheriff directed the bright ray at the college student's eyes. "Tell me how you did it!"

Alex uplifted a palm to cut the annoying glare. "Easy-peasy lemon squeezy. You better reprimand your IT staff for not staying on top of the server security updates. How 'bout you redirect that light onto the keys instead of in my face?" After the Dell booted to the desktop, he plugged in a USB drive. "Grandpa Bill sent me a carton full of notebooks. To keep active during his retirement, he tried to solve cold cases. Whenever my grandfather discovered anything useful, he'd anonymously tip off the police. My parents claim he died in his sleep. Do you believe that?"

"Bill was eighty and unwell. The death certificate says respiratory failure."

"Too vague." Alex input a password. "We all stop breathing at some point."

Davis thumbed the new transdermal patch on his upper arm in a wasted effort to infuse a higher dosage of nicotine. *Big Pharma must manufacture a patch for alcohol.* "No one lives forever. That's a sad fact."

"Sheriff, when you see what I've got, you might change your mind about how he died and run for your life. My grandfather said to trust you. I pray to God he's right." Alex clicked on an icon. A worldview map dominated the screen.

Roy squinted. "What are all these green dots?"

Alex kept his response straightforward, not elaborating on the art and science of data visualization. "I entered the material from my grandpa's notebooks into my database. He provided me with a set of parameters to filter the data. A, there was no motive for killing the victim. B, a collective of bad actors participated, notably after the dirty work took place. C, these aren't your garden-variety homicides. Think crucifixion or evisceration by a dessert spoon. And D, the murders occurred at regular intervals over a long period."

Davis contemplated the suspects he had seen in the white plumber's van, the indistinct shoe prints around Barton's body, the person who blew off the Korean's head, and the article Bill gave him regarding the woman stabbed in Anchorage. After he took Luke Bell on the Copper Queen Mine's "Haunted Tour," he forgot to call the Alaska State Troopers for more information. "What are these blue spots?"

The college student simpered, outwardly sheepish, inwardly proud. "I also hacked into the International Criminal Police Organization databases."

"You got into Interpol?"

"Yes, sir. Had to barter with a crazy Russian on Onionland to find a backdoor. For access into the FBI, I. . .um. . .never mind. The blue dots are in addition to the slayings my grandfather figured out on his own."

"Step away from the touchpad," Roy commanded. His finger revolved the globe on its axis, zooming in on various green and blue clusters. Bisbee, Arizona, had two green dots: Daniel Barton – Asphyxiation by Hand – 11/21/2017 and an older entry, Helen Davis – Battery by Golf Club – 5/12/1982. "Only one individual was linked to the Davis case. Your data is incorrect."

Alex, mildly offended, retorted, "No, it's not. The digital FBI file stated they found two sets of footmarks near your sister. Didn't the paper file show this?"

Roy plopped down on the eroded grave curb and hung his head. Alex put away the computer and took a seat beside him. Their exhalations—illuminated by a Wolf Moon—combined and dissipated.

"Sheriff, I know this is a lot to absorb. Something quite strange and very dangerous is happening. These homicides go back over a century." Alex took out his grandpa's letter. "Turn on the flashlight." He pointed to an inked-out line. "See this?"

Davis saw a scratched-out mistake.

"Hold the light behind the page."

Roy read the words "Murder for fun – a club?" and switched off the penlight. "You and Bill are—I mean, *Bill was*, either delusional or. . . ." He massaged his forehead and sighed. *Such a stupid time to stop drinking and smoking.*

"What do we do?" Alex circled his family's gravesite waving his hands. "This is huge!"

"First off, I'll exhume your grandfather and get the medical examiner to do a thorough exam—specifically, a toxicology report."

"An official autopsy may attract the *wrong* species of bee. We could get stung." Alex gathered up the assortment of sprays and funeral wreaths from the grave and put the tributes to the side. "While playing international spy, I noticed hundreds of files had been tampered with. I have complete confidence a syndicate of this magnitude is capable of cracking any firewall and deleting or modifying all incriminating records."

"Organized crime? As in, La Cosa Nostra?"

"In general, the Sicilian and American Mafias kill for money, power, or revenge. Thousands of people are dying for no good reason. Sheriff, what we've got here is some kind of sick game."

"Did your grandfather discuss any of this with you electronically?"

"Negative. He used the U.S. Mail to send the letter asking me to hack into your servers and to ship the container of notebooks. The return addresses were phony. I used an off-campus pay phone to inform my granddad that somebody besides Kim Jin-ho choked Daniel Barton to death."

"Great. Untraceable to him or to you."

Alex crossed his arms. "A skillful hunter can track down an individual tiger by the shape of its footprints, the trails it frequents, and the sounds he or she makes. Claw marks indicate the trees in which the big cat eats and sleeps. A tracker even analyzes fresh scat. The stalker learns to think like the animal, imagining where it is and what they are doing. With Big Brother watching our every move, there are no places on the planet left to hide." He stepped behind the vandalized cherub, coming forth carrying a shovel, a spade, and a pickax.

"What are those for?" The sheriff felt sure the reply could cost him his job or, worse, his soul.

Hill threw the rusty spade. Davis' palm smarted catching the straight-edged tool.

"It's better to know the truth—even if it hurts."

Alex shucked his jacket and scooped up clumps of earth with the angled blade.

"Wait. I have a tarp in my truck to put the dirt on."

An excavator had tilled the rocks and clay, easing the men's task. Roy's spade struck wood first. At the bottom of the three-foot-deep hole, they used their hands to sweep the soil off the seven-foot-long box. When Roy returned from the Chevy with a crowbar, he heard Alex sniffling. Salty tears streaked the varnished mahogany.

The sheriff stretched out his palm. "Come outta there, son. I got this."

"No, this is my family, and it's my idea." Alex straddled the casket's lower lid. "Pass me the pry bar." He snapped the upper lid's lock and swung up the top. With the satin overthrow peeled away, William Hill (apart from the loam sprinkling his pressed detective's uniform) looked as he had earlier that day—dead. Alex took Roy's multi-tool. He opened the small pair of scissors, snipped hair from the back of his grandfather's head, and dropped the filaments into an envelope. Alex unfolded the stiff fingers and groaned. "Not much here. The mortician clipped his nails at the funeral parlor."

"That's okay. We have the hair samples."

Angst aged the boy's face as he accessed the larger blade. "I can't get the— Sorry, but I—" A strangled noise originated from somewhere deep in his larynx.

Roy pulled Alex onto the plastic tarpaulin and dropped into Bill's final resting place. The sheriff whispered, "Forgive me, pal," and carved out his old friend's eyeball.

The notch in the landscape filled faster than it had emptied. To the casual eye, once the withered flowers were arranged atop the earthen tumulus, the surface appeared untouched.

Chapter Eleven

Saturday—December 9, 2017

OLIVIA STEWART STEERED THE 2002 GREEN HONDA ACCORD alongside her other automobile, the red Ford Mustang, and shifted into park. Motor idling, Stewart sat for a moment admiring the Boss 9's racing tires and menacing front spoiler. "What a magnificent beast," she murmured. *Perfect, except for that damn crack in the hood scoop.*

Olivia had avoided imprisonment by escaping to Mexico. This getaway entailed a short journey in the Toyota Camry through the Naco Port of Entry; a longer, bumpier ride on a stolen Kawasaki dirt bike to Agua Prieta; a stifling bus hop to the distant coastal town of Matamoros; and a nighttime cruise across the Gulf on an American smuggler's go-fast boat. Stateside, Olivia chartered a flight from Galveston to Alamosa. Finally, after she purchased the Honda with cash, a leisurely hour drive home.

The Arizona mission was a disaster. The Korean lay on a slab in the Tucson city morgue. *My Patron and my responsibility. The Curator will skin me alive and hang my corpse up for the buzzards to peck my eyes out.* Stewart turned the ignition key to off and got out of her latest commuter car. For all she knew, her previous vehicle, the Camry, might still be burning in the

Sonoran Desert. *The day of reckoning with Morrigan needs to wait.*

Olivia ached to wash off the road-stink from her crappy trip. When the garage door closed, she let Kasha out of the cat carrier. The one-eyed Siamese, resentful his master had left him cooped up at the all-inclusive pet resort, slunk away.

At nine thousand feet, the temperature in Creede, Colorado, plummeted to single digits as rock ridges swallowed the sun. Inside the thawing house, a modest-sized log cabin fronted by a babbling brook and backed by tall, craggy cliffs, Stewart lit candles while the bathtub filled with hot water. She showered, then lowered herself into the soapsuds. The imported cognac further heated her tummy and lightened her dark mood. Kasha (easy to forgive) catnapped on the tub's rim.

Olivia closed her own eyelids. She pictured Park Jin-ho staggering to his SUV; Leroy Davis, the nosey sheriff, pulling the Korean over; the rifle scope's crosshairs centering on the target— Here is the moment Stewart's eyes opened in puzzlement, the point when she committed to squeezing the trigger. *Should I have shot the sheriff rather than my client? Should I have killed them both, or neither one? And that old detective? Why can't I stop going over what I did to him?* The Handler seldom rethought her actions or harbored any feelings of self-reproach. *I obeyed orders. I followed protocol. What the hell is the matter with me?* She sank below the steaming surface, blowing bubbles out of her nostrils.

Named by the state of Utah, Olivia Stewart (no one is privy to the names written on her birth certificate as no known documentation exists from the day of her creation) grew up in a series of Midwest foster homes. Unadoptable as an infant, her earliest childhood memories were of living on a hog farm south of Salt Lake City. The biddy who "encouraged" Olivia to call her "Ma" clothed herself in pastel, ankle-length dresses and carried the Book of Mormon wherever she went (Ardeth had never traveled fifty miles from her birthplace). The man who each morning draped himself in a black rubber apron, unless at worship in the meetinghouse, made Olivia hold the pigs as he hit them between the ears with a large, wooden mallet. When the young lady blossomed, the jealous wife returned her to the Children's Bureau.

In Kansas, this time on a three-hundred-acre corn farm, Stewart's foster parents had an older son and daughter. The girl ridiculed Olivia for her "dirty skin" and "chinky eyes." The boy threw stones at his "fugly" foster sister until she clubbed him on the head with a rusty sickle. Because the hooklike blade had dulled over the years, the farmers' son merely required a tetanus shot and forty-three stitches.

Olivia relocated from state to state, county to county, and from home to home, only staying a month or so in any one school. Her thirteen foster families found her peculiar. The gangly girl often listened to her state-certified caregivers discussing her "inferior" attributes behind closed doors. *"That odd duck's damaged goods!"*

Olivia Stewart's teenage years molded her into the confident, self-reliant woman she is today. In the hot and humid summer of 1998, the Children's Bureau loaded her aboard a Greyhound with an "INDEPENDENCE – MO" destination sign on the front. The Allens picked up their new charge from the bus station and put her in "Lily's old bedroom." Whenever Olivia asked her custodians about Lily, they deftly changed the conversation.

Professor Allen had built a special room in the basement. He enjoyed dragging "Livvy" downstairs to his "man cave." On the L-shaped sectional sofa, as Mrs. Allen darned socks in the attic sewing room, the two (along with Tigger the cat) watched cable "documentaries" on the brand-new Sony Trinitron. Marcus, the name her foster father desired to be called during these viewing sessions, commanded the remote. He flicked through the Skinamax channels, stopping each time he came upon cheesy softcore porn, principally movies featuring Marilyn Chambers. The fifty-four-year-old man got under the fifteen-year-old girl's skin with inappropriate questions such as, "Livvy, are you enjoying what they are doing to each other?" or "Do you think you would ever like to try that, Liv?"

For three months, Olivia used humor or bathroom break excuses to rebuff or evade Marcus' increasingly lecherous advances. Then in the fall, the week after classes commenced at her Catholic high school, Professor Allen stepped over the thin line drawn in the sand. He slid his sweaty hand beneath his foster child's plaid skirt.

Olivia made two moves to incapacitate the man she now visualized as the "enemy," each spontaneous and each with no thought of consequence. First, she drove her elbow into the six-inch tent pole rising from his crotch. Second, as Marcus' head tilted backward and his lips split in a primal scream, the girl swung her arm into his throat. As her foster father turtle-walked across the waxed tiles, she kicked him onto his back and crammed the Sony remote into his snapping beak. Mrs. Allen, hearing a noise akin to a barnyard rooster drowning in a pail of peanut butter, descended the cellar stairs calling her husband's name. Stewart slid a broom handle through the wooden balusters to trip the silent accomplice. She lashed her half-conscious foster parents to a support column with an electrical cord and used lawnmower gasoline to burn the house and its two sleazeball occupants (she took Tigger with her) to the foundation.

On the run from the law, Olivia melded into the torn fabric of society. For a short while, she scraped by on the streets of Kansas City—rough for a wanted girl of her height and mixed ethnicity to remain unnoticed. Stewart hitched west to

Colorado. During the summer, she bounced between Aspen and Vail, breaking into vacant vacation homes and raiding the pantries for cans of soup and boxes of mac and cheese. As the young woman lay awake underneath someone else's sheets, she erased the hopeless past and concentrated on building a bright future.

At the first flakes of winter, Olivia followed the migrating snowbirds down the mountain to southern Arizona. In Yuma's fertile fields, she bent her back with other illegals picking cantaloupes and watermelons. Nobody looked at the hardworking girl sideways or challenged her history. She learned basic Spanish and, of vital pertinence, how to stay free.

One night, another fieldworker knocked on Stewart's trailer. Gabriela told Olivia how, after quitting time, her supervisors baited her with "promises of a promotion" to the cooling plant. Among the crates of fruits and vegetables, no talk of advancement could be heard, only shrieks. Gabriela pulled up her lip to reveal the bloody gap in her once lovely smile. "I'm scared they'll kill me!"

Olivia grasped the weeping woman's hands, and avowed, "These vermin shall harm you no more. Tell me who did this to you."

The laborers assigned ribald nicknames to their *jefes*. From Gabriela's descriptions, Olivia singled out *"El Conejo,"* a bucktooth Caucasian male with carrot-shaped ears, and *"Comedor de Mierda,"* a Hispanic male whose teeth resembled a cob of Indian corn.

When Gabriela attempted to reward her champion, Olivia pushed the crumpled dollars away. "Leave the state. The police will not let this go."

At sunrise, Olivia waited by a row of liquid fertilizer storage tanks. She knew the supervisors began their day with a stand-up meeting to divvy up tasks. Connor Evans parked his

Chevrolet Silverado crew cab next to the green portable toilet and plunged inside. Before the man unbuckled his belt, Stewart yanked the plastic door open and used her harvest machete to reap *El Conejo's* blighted melon from his long stem of neck.

Minutes later, Esteban Gómez pedaled up on a mountain bike. *Comedor de Mierda* peered in his co-supervisor's truck and yelled for Evans. He dropped the bicycle and limped to the honey bucket's half-open door. Esteban wailed, *"Cara de muerto!"* and turned to flee.

Olivia vaulted from behind the chemical closet and nabbed Gómez's collar. The fourteen-inch cleaver arced upward in the seam of his spread legs. A fold in Esteban's baggy dungarees deflected the blade from her intended destination. In lieu of cropping his twig and berries, the honed edge slashed deep into his fleshy thigh. Stewart rinsed off the carotid and femoral blood covering her forearms under an outdoor spigot. She let the machete sink into a vat of high-phosphorus bat guano.

During the rest of her teens and early twenties, Olivia moved from community to community. Sometimes she purged the wicked, but in most cases, she used her street smarts to hustle the wealthy. A Holocaust survivor/Nazi hunter in Oklahoma City specialized in forged documents. From the moment Olivia Stewart stepped out of his gleaming Airstream Overlander, her public persona was stapled to the forgettable name of the late Katherine Knight. These falsified papers enabled the reincarnated woman to secure a college degree in business and to buy the log cabin in Creede.

Two years later, Olivia had buried a plastic pickle jar full of Gold Eagle coins on a trail above the one-hundred-foot-high North Clear Creek Falls when she heard footsteps. She toed leaves onto the hole and fingered her pocket pistol, a semiautomatic Beretta Jetfire.

A female walking a toy dog on a long, blue retractable leash appeared over the ridge. She seemed innocuous, so Stewart switched on the weapon's safety, keeping her hand in her pants.

"Good day, to you!" the dog walker called. Actress Glenn Close's doppelgänger wore leopard print leggings and a red "BIG HEART IN A LITTLE PACKAGE" pullover. A pricey DSLR hung from a camera strap.

"Hi," Olivia greeted. She raised her free fingers, unable to see the eyes shielded by designer sunglasses.

The diminutive woman cradled the Shih Tzu. "My baby boy is pooped. Is this the footpath to the overlook? I am dying to try out my new wide-angle lens."

Stewart pointed eastward. "It's by that stand of trees. What's his name?"

"This sweet bundle of joy is Fluffy." The photographer stroked his teensy head. "Well, off we go to take pictures of the waterfall!" As she placed the animal on the ground, the tether's hook came undone.

Olivia, watching Fluffy scamper into a field of tall prairie grass, saw a blur of blue pass over her chin, too quick to get her thumbs under the cord. Stewart's left hand clawed at the snare while her right hand groped for the Beretta—*gone.* The pressure on her trachea abated; however, the force of the gun pressing against her skull strengthened.

"Ms. Stewart, I am letting you go. Will you stay still?"

Olivia, her sight blotchy with black speckles, could only nod in the affirmative. *Did she say my name?*

"Good girl." The woman released the noose, and commanded, "Turn to me, please."

The middle-aged female aiming the Jetfire reminded Olivia of one of her foster mothers. *Wichita? Akron? No. . .her name shall come to me later—or never. How did this gnome get the drop on me?* She gulped in air. "Who are you?"

"Morrigan, the Celtic goddess of fate, war, and death."

What did she just say? "What?"

"You heard me." The "Queen of Demons" twirled the trigger guard around her forefinger before returning the pistol to Stewart. "And what's our lesson for today?"

This bitch is out of her mind. Olivia shrugged. "Next time, bring bug spray?"

"Trust no one, no matter how virtuous their demeanor." Morrigan put two fingers between her compressed lips and whistled. Fluffy's flat snout parted the June grass. The dog romped along the pathway and dived into her outstretched arms. "How much gold did you hide away?"

Is my gun still loaded? "What gold? I'm out for a hike."

"How many people have you murdered? Five, ten...twenty? *Over twenty?*"

Stewart tipped up the Beretta's barrel to check for a bullet. She snapped the cylinder down, cocked the hammer, and flipped off the safety. "Nice talking to you, but I must be going."

When Olivia arrived home, she found a compact, bearded male seated at her kitchen table. A tweed flat cap rested on the tablecloth next to a breathing bottle of wine and two glasses. She aimed the Jetfire at his face, feeling foolish asking, "How did you break in?"

The man showed her a lock picking tool. "I fed Kasha. Your cat wouldn't quit pestering me. Have you thought about shelling out for an automatic pet food dispenser?"

Stewart, her back vulnerable to the dark foyer, repositioned herself in front of the refrigerator. The clingy feline jumped up on the counter and rubbed his head against her shoulder. "And the burglar alarm?"

He fished a wire cutter from his windbreaker. "Invest in cellular monitoring."

"Today has been a very trying day. Why are you in my kitchen?"

"Morrigan notified me you passed the initial test."

She kneaded the purple marks on her throat and winced. "I failed."

"You didn't receive an A," he agreed. "Nor did you earn an F."

"Your psycho friend outwitted me."

"And why beholdest thou the mote that is in thy brother's eye, but considerest not the beam that is in thine own eye?"

"I hate to be the one to tell you," Olivia muttered, "I also flunked out of Bible studies."

"The parable means—"

"I understand what the fuck it means," she growled. "Get to the point."

The man moved his hat and centered a bowling bag on the tabletop. His eyes glued to hers, he removed a weighty gold bar and a compact submachine gun. An overhead pendant lamp set the precious metal ablaze. The Uzi deposited black oil stains on the white linen. He decanted the wine into the large glasses. "Sit. Any cheese to pair with this Bordeaux?"

"No, and I'll stand if it's okay with you."

"Suit yourself." The man swirled the red liquid and inhaled the tannic acids. "Only the best for you. After such a hard upbringing, I don't blame you one bit. You deserve everything life has to give." Her unwanted visitor quaffed the wine and poured himself another glass.

Olivia opened the fridge—*he wants me to go for the Uzi*—and rolled a package of goat cheese across the table. She withdrew a cheese knife from the walnut block, pausing for a heartbeat before placing the handle in his palm.

He sliced the *chèvre* with the forked blade. "Ms. Stewart, I am here to offer you a job."

Olivia's stomach grumbled. She'd only eaten an energy bar since lunch. "My name is Katherine Knight, and I'm doing just fine, thank you."

"Extortions, shakedowns, flimflams. Are con games your solitary reason for living? You made a tidy fortune, yet working alone, you have no safety net. With us, the sky is the limit. Our big umbrella will keep you nice and dry in any storm." He thumbed the white cheese into his mouth.

"You've got the lowdown on me. What's your story? Who's this 'us'?"

The man shifted in the ladder-back chair. "Ms. Stewart, do you want the job or not?"

"Not knowing my duties?"

His Vandyke dipped to the gold bullion, then drifted to the Israeli submachine gun. "Choose."

"I'm the one holding your fate in my hand." She grinned. "I'll take whatever I want."

"Are you sure you're the one in control?"

When the Beretta's firing pin hit Morrigan's dud, Olivia grabbed for the 25-round Uzi. The Accountant drove the 12.4 kilograms of gold off the table, hitting her in the thighs and smashing her against the refrigerator door. Stewart lurched frontward, slumping in submission as the submachine gun poked her in the chest.

The senior 57 member took her arm and helped her up. "You excelled at the second test by going for the gun knowing you would most likely be cut in half. Morrigan will fill you in with the details of your employment and sign you up for training. Good luck and good hunting!" He left the half million in gold, walking away with the unloaded weapon.

Olivia finished the glass of cognac and reached between her waterlogged feet to pull the plug out of the bottom of the tub. The last of the lukewarm water formed a whirlpool draining into the hole. As she dried herself and slid into a bathrobe, Kasha leapt down and ran to the kitchen. Stewart shook dry food into the cat's bowl, double-checked the doors and windows, set the top-of-the-line alarm to detect motion, laid the TEC-9 semiautomatic pistol underneath her pillow, and slipped below the cold sheets. In the blackness of Olivia's dream, pink piglets squealed as she led them to slaughter.

Sunday—December 10, 2017

Tom stared from the window of his Hunts Point walk-up. A woman lay on the sidewalk with her leg bent at an unnatural angle. Out on the boulevard, a purse snatcher sprinted through traffic. Whenever he tugged the shade down, it shot back up.

At the small kitchen table, Hayden viewed the Metropolitan Transportation Authority surveillance video for the hundredth time on his MacBook. In that the placement of the camera was high and the distance great, the image lacked sufficient resolution to make out more than basic physical characteristics. Still, he identified the mustached male wrestling with the female police officer at the Lafayette Avenue Station.

After the murder, his mind galloping in circles and his nerves fried, Tom stuffed clothes in a satchel and locked the door to his Park Avenue apartment. Following a nauseating cab ride to the Bronx, he had paid the vampirish superintendent a month's rent in twenties for this fleabag studio. To keep up appearances, on Friday, the equity trader had headed into the Stock Exchange as usual, leaving at noon with complaints of a headache. Over the long weekend, he scoured the internet for articles pertaining to the "Manhunt for Cop Killer."

The terms "Computer-Enhanced Images" and "Facial Recognition Technologies" sent Hayden into a tailspin. *I should have been more cautious,* he thought. *Why did I spend so much time riding the subway? My face must be written on the hard drives of thousands of security camera systems.*

Tom launched the Tor Browser, input the 57 website IP address, and selected "1" to initiate a secure communication with his Handler. He typed "Is it normal for me to feel," hesitated, then backspaced over the characters. Hayden pondered why the aspect of filling in the blank field intimidated him. He had no difficulties composing formal business emails or concocting snide comments when trolling social media posts. Tom watched his hand write "Tanda" on the scratchpad he kept handy for recording ideas. He bolded the letters and pronounced her name aloud. The man, liking the way the word rolled off his tongue, enunciated the woman's name drawing out the vowels. "In Central Park, she told me Tanda stands for the Seer of Life and Death."

Tom didn't trust people and liked them even less. Since his mother discovered Fins the goldfish in the closet (she spanked him and flushed his pet down the toilet), he had no use for animals other than as a source of protein. Hayden wadded the scrap of paper and fired it at the wastebasket. He missed.

Many years ago, during the summer Tom graduated from high school, a girl had asked him on a date. Mary and Tom worked at the same supermarket, she as a bagger and he as a stock boy. Mary was enthusiastic to see a popular rom-com playing at the local movie theater. She gave her coworker her telephone number and home address, requesting that he pick her up at seven o'clock. Tom borrowed his father's Chrysler; however, without a road map, he became lost during the first mile. The frustrated boy turned the Concorde around and drove home to an empty house. Tom went straight to bed, not phoning Mary that night or making amends the next day. After a week of no-shows, the grocery store manager crossed "Thomas Hayden" off the staffing list. The teenager's love life miscarried before the fetus had a fighting chance to suck in oxygen.

Hayden stretched his arm between the stove and refrigerator to snag the ball of paper. On his elbows and knees, he uncurled the square, pressed the edges against the floor, and whispered, "Tanda." Inspired, Tom returned to his laptop and translated his thoughts into words.

Monday—December 11, 2017

As Nora entered Roy's office, she saw his feet positioned on either side of the desk drawer. He used all his might to tug the handle with both hands. When the bullet jamming the slider broke free, the bin shot from the desk, spilling office supplies and impelling the seated man across the parquet floor and into the ribbed steam radiator.

After the chief deputy stopped laughing, she inquired, "What's in that drawer that's so valuable?"

The sheriff opened the Nicorette box and shoveled a handful of fruit-flavored gum into his mouth.

"You're also on the nicotine patch. Aren't you worried you'll overdose?"

Roy brandished his crossed forefingers. "I need as much ammunition as I can get to battle the furry, little gremlins chasing each other inside my head." He crouched under the desk and held up an ancient bullet. "Wowee!" Davis passed the spent slug to Clarke for her inspection. "This old desk got between a man with a badge and the Clanton brothers!"

She hefted the deadly weight, and countered, "Or blocked Dudley Do-Right from shooting himself in the big toe."

"Don't mock my new talisman!" Roy kissed the .45 and dropped the lead casting into his pocket.

Nora lay a color photograph of an ID card on the table. "Kim Jin-ho is de facto Park Jin-ho. Seven days ago, his wife reported him as missing to the Seoul police. He was a thirty-eight-year-old tax attorney employed by a big Korean bank."

"And?"

"Pretty ordinary. Married for seven years and has a young daughter. Traveled for work, mainly staying in South Korea."

"So, why was Park in our town running people over?"

"His wife," Nora reviewed her notes, "Sun-young, says Jin-ho recently returned from a business trip. An emergency came up—he had to leave again. She had no prior knowledge her husband flew to the United States or why. Sun-young received a 'Just landed' text from Jin-ho the morning after he left, then nada."

Deputy Drake stepped into the room and handed Clarke a printout. Her brow furrowed reading the list of air flights. "Out of the past three years, Park took a plane six separate times to five different countries: Saint Petersburg, Mexico City, Cairo, and Varanasi. The final two were to Los Angeles and Las Vegas. Twice a year, seven days each outing. Justin's a wizard for sorting this out. Our dead Korean adopted a new alias for every trip. He always used Jin-ho for the given name, but made up diverse family names."

The sheriff wanted to pass on the sinister results of Bill and Alex Hill's dark study to his chief deputy, yet he feared it could land her on thin ice. On the Q.T., Roy had submitted Bill's hair and vitreous humour specimens to an old college schoolmate. He waited to hear the results of the toxicology tests.

The Alaska State Troopers had little new information to share concerning Megan Guthrie's stabbing. A priest noticed a blond female speaking to the Lost Nickel Saloon bartender on the evening of the murder. Professionals cleaned the room at the Falling Water Inn, leaving no physical evidence. The woman who had checked in, the current suspect, Natalie Bailey, did not reside at the address connected to her credit card.

Roy felt trapped, afraid to look backward, afraid to move forward, and afraid to stand still. *I need a plan of action.* He slid a hand into his trouser pocket. The lucky bullet ministered no succor. "What would you do?"

Nora watched the indecipherable skein of sentiments ripple across her boss' face. Not once had she seen him so indecisive. *He knows something I don't. Or. . .he's losing it.* "I'd begin by checking if the dates of his excursions to these cities coincide with any local homicides."

"That's a place to start." The horizontal compartment slid into the desk with ease; nonetheless, the repair job gave the sheriff no satisfaction. The chief deputy turned the doorknob. "Nora!"

When he blinked and turned away, she was at a loss. "What's wrong?"

"It's all good." Roy tossed the junk back in the drawer and slammed it shut.

Chapter Twelve

Thursday—December 14, 2017

Olivia entered the French bistro and strolled past the host stand. The maître d', a Napoleonic man in a too-tight blue blazer, called after her, "May I help you, ma'am? Do you have a reservation?"

"I'm meeting someone," she snapped, and walked past the bar. In a small, private room lit by a gaudy chandelier, the Handler spotted the Patron who had demanded this rendezvous.

At a table set for two, Thomas Hayden held out a bouquet of wildflowers and, acting as though he also intended to give her a hug, uttered, "Tanda, thank you for coming. I wasn't convinced you would."

Olivia grabbed the nosegay of purple marsh rosemary, yellow billy balls, and pink dianthus. "What are these for?"

Tom fidgeted with the knot of his tie. "Anybody can buy a dozen red roses. I picked these myself."

She cast the colorful posies onto the tablecloth. "When we first met, I told you we'd never again see each other in person. This meeting is highly irregular *and asinine* for the both of us."

His cheeks dropped. "I just thought—"

"Eh!" Stewart pressed a forefinger to her lips. She scanned the space for hidden cameras, wondering why she was there.

Hayden's secure message, "I'm worried the cops will ram down my door. Can't work during the day. Can't sleep at night. Tanda, I need to see you!" wasn't enough impetus for her to fly two thousand miles to hear his sob story. *And what's with all these flowers?*

Tom pulled out a chair. "Please. We'll talk business later." After both were seated (she under protest), he clicked his fingers. A waiter with a white cloth over one arm glided into the room. "Please bring a container to put these flowers in and a bottle of your finest Cabernet."

With tap water filling the vase and their glasses red with wine (Tom's lips barely touched his), Olivia perused the menu. "I'm tired and hungry. A colicky baby cried during the entire flight. Little brat kept kicking my seat. The airlines should pack the sniveling kids and the sneezing old farts with the animals in the luggage compartment."

Tom chuckled. "Wuh, wuh, whaaaa! Worse than nails on a chalkboard. Are you a mother?"

"Mr. Hayden, I don't share personal information with clients."

"So, no kids?"

"Mr. Hayden."

"Call me Tom. To you, I'm an open book. Thus far, you're a total mystery to me."

"We had to run a background investigation to evaluate your worthiness. There is no requirement for you to know anything about me. I can only give you my professional support."

When the headwaiter returned, both diners ordered rare red meat. As the porterhouse steaks broiled, Olivia checked her watch and Tom checked out Olivia.

Roy was in the backyard giving Pancho a bath when he received this text message from Maria: *Picked up a pizza. Be there in 5.* He tagged the thumbs-up emoji. Davis, sensing the reply needed a human touch, added: *Drive carefully.* "That sounds like I think she's an idiot." He sent Maria a cute photo of the sudsy dog.

Indoors, Roy bustled about the living room and kitchen rearranging the clutter. Then, noticing his muddy legs, he surmised a shower might be a wiser use of the minutes remaining ahead of her arrival. Aside from Nora dropping by to shoot the shit (in truth, she felt duty bound to verify he hadn't hung himself from the ceiling fan), Roy had never invited a woman across the threshold of his trailer. If he scored at RJ's Roadhouse, he took the lucky lady to a motel, to her place, or, in his fledgling days, into his Plymouth Valiant's back seat.

The doorbell chimed before Davis finished toweling behind his ears. He hastened to the door shimmying into blue jeans while sliding a shirt over his wet shoulders. Maria balanced on the stoop—a teetering stack of cinderblocks—holding a Rudy's Pizza box and a six-pack of Diet Pepsi.

Roy unlocked the screen door and accepted the pie. "Come in. I wasn't expecting you, so. . . ."

Maria set foot in the living area—not as deplorable as she had conjectured. From the outside, the mobile home, with its faded green paint and darkening orange rust stains, could double as the movie set from *Deliverance*. Inside the tin can, not even a dry cleaners' complimentary calendar adorned the off-white walls. The beige carpets were vacuumed and, barring the stale scent of cigarette smoke, the air was breathable. A dated couch and easy chair (evidently bought at a consignment shop or scrounged off a curb on garbage day) furnished the unpretentious room. "Mind if I take a look around?"

"There's not a lot to see. I'll wrangle up plates and glasses." Roy's eyes followed her down the narrow hallway to the rear. *She's deciding if she should stay or, more logically, if she should run screaming.*

Maria pushed the first door and entered a small bedroom. Manila folders fanned a bed and 8x10 photographs covered the walls. *These must be part of his work.* She gave in to human nature and moved closer. *Dios mío!* The glossy prints taped to the wood paneling soured her stomach, yet the nurse found turning away impossible. Nora had spilled what she knew of the sheriff's past. *This dead girl is his older sister. Helen.*

Flores circuited the master bedroom. A police manual, *Reasonable Use of Force in the Age of Social Media*, rested on the nightstand. The coffin-sized bathroom was spotless, the shower stall mold-free. No prescription pills stocked the medicine cabinet, only two economy-size bottles of Excedrin.

Roy watched Maria poke beneath the kitchen sink and in the refrigerator. "Find anything good?"

She pawed through the trash. "Not so far."

"After dinner, you can check the garbage bins out back."

"Thanks, I will." Maria took an egg timer from the stove and placed it on the table. "Shall I let Pancho join us?"

"He's still air-drying."

She opened the door. "I've always been partial to the fragrance of wet fur." Jubilant to be with his pack, the soggy canine shook water onto the melamine cabinets. Pancho laid his big head on Maria's shoes. "He looks fierce, but he's really very gentle."

"Panch is taking you under his wing. I learned that my neighbor's husband raised him as a police dog. He responds to Dutch. Get a load of this!" Roy lifted his right fist, curling the bicep inward. "Zit!" The German shepherd sat. Now, he upraised an arm in one fluid motion and held the palm up. The K-9 lay down and awaited his next instructions.

Maria clapped. "Smart! Does he, umm, attack?"

"The trigger word is," the sheriff concealed his mouth, "'s-t-e-l-l-e-n.'" He envisioned the serrated knife in Park Jin-ho's hand. "Means bite. I haven't tried that command."

"Let's pray you never do." She took a seat across from him and dished out two servings of wood-fired pizza.

"What's the timer for?"

Maria turned the plastic dial to 60. "Roy, you've got one hour to tell me everything about yourself. The whole enchilada. Don't waste a second of this opportunity."

Davis attempted a lame joke. "Is this what's known as speed dating?"

Pancho sprang to his feet when she stood abruptly. "I'm way too old for this."

"It's just—"

"Bill and Nora say you're broken. That it's my duty to fix you. They swear you're worth the effort. Are you?"

The bell dinged sixty minutes later, but the man spoke for another one hundred and twenty. He told her of his murdered sister, his distraught parents, the killing fields in Iraq, the reason he entered into law enforcement, and of greater salience, why, at his age, he still lived alone. By now, night had fallen, and the pizza's congealed lumps of mozzarella cheese required reheating. As the propane oven hissed, Roy prepared himself for Maria's reaction.

Friday—December 15, 2017

Olivia sat on the mattress, staring out of the hotel's floor-to-ceiling windows. Beneath a gray sky, office workers in an adjacent sky-high building woke sleeping computers and drank strong coffee to keep their own brains online. If she saw them, she figured they saw her too. The man in the king-sized bed moaned, snorted, and reverted to regulated breathing. *Not too bad for a cherry boy,* Stewart thought. She backtracked around the room to retrieve her clothes. *However, he needs to comprehend that real life is nothing like those morose pornos he watches on the dark web.* A mislaid shoe lay below a chair. *What might my boss think of me "deflowering" a Patron?*

Whereas Olivia was no longer frightened Morrigan would send one of her henchmen to drop her into the nearest lime pit, she understood her actions had been careless. Not ever, under any condition, could she meet with Thomas Hayden again.

Prior to the Handler's impromptu trip to New York City, the Curator had spoken to her via video chat. To Olivia's surprise, Morrigan hadn't been threatening or even peeved. She had only lavished accolades upon her assistant. "Thank you for preventing that lush from talking to the police. We're also grateful you took on that side job while you were stationed in Bisbee. Why didn't the flatfoot while away his golden years playing bingo instead of meddling in other people's affairs?"

"Do you regret having me take out the ex-detective?"

"Not at all." The Curator frowned. "Do you?"

"No."

"Upper management has been keeping tabs on you. I've heard you may be promoted."

There was no mention of Olivia's decision to let Sheriff Davis live. She received a large cryptocurrency bonus and an additional member to oversee, a child psychiatrist from San Diego, California. Apparently, the Patron's customary Handler had vanished.

"It won't take long for us to find him," her manager promised, before terminating the secure connection.

Since Olivia had incinerated her final set of foster parents, she had slept with many men and woman—never twice or for anything beyond physical pleasure. She slipped into the wrinkled dress, strapped on her pumps, and stood by the bed.

Tom looks so peaceful. Do I look this angelic when I sleep? The Handler pondered why she had bared herself to this particular liability. Olivia restrained her fingers from sweeping a stray lock of hair from his brow. *Should I leave Tom a note? What can I say? Great time last night. Sorry, but I had to— Girl, stop, stop, stop. He's a client. Are your hormones out of whack?*

As Stewart waited for the elevator, she jammed the flower arrangement inside the trash receptacle.

On the way to the bathroom, Maria stubbed her two-ounce little toe on a ten-pound dumbbell protruding from underneath the bed. She hopped about the bedroom on one foot biting the web of her hand. By her effort to suppress a yowl of agony, the giant continued to snore.

The clacking '70s flip clock swiveled Flores' head. 4:35 a.m. *Why is everything in this place so old?* She gathered her clothes and, stepping into her panties, paused. The nurse perched on a rush-seat Shaker chair—*this might actually be a collectible antique*—clutching her things. *This bedroom breeds depression. And that spare bedroom down the hall, the room with the pictures of his murdered sister plastered to the walls? That tomb ought to be sealed shut until hell freezes over. Somebody should douse this double-wide with gasoline and set it on fire.* Maria contemplated the man hogging the blanket. *And that somebody lighting the match isn't going to be me.*

Maria recollected Roy's expression once the mental dam collapsed—an endless chain of words gushing from his mouth. She had prompted him forward with "How did that make you feel?" or "What did you do then?" but overall, Maria gave Roy her ear. The sheriff's life story contained too much dolor for her easy digestion.

"Some mornings," Roy disclosed to Maria, "I wake full of hope. As the hours drag by, I wage war with an onslaught of despair. Other days begin deep in despair and, somewhere along the way, hope throws me a life preserver. Most of the time, I feel like," he wiped his eyes with a shirtsleeve, "Sisyphus."

The boy had become a man, yet each day the man pushed the same boulder up the same hill only to have the damned thing roll back down and flatten him. His sister's slaying defined his every conscious moment and yielded ripe fodder for his reoccurring nightmares.

Flores had always been tempted and seduced by the wrong kind of men. Her last boyfriend, a U.S. Border Patrol Agent born with the slick name of Thorn Ravensong, became a thorn in her side. Ravensong got a blast out of provoking immigrants standing on the Mexican borderline, at that time, X-shaped barricades designed to stop vehicles, not people. The agent slandered the men's mothers, wives, girlfriends, sisters, and daughters. When the outraged migrants crossed the line to defend their family honor, Thorn administered a beat down with "Lucille" (a riot club he named after a barbed wire-wrapped baseball bat featured on a hit TV series).

Whenever a case of Corona Extras loosened the bully's coarse tongue, he loved to give his lady a blow-by-blow accounting of the day's events. At first, Maria thought Thorn jested or exaggerated. The border agent demonstrated he wasn't doing either by showing her a series of atrocious pictures saved on his phone. When Maria failed to change her hotheaded boyfriend, she realized it was she who needed to evolve. *How can anyone be attracted to someone so reprehensible?* Flores left Ravensong while she still had an ounce of self-respect and her two front teeth.

The series of men before the border guard had likewise proved to be of no worth. *Such a bunch of macho a-holes.*

Maria's gaze swung again to Roy. *Was tonight a mercy fuck? Or does being with him mean something more?*

She saw the German shepherd watching her from the doorway. As the dog lifted his muzzle to whine, Maria coaxed, "Come here, boy." He padded to her side and sat still as she rubbed the soft fur under his collar. "What did I get myself into, Pancho?" The bed frame sagged as the big animal bounded atop the mattress and lay at his master's feet.

Chilled, Flores stood and placed her garments on the slat-backed chair. She crawled back into the bed, shoved Roy onto his side, and wrapped her arm around his warm chest. It took Maria many clacks of the flip clock to nod off. She dreamed of a rusty trailer blazing in the desert.

Monday—December 18, 2017

Alex pulled up the bottom sheet and probed for the slit in the mattress' fabric cover. He wedged his hand inside the foam core and extracted a cell phone. At Hopscotch Liquors, Hill had purchased five burner phones from a sketchy bloke selling electronics out of the trunk of his car. The banged-up prepaids (undoubtedly hot) worked and had adequate minutes. He pressed the green button on a Nokia, squirming as it powered up.

The college student itched to ask Sheriff Davis about his grandfather's toxicology tests—*petrified they were positive*—and he wanted to inform him of the recent killing of a New York City Transit cop. Alex also longed to talk to—*and empathize with*—somebody else who knew William Hill and the enigmas he had exposed. Decent people were being slain for no reason other than for some sociopath's personal gratification.

After Alex returned with his parents to Savannah and headed back to Georgia Tech, he had programmed his software tools to fine-tune the parameters of the abstract visualization dataset. Drawn to the newer homicides, the computer science major modeled the color-coding to duplicate the legend on an earthquake map: cool blue for the older dates ranging to red hot for the latest. Hill nicknamed the globe revolving on his Dell's screen "Planet Death" or, if he had inhaled copious amounts of Acapulco Gold out of his roommate's ceramic Yoda bong, "Grandpa Bill's Orb of Wicked Wonder." When the toker came down from his THC high, neither of these appellations seemed especially funny.

Alex had given Roy the telephone number to the prepaid phone his grandfather had sent him. A week had rolled by, and the cell phone hadn't beeped once. Unnerved, he crushed the questionable device under a chair leg. The Cochise County website listed a general number for Roy Davis. Hill dialed the ten digits and pushed the Nokia to his ear.

A woman answered. "Cochise County Sheriff's Office. How may I direct your call?"

"Sheriff Davis, please."

Marge Connors asked, "And what is this referring to?"

"I'm. . .he left me a voicemail."

"Your name?"

Alex, going backward to the evening they shared at the Evergreen Cemetery, tried to picture any noteworthy memorials or monuments Roy might have seen as well. *The big mausoleum with the columns had "Kosok" written across the top. What was the first name?* He had read the bronze plaque, but it had been dark and. . . . "Andy. Andrew Kosok."

Marge jumped back on the line after four minutes of staticky hold music. "Mr. Kosok, what is your phone number? Sheriff Davis will call you tonight."

Rachel Martin logged in to the 57 portal. She gnawed her fingernails while she waited for the meeting to start. Once long and elegant, the unpainted nails were cut to the quick. Martin speculated on who the organization had appointed as her new Handler. *Male or female? It doesn't matter.* She spit out a sliver of keratin. *They're all the same—gasbags who think they know what I want. Those pencil pushers know diddly-squat.*

Rachel's last Handler, fat and ugly Howard Grossman—*God, such a perfect name for a flat-headed man*—lay mummifying below a cubic yard of aridisol at a primitive campground outside Borrego Springs. *Howie shouldn't have*—

A woman's face, her porcelain skin as smooth and as white as a toilet bowl, appeared in the video chat window. "Good morning, Rachel," Olivia greeted in a British cadence.

"Great avatar," Martin said with sarcasm.

"Thanks. It's wonderful to meet you. My name is Lorelei. I'm taking over as your Handler."

"Oh, the siren who lures men to their deaths. Nice, although I prefer a German accent."

The laughter squeezing from the laptop's micro speaker sounded tinny. "Ah, you're well versed in Germanic mythology. I can already tell how much fun it will be for us to work together. I'd open up about myself, however, revealing my true identity is against company regulations."

"The only time we get to interact physically with our Handler is during the initial 'sales pitch.' I met Howie at the San Diego Safari Park with a man who called himself the Accountant. After a catered lunch in a hospitality tent, the Accountant shot the server in the forehead. Claimed the guy was an informant. He showed me a recording device in a bag of ice. Nobody fooled me with that old parlor trick. Hilarious! Do you aim to bullshit me too?"

"No," Stewart assured. "Your file says you've been with us for four years and have successfully completed all four vacations. Congratulations on your achievements! You finished your trip three weeks ago?"

"Anchorage was marvelous. I've been so relaxed since I came home. No more migraines. No more insomnia. Looking forward to next year."

"Made any plans?"

"Not yet. Still catching up with work."

"Patients at your practice? The children?"

The psychiatrist smiled. "It's a labor of love. The youth are our future."

"Contact me if you need my assistance. That's my job. On the last holiday, you gave your male Sentinel a low rating. Your comment stated: 'Jack is surly and insolent.' Was there a problem with his performance?"

"Lorelei, I may have been overzealous when I filled out the survey. Under the circumstances, I understand the basis for Jack's stress."

"The Sentinels had to break into your hotel room. Jack and Jill found you passed out on the floor drenched in the Pawn's blood."

"Just relaxing after a little me time. No need for them to barge in like the Bobbsey Twins."

Olivia peered into the she-cat's hooded eyes. *This woman is now my headache. I am dealing with an unknown quantity.* "Rachel, do you know what happened to your former Handler?"

"Howie?"

"Yes, Howard Grossman."

Martin dug a fleck of desert dust from underneath her ring finger's ragged nail. She stared at the webcam. "Lorelei, I wish I could be of help, but I've no idea where Howie ran off to."

Alex had kicked off another round of foosball when the Nokia rang. He begged pardon from his dormmates, left the rowdy common area, and sat halfway down the stairwell. The telephone number on the cell phone's screen might be the call he anticipated, the device's previous owner, one of his or her contacts, a wrong number, or a psychopath on his way up the stairs toting a fire ax. "Hello?"

A gravelly voice asked, "Can you talk?"

"I'm by myself and using a disposable."

"Me too," Roy said. "You shouldn't phone me at the Sheriff's Office."

"I had no better way of getting ahold of you. Do you have the results from my grandfather's tissue sample?"

"Just heard back. The toxicology reports indicate high levels of saxitoxin."

"What's that?"

"Saxitoxin is a neurotoxin. Poisoning can occur from eating shellfish contaminated by algal blooms. This concentrated substance was in all likelihood synthesized in a military lab. The toxin induces respiratory failure through paralysis. An ingested dose the size of a grain of sand is enough to kill an average-sized man. The saxitoxin might have been administered as an aerosol."

"Someone murdered my grandpa?"

"'Fraid so. Presumably the same person who shot Park Jin-ho. My condolences." Roy waited for Alex to take in this news, thinking he may hear bawling.

The young adult rallied in short order. "How does a civilian get their hands on a neurotoxin?"

The kid's smart as a whip, Davis thought, *and he's got backbone.* "Nixon banned biological warfare in 1969. Congress later discovered the CIA kept a secret stash. Other countries, Russia and North Korea for example, stockpile all kinds of bad shit."

"Bad shit happens to good people."

"The world's been that way since the first man ate from the tree of knowledge."

"Sheriff Davis, are you religious? My parents raised me Baptist."

Roy recalled scrubbing the innocent Kurdish chief's gray gloop from his beige combat uniform and seeing the bloated corpses of immigrant families blackening below the Sonoran sun. He had seen enough bad shit to last several lifetimes. "In this line of work, it's hard for me to imagine God as anything other than dead."

Alex heard a door open and close. "Hold on a sec." He stalled until the jabbering girls were out of earshot. "There's an item you must look into. In New York City, a male pushed a female undercover transit cop onto the subway tracks."

"The Big Apple is worming with scumbags and screwballs."

"You ever hear of the dark web?"

"Alex, I may not be a millennial, but I'm not a Neanderthal. Our office works with numerous governmental agencies to squash the cockroaches who believe they can run free under the cloak of anonymity. Onionland ain't so dark when we shine a laser beam into the cracks and crevices."

"Sheriff, I uploaded a folder of subway security system files to the darknet. Compare these suspects to the ones who stabbed the bartender in Anchorage. Standby, I'm texting you the address."

"Son, I cannot provide protection if you keep breaking into every server on the internet."

"No hacking necessary, sir. The Metro Transit Police posted the videos on YouTube. Use the Tor Browser to remain incognito."

"Thanks."

"What's our plan?"

"The plan is, Alex, you're gonna hit the books to honor your grandfather's memory."

"They poisoned him. *Your friend.* Aren't you furious? Don't you want retribution?"

"Hell yeah! Those motherfuckers did their damnedest to toast my dog and me. An eye for an eye and a tooth for a tooth? I'll be the first in line to uphold Hammurabi's Code, but," Roy raked the stubble stippling his chin, "the immensity of the organization we're up against is overwhelming. I can't worry about your welfare and also do my job."

"Sheriff, you need me. We're the only people who know what those cutthroats are doing!"

"Cool your jets. I'll call you."

"Use a new phone every time we speak."

"Will do. Goodbye, Alex. Stay safe."

"Hey, Sheriff. God isn't dead...just hibernating during a long, cold winter. When God emerges from the cave, he *or she* shall be mighty pissed at the mess we've made."

Chapter Thirteen

Tuesday—December 19, 2017

OLIVIA STEWART SAT AT A SPARTAN PINE DESK in her log cabin's airy loft. She pinged her manager via a secure connection: *Got a minute?*

What's happening?

Any news on Howard Grossman?

No.

Olivia stared intently at the computer monitor. Did the two letters mean "Nothing to report, still searching for Rachel Martin's Handler," or did the curt response signify "Howie's dead, mind your own damn business!"? Conversing with the Curator felt like tiptoeing on eggshells. *I met with my new Patron.*

Good.

Stewart, wanting to appear positive, yet gain insight into her latest client's inner nature, typed: *Rachel Martin didn't believe the Accountant killed the server at her Onboarding Conclave. Thought we tried to bamboozle her into signing.*

No hoax that time.

I read the recap of her vacation. The Sentinels documented a problem. Martin conked out in the hotel room after accomplishing her mission. They had to break in and extract her.

The doctor is a high-paying customer. Prominent in society. Are you capable of managing her, or should we find someone up to the job?

When they had last conferred, the Curator showered the Handler with praise for her work. Olivia had received a nice bonus and talk of a promotion. Today, Morrigan's clipped words made her sweat bullets. *Everything's going well. I apologize for bothering you.*

Anything else?

No. Thanks. Upon ending the messaging session, the program permanently deleted the text thread.

Olivia never had the occasion to pose the central questions she absolutely needed answers to: "Is Rachel Martin the cause of Howie Grossman's disappearance?" and "Am I in grave danger?"

In the spare bedroom, Roy made one more side-by-side comparison of William Hill's screenshot of Megan Guthrie's suspected murderers and the subway video Alex Hill uploaded to the darknet. In the pixelated image, a stumpy, bald male and a willowy, red-haired female accompanied a short, black-haired *male?* through the Falling Water Inn's lobby.

The Lafayette Avenue Station security clip exhibited a man and woman (physically similar to the bartender's killers) hoisting a mustached male dressed in janitor's overalls (the person who fought with the female Metro Transit Police officer) onto the subway platform. The subway couple's ski masks hindered the sheriff's ability to match their facial features to the couple at the inn. Davis' intestines knotted as they ofttimes did when too much shit sluiced in from too many sources. *I can feel it in my bones. Those are the....* "Same two people!"

On the bathroom toilet, Roy correlated the dates. *I noticed two guys in a plumber's van on the morning Park Jin-ho hit Daniel*

Barton with his car. They seemed to be following Jin-ho. Saw their faces, definitely both male...not the man and woman who assisted the killers in Anchorage and New York City. Maybe, those men aren't part of this whole mess. Hell, I know they are. The barmaid, Megan Guthrie, was stabbed a week after Barton, the bicyclist, was choked. Sharon Moore, the subway policewoman? He counted on his fingers. *Nine days later, the subway train mowed her down. The fat guy and the ginger gal had enough time to be in both Alaska and New York. Who shot Park in the head and set his truck on fire? The goons in the white van? Could be, but I didn't see two men. Only one, possibly a woman. The gingernut? Ginger would be in New York with Fatso. A fifth person? Another female?*

Davis flushed some of his anxiety down the bowl, washed up, and went to get a beer. The refrigerator only cooled two cans of Diet Pepsi. He recalled the priest's Serenity Prayer at William Hill's funeral. *God, grant me the serenity to accept the things I cannot change, the courage to change the things I can, and the wisdom to...to.... That's the hitch. I haven't the brainpower to understand the difference.*

Roy let Pancho outdoors and tossed a tennis ball to the far corner of the yard. The dog never tired of this game, and his master enjoyed lobbing the toy even if playtime soaked his hand in slobber. *Let's sum it up. The three people murdered were: Daniel Barton, Megan Guthrie, and Sharon Moore. Trades? A divorced mortgage broker, a single barkeep, and a married undercover cop. Now for the suspects. Attempted homicide of Daniel Barton by Park Jin-ho, completed by Van Guy Number One and Van Guy Number Two. Somebody using the alias of Natalie Bailey skewered Megan Guthrie. Fatso and Ginger helped him or her to escape. This twosome also aided the man who killed the subway police officer—the Janitor. And the woman who bumped off Park? We'll refer to her as Toyota for now. Toyota coulda shot me. Why not?*

Under the azure sky, the fuzzy, greenish sphere in his wet palm reminded Roy of Alex's computerized globe and the homicidal dots covering every continent. He threw the tennis ball to Pancho. *I should write this down.* The sheriff climbed into the mobile home, opened a cold soda, entered the second bedroom, and began a new link analysis chart on the only empty wall.

Wednesday—December 20, 2017

In the garage of her house in Creede, Olivia scrolled through Tom's messages. He texted her constantly at all hours of the day. She hadn't replied to any of them. In the beginning, the theme of the requests remained needy, but passive: *Phone me. I must see you again. When can we meet?* Now, the capitalized words left no doubt as to the man's state of mind: WHY AREN'T YOU CALLING ME BACK? DON'T YOU WANT TO SEE ME AGAIN? WHERE THE FUCK ARE YOU?

The toned-down declaration from minutes ago appealed: *Didn't you think we had something special?*

Stewart packed the cell phones she used to communicate with Hayden and her other clients into a cardboard carton. She hesitated to close the corrugated flaps. *Do we have something special? How will I know?*

Olivia sat in the center of the garage, drew her heels up to her body, rested her palms on her knees, and in the Burmese position, shut her eyelids. The Handler used Transcendental Meditation whenever her job or outside influences encumbered her, and Thomas Hayden had become a burden she had not before encountered.

Olivia focused on her breath, reiterating her single-word mantra. *Squirmles, Squirmles, Squirmles. . . .* Squirmles had been her googly-eyed pet during an extended stay at one of the foster homes. A cleverly concealed string brought the green, furry, wormlike toy to life, pure magic for a child without a stitch to call her own. The woman's pulse moderated as her mind's eye watched little Squirmles dart and dance through her tiny fingers. *Squirmles, Squirmles, Squirmles.* The vision morphed from a goofy worm's face to a handsome man's face. *Tom, Tom, Tom. . .fuck, Fuck, FUCK!*

Olivia dug into the assortment of cell phones, found Tom's, and typed a wrathful reply: *Nothing took place between us! Please be professional!* She threw the iPhone inside the moving box and double-taped the lid.

Thursday—December 21, 2017

Nora entered Roy's office and closed the door. She stomped to and fro, huffing, puffing, and waving sheets of paper.

Davis wondered if it ever came to a throwdown, would Clarke come out on top in a hand-to-hand fistfight? *Probably in the first round—unless I fought dirty.* "What now?"

"I'm so. . .ugh. . .upset!" The chief deputy leaned over the computer screen. "Go to YouTube and type in 'Arizona Sheriff Shoots Unarmed Man.'" She laid a printout on the desk. "On the way to give you this report, I heard the TV in the breakroom. Christ on a cracker. . .it's all over the news!"

Roy, dreading what he might see, launched the video and enlarged the dim image to full screen. He watched himself approach a black Ford Expedition, recognizing his own keyed up voice shout, "Cochise County Sheriff's Office! Sir, shut off the engine and put your hands out the window!" Park Jin-ho ignored his directive. Davis tapped pause. "Who shot this?"

"The bike rider Park almost turned into pavement pizza."

"Our eyewitness vamoosed after the accident. We never discovered where the kid lived."

"It only took him minutes to upload the video to the infobahn."

"I followed procedures." Roy juggled his lucky bullet. "You can hear me announce myself. Reached for my TASER, not my Colt. Did everything on the up-and-up."

"Hit play," Nora instructed.

In the handheld clip, the sheriff rapped on the SUV's window, motioning for the motorist to crank down the glass. Roy grabbed for an object on his duty belt and dragged the driver out of the truck. Jin-ho's body jerked as a bullet struck his shoulder. Reddish mist sprayed from the Korean's head as both men slid below the Ford's hood. The point of view tilted to the ground and ended.

Davis pounded the tabletop. "That's what happened!"

Nora gestured at the monitor. "Read the remarks."

The video already had a million views and three thousand comments, most defamatory. Roy glossed over the shorter outcries—":-(" and "This makes me sick!" or "FUCKTHEPOLICE!"—going straight to the meatier castigations.

"The dude had his hands up! Murder!"

"Deputy Dipshit should not have been given a badge or a gun!"

"Train peace officers not to panic under pressure."

"Unlawful use of deadly force. Fry Barney Fife in hot oil."

"Another unarmed Asian shot by police. Would the cops have killed Park Jin-ho if he was white?"

"Put the Nazi swine in prison for life. Better yet, give the pig the electric chair!"

"Law enforcement can't be the judge, jury, and executioner. Penance is for the Will of God."

"Gunned down like an animal because of the color of his skin."

"Stupidity is no excuse to shoot anyone!"

"Park Jin-ho's sole crime was being Asian in America."

"The lies don't add up! Call the Internal Affairs Hotline!"

"Coward with a GUN. Run Coward RUN!!!"

This last upbraiding boiled the sheriff's blood. "Where's the rest of the recording? The part with Park clutching a knife and Pancho biting his arm? And the shooter? I can't see the goddamn shooter!"

The ringing telephone drowned out Nora's unhelpful comeback.

Roy jabbed the speakerphone button. "Yes, Marge."

"Clay Cooper from the *Sierra Vista Herald* is on the line, and a writer from the *Douglas Sun-Times* is on hold."

"Put Clay on. Notify the other fella I'll get to him next."

The dispatcher sounded out of breath. "Sheriff, the phones are lighting up like a Christmas tree. Transferring Mr. Cooper now."

Roy heard a click, and asked, "How you been, Clay?"

Cooper cleared his throat. "*I* got a bit of phlegm; however, it appears *you* stepped in a tar pit."

"Nothing sticking to this old dinosaur's bones. Can I assume this call concerns Park Jin-ho?"

"How did you guess?"

"Is this conversation on the record?"

"Everything's on the record, 'cept, if it ain't."

"Look, Clay. We go back to high school. You read the medical examiner's report. Dr. Jensen stated the shot killing Park Jin-ho came from a high-powered rifle located fifty yards distant. I didn't fire my gun, nor did I have time to arm my TASER. My dog kept Park from disemboweling me. Someone else blew his brains out. You watched the video?"

"A thousand times in slo-mo. Due to the illumination and the viewpoint, it's challenging to see who did what to whom. Still, I get why the 'hands up, don't shoot' activists are up in arms. When is your department going to get body-worn cameras?"

"They're on order! Jin-ho was implicated in the Daniel Barton hit-and-run. Another person, or persons, strangled Barton after Park whanged him with a rent-a-car."

"Any reason why you withheld this information from the press?"

"To protect the investigation, that detail is classified. Buddy, you can't publish what I just let slip."

"Sheriff, give me something. Can you comment on Frederick Morales?"

"What of Freddie?"

"The man standing in the way of your reelection fired up a Twitterstorm. Haven't you seen what he's saying?"

"No, Clay. I'm busy solving crimes and putting criminals behind bars. What's that birdbrain tweeting about this time?"

"Morales says you're a drunk who murdered an unarmed man in cold blood. He's awarded you a nickname."

"And what, pray tell, may that be?"

"Dirty Davis."

Roy snickered. "That's the best Freddie came up with? How about 'Rapin' Roy' or 'Douchey Davis'? Clay, I stopped drinking, and none of that other shit is even remotely true. Dr. Jensen can testify the bullet wasn't shot from my Colt."

The journalist coughed. "Sheriff, the public couldn't give a hoot about what you or Jensen testifies to. In today's divisive climate, fake news is the only news that counts. And the more contentious the headline, the more folks want to read the crap written below."

"Clay, what are you going to write? What really happened or complete hogwash?"

"As my pappy before me and his pappy before him, I stick with the truth. Always have and always will. It's a sin all of God's children weren't born this honest."

"Hallelujah and amen. An ink slinger from the Sun-Times is on line two." Roy mustered up the image of Alex's spinning Planet of Death. *Perhaps, if I'm lucky, Clay shall get the scoop of a lifetime and a guaranteed Pulitzer Prize in Investigative Reporting.* "Allow me a couple of days and I'll—"

Cooper interrupted. "Frederick Morales is giving a televised press conference. You might—"

Davis dropped the handset into the cradle and rushed to the breakroom. He snatched the TV remote out of Justin Drake's hand and flicked through the local stations, stopping on channel 15. Morales stood on the top step of the Superior Court building. The semicircular plaza teemed with reporters, townspeople, and tourists. From the camera's upward perspective, the hunky Sierra Vista Police Department corporal gave the illusion he was guarding the courthouse's Art Deco doors against invading marauders. *Jeez, the smug bastard looks impressive on the big screen. Let's hear how the jack off sounds.* Roy increased the volume.

"—warrants a full inquiry by the district attorney into the wrongful death of Park Jin-ho. In my twenty years as an officer of the law, I've brought hundreds of criminals to justice and have participated in dozens of special task forces. Never have I seen such blatant contempt for the rules of our land." Freddie directed his hypnotic stare into the zooming telephoto lens. "Sheriff Davis, I hold you personally responsible for this loving father's unnecessary death. The God-fearing taxpayers of this fine county and our South Korean brothers and sisters implore you to do the honorable thing. We petition for you to resign from governmental office. Check yourself into a drug and alcohol rehab center. Get help now! Come clean! Tell us why you shot Mr. Park!" The corporal tented his fingers. "Now, I'll be glad to take your questions." He waved his hand at a hirsute man in the front row.

The hipster displayed a red, yellow, and green "HAPPY 420" sign. "When will marijuana be legal for recreational use in the state of Arizona?"

Morales scribed the air with an imaginary pen. "Write your congressman or congresswoman. They can submit a proposition on the next ballot." He signaled a dowdy woman with an infant strapped to her chest.

The red-faced mother yelled, "Why can't you stop Mexican wastewater from discharging into the Santa Cruz River? Raw sewage gives my baby runny bowels."

One of the deputies in the breakroom laughed so hard he sloshed coffee onto his boots.

Freddie did a fair to middling job of hiding his annoyance. "Again, that's a political issue. Any questions specific to the Park Jin-ho case?" The officer leveled his palm over his eyes and pointed into the audience. "You there in the blue shirt with the press pass."

"Rex Harjo, *Douglas Sun-Times*. Corporal Morales, are you suggesting the Cochise County Sheriff's Office and the Pima County Medical Examiner's Office concealed or tampered with evidence?"

"Mr. Harjo, as every good citizen with a nose can smell, something is rotten here in Bisbee. Regardless of Sheriff Davis' obvious misconduct, it is not for me to place him where he belongs—in a jail cell. Our district attorney and internal affairs must arrive at that conclusion on their own. Thank you, and have a great afternoon."

Roy realized the breakroom had filled to capacity. "Clarke, Drake. Come with me!" The sheriff corralled the chief deputy and information specialist into his office. He yanked the doorknob forcefully enough to fracture the name stenciled on the door's frosted pane of glass.

Nora folded her arms. "That halfwit's got jack shit. The ME's report will stand up in any court of law. Freddie's blowing smoke up your wazoo to make himself look electable. Right, Justin?"

Roy concentrated his hostility upon the new guy. "What were you discussing with Morales at Dot's Diner?"

"A month ago?" Deputy Drake's face went blank as he scanned his memory banks. "Freddie asked me how I liked the job. I said I just started, and the work was fine."

"That's all?"

"I told him you and I had had little contact since the swearing-in ceremony."

"Sorry about that, Justin. I've been up to my pits in frackle nackle. Marge can set up monthly one-on-ones on my calendar. But first, who posted that video?"

"The boy's name is Owen Collins. He's over in Huachuca Terrace. I'll write down the full address."

A half hour later, Chief Deputy Clarke parked her department-issued Chevy Tahoe in front of the humble single-family home on Vista Drive. A brown Hyundai slumbered under cover of an attached carport. Pink flamingos waded in the kiddie pool's greenish water. Across the lane, girls on a trampoline stopped bouncing to gawk at the law officers walking up their neighbor's driveway.

Nora kicked a soccer ball from the brick walkway. "Sheriff, will you keep your cool? He's only a kid."

Roy, his rejoinder a grinding of teeth, stepped onto the "Wipe Your Paws" welcome mat and rang the doorbell.

A fair-skinned female in a printed cotton housedress opened the door. Her eyes widened in distress. "Did something happen to one of my sons?"

Nora shaded her brow to see through the screening. "Does Owen Collins live here?"

The woman nodded. "Owen's out taking his younger brother to the. . .oh, there he is. You had me worried."

A teenager on a banana-yellow BMX rode into the yard and dropped the bicycle next to the flamboyance of long-legged plastic birds. When the lanky boy caught sight of the official vehicle and the pair of armed deputies, he wrapped his fingers around the handlebars and swung a leg over the seat.

"Hold up!" Roy hollered. "We just want to talk to you!"

Owen's mother put her foot down. "Put your bike away and come inside!"

After the adolescent rolled the human-powered transport beneath the wall-less shed and locked the frame to a pole, the woman received the officers into the small living room. She stretched out her hand. "I'm Charlotte, Owen's mom."

"This is Sheriff Davis," Nora introduced, "and I'm Chief Deputy Clarke."

Charlotte indicated a dark couch pushed under a bright window. "Have a seat. May I get you some lemonade?" When both of her guests responded in the negative, she sat in a pomade-stained recliner. "Why are you here?"

Clarke took out a pad and pen. "We need to ask Owen about the video he uploaded to YouTube."

The mother turned to her eldest in confusion. "What video?" The stone-faced high school senior tugged a cell phone from his pocket and pressed his shoulders against the wall.

"On December third," Davis said, "a man aimed to run your boy over. I stopped him in time, but when I tried to make the arrest, somebody shot him dead."

"Dead? That's—" Charlotte stood and put her hands on her hips. "Owen, why in the world didn't you tell me?" The teenager stuck out his lip and shrugged. "Ever since his father ran away with my maid of honor, my son has been unmanageable. At school, he's barely passing—Ds and Fs. Lies...cheats. Last week I found a baggie of pills and a roll of bills hidden in his sock drawer. As a single mom, I don't know what to do. Owen is a talented artist. The College of Fine Arts awarded him a full scholarship. Now, my son is either moping in his room waiting for his deadbeat dad to come by or he's running wild with his so-called friends getting in all kinds of mischief."

Roy couldn't count the busloads of kids he had sent packing to Cochise County Juvenile Detention. "The teenage years are rough. Owen, why didn't you inform the police you made a video? It might have helped with our investigation."

The boy goggled at the sheriff. "Omigod! You're the cop in the video I shot! Is that big German shepherd out in the truck?"

"No. My dog is at home. Pancho is a former K-9. He rode with me that evening. Can I show you some pics?"

"Okay. Is Pancho named for that badass Mexican general?"

"Yep. The one and only Pancho Villa." When Owen finished viewing photographs of Pancho fetching a tennis ball, eating jumbo pig ears, and sleeping on his back, Roy queued up the YouTube clip. "Mrs. Collins, I must caution you, these images are extremely graphic."

Charlotte, watching the top of Park Jin-ho's head fly off, gasped. "Did you shoot him?"

"Sheriff Davis' handgun was still in its holster." Clarke touched her own service weapon. "Only a rifle inflicts that amount of damage."

Owen blurted, "Mom, everyone thinks the sheriff intentionally killed the driver." Antsy, he picked at a pimple on his chin. "After I stopped recording—"

Roy leaned forward. "Who did you see, son? You won't get in any trouble if you speak the truth."

"Tell him," his mother beseeched. "He saved your life!"

"When I heard the gunshots, I freaked out. I hid behind Old Man Wilson's pedo-mobile and—"

"Owen, quit saying that!" Charlotte scolded. "Father Wilson has always been kind to you."

"Mom, the neighborhood kids are terrified of him. They say he chains altar boys to an iron cross in his tool shed."

The chief deputy raised her palm. "Unsubstantiated claims were alleged against Mr. Wilson." She exhaled. "We *have* confirmed he's not ordained."

The sheriff guided the dialog back onto the right track. "Owen, what did you observe from Mr. Wilson's ice cream truck?"

"A woman."

"Where?" Nora asked. "What did she do?"

"She lay across the hood of a car holding a long gun. The kind the kids shoot up the schools with."

"An assault rifle?"

"With a scope." The teenager spread his thumb and index finger apart. "A short one."

Clarke lifted her eyebrows when Davis made eye contact. "Owen, do you remember the make and model of her automobile? Color? New or old?"

"Old. From before I was born. It had three circles on the front grill. Toyota? Gray or silver. Not sure of the model. Four doors. . .and a ball-shaped thingy on the antenna. A smiley face."

Nora rounded her fingers. "The white Jack in the Box head with the yellow hat?"

"Uh-huh. In grade school, I wanted my dad to buy one for Mom's car. He got angry. Said it was a waste of money."

"Too stingy to spend a dime on his own flesh and blood," Charlotte squawked, "but has enough cash to fly that floozy to Cancún first class!"

Owen closed his eyes and tongued the lining of his cheek. "The license plates had white mountains on a green background. The last three letters were 'AWR.'"

"That's Colorado," Nora established. "Did you see the woman's face? Was the shooter older or younger than your mother?"

"A few years younger? As she stood up, I got a good look. Pretty? I mean, nowhere as pretty as you, Deputy Clarke."

Roy grinned inwardly. "Can you describe her hair color and length? Weight and height? Her complexion—light or dark? Any visible tattoos?"

"She wore a leather jacket and long pants. Skinny, not as tall as your partner. *Jesus.* Did you play professional basketball?"

Nora blushed. "After the Marines, I shot hoops in college. A torn ACL and the handicap of being four inches shorter than the average WNBA player killed my dreams for the draft."

"Her hair and skin tone?" Owen chewed his upper lip. "Kinda difficult to put across in words. I can draw a picture if you want."

Heaps of clothes, notebooks, video game components, snack wrappers, and soda bottles littered the typical teenager's bedroom. A wooden drafting table sprouted triumphantly from the landfill, its slanted surface as neat as a pin.

Charlotte pinched her nostrils. "Owen, pull the blinds and open a window, please." She toed a bag spilling with trash. "What a pigsty. I tell my son to clean his room, but his ears are plugged with wax."

The aspiring artist sat on a stool before the desk and turned on an adjustable lamp. He grasped a drawing pad, gripped a pencil, and sketched an oval. Owen drew quickly, often shading the graphite with his thumb. Twenty minutes later, he presented the finished black-and-white masterpiece.

Sheriff Davis lifted the lifelike portrait. The beautiful woman's eyes drilled into his own.

Chief Deputy Clarke led the lad to the backyard and clasped both of his shoulders. "Owen, I must be blunt with you. Your dad's a dirtbag. He's not coming back and, if he does, he'll let you down again and again. I know. My father was cast in the same mold. Your mom loves you. Stop giving her grief. You have a God-given gift, and you've been granted a single shot to succeed—your scholarship. Go to art school and graduate with honors." Nora smiled and slapped his cheek with a gentle hand. "Don't screw this up, okay, pal? Someday, I'd like to see your paintings hanging beside the *Mona Lisa*."

Outside the Collins' domicile and inside the green-and-black law enforcement vehicle, Roy asked Nora, "Did you scare the kid straight?"

"I gave Owen the same tough love I give you. You're welcome, by the way." She withdrew a sheaf of papers from the glove box. "Read the rundown Deputy Drake put together. It's a bucket list for a nutcase."

"Why didn't you show this to me?" He moved the rows of small font closer to his face. "Ah, I plum forgot to schedule a checkup with the ophthalmologist."

"Boss, I placed the report on your desk this morning. Then, a fat turd named Freddie Morales clogged the toilet. Are you able to read any of this or shall I provide you with an executive summary?"

Davis returned the spreadsheet and put on his shades. "Please, sum it up."

"Justin learned from airline flight manifests that Park Jin-ho took two one-week trips each year for the last three years. He used various false names every time. We know the cities Jin-ho flew to, and we're fairly certain of his activities."

"This was before he drove into Bisbee and made a run at two bicyclists?"

"10-4. It's as if someone sent Park on a scavenger hunt. Instead of collecting an orange tree leaf or a purple hair clip, he carried a list of unusual ways to kill people. In early 2015, using the alias Jung Jin-ho, he traveled to Saint Petersburg, Russia. On a tour of the Winter Palace, he offered a cup of strychnine-laced tea to a Polish widow."

Roy rubbed his Adam's apple. "Horrible way to go."

"I hope I croak in my sleep or get smushed by a falling meteorite. Later that year, as Choi Jin-ho, he visited *Neza-Chalco-Ixta*, a mega-slum in Mexico City. Park used a car battery to electrocute a woman selling black-market gasoline. Multiple burns covered her chest and back."

"Torture?" He frowned. "I heard automotive cells have enough amperage but lack the volts to stop a healthy human heart."

"A standard twelve-volt DieHard can't deliver more than a bad shock or a second-degree burn. The sadistic fuck operated a separate electrical device. Something called a *picana*. Picture a souped-up cattle prod—high voltage, low current."

The sheriff pinched his jowl. "You'd think a lone Asian male would stand out."

"He did. The Federales interviewed a gang member who saw a foreigner matching Park's description near the murder scene."

"I'm reluctant to ask about 2016."

"That summer, on a jaunt to Cairo, Egypt, Park identified himself as Shin Jin-ho. At the Ramses Luxury Resort and Spa, he put a pneumatic framing nailer to unholy use. Have you watched any of the *Hellraisers*?"

"The horror flicks where that ghoul in the black leather frock harvests human souls? What's his name again?"

"Pinhead is a Cenobite. A swimming pool service technician found an elderly Brit floating in the hotel's hot tub. Hundreds of ten-penny nails were driven into his shaved head. Seven months later, our same killer, Yoon Jin-ho popped up in Varanasi, India, to drown a Hindu yogi bathing in the Ganges."

Roy mused. "Park Jin-ho used four different methods to dispatch four different strangers before he rode into our one-horse town. Using an automobile to run somebody down seems the easiest means of them all, yet he bungled both times."

"Individuals collaborated with Jin-ho while he was in Bisbee. Is it your opinion Park had help during his other homicidal holidays?"

"Can't say." The sheriff did not want to drag his chief deputy deeper into the quagmire. He studied Owen Collins' drawing. *I've got a face and part of a Colorado license plate number.* "You guys did a bang-up job on this report. Thanks."

Chapter Fourteen

Friday—December 22, 2017

THE WALL OF SECURITY CAMERAS AT THE NACO PORT OF ENTRY captured an image of the female illustrated in Owen Collins' exceptional portraiture leaving the United States on December third. On the Mexican side, a Kawasaki off-road motorcycle was hot-wired shortly after the Federales discovered the scorched remains of a Toyota Camry. Now, the sheriff possessed an actual photograph of the murderer he hunted, as well as the missing four digits of her vehicle's license plate. The problem was, as fate would have it, the automobile's license plates were not registered to a Toyota Camry. They belonged to a BMW X5 that had been cubed in a car crusher seven months earlier.

Roy needed a break in the investigation. Yesterday, he sent the woman's photo and left a message with the one person who could help. The interminable waiting ended with his burner phone, a Samsung Galaxy, buzzing. Davis nearly declined the call in his haste to respond.

Alex whooped in his ear. "Sheriff Davis, I located her! Well, sort of."

"Calm down, son." Roy felt his own pulse speed up. "We should refrain from using our names on an open connection."

"My fault. I was just— Hey, what's that howling?"

"Pancho. He wants to go outside."

"You've got a dog?"

"Is it that strange I have a pet? Shake a leg and tell me what you dug up!" The sheriff visualized the grave they had excavated in Evergreen Cemetery. "Sorry for using that turn of phrase."

Hill batted aside the faux pas. "When you said the Camry had rusty fenders, I examined a map of the salt belt. The states neighboring Arizona with high levels of corrosion are north and northeast—Utah, Colorado, and Kansas. Because the stolen plates were registered in Colorado, I started there. I intended to hack into tollbooth security; however, cameras are only installed on the turnpikes around Denver and, anyway, it would be—"

Davis cut in. "Like looking for a needle in a haystack."

"A pin in a field full of alfalfa. Besides, I have a full plate cramming for a Hoare Logic and Model Checking quiz. I promised Grandpa Bill I wouldn't flunk out during my freshman year."

"Alex, I cannot handle the thought of you bagging groceries for the rest of your life."

"No worries. I came across the answers to the previous year's exam. Last night, I put on my thinking cap and slid into a pair of your hot lady friend's high heels."

"That 'lady' is not my friend." Roy's spirit leapt from his chest as he pictured Maria's dazzling smile. "She's a professional killer."

"Don't become buried in semantics. The Toyota's driver had to buy the vehicle someplace, correct? And as you said, the lady is a pro. She'd be careful. A used car lot has too much paperwork to complete, and grand theft auto gets you pulled over by the po-po. Her best option? Carry out the transaction with a private seller using cash money."

"On Autotrader?"

"Tried that," the college student said. "I hit pay dirt on Craigslist."

"Doesn't the database administrator delete the advertisements when the item is sold?"

"The ads automatically expire after a week and—*pop!*—they dematerialize into the Upside Down. Have you heard of the Wayback Machine?"

The sheriff ran his fingers through his remaining hair. "If I could return to my boyhood, I'd do things much differently."

"My dad regrets not flossing when he was my age. You can't undo a root canal, but *you can* go back in time in cyberspace. I'm sending you a link to a public notice I found in the Internet Archives."

Roy clicked on the URL landing on a Craigslist Pueblo listing for a 1999 gray Toyota Camry LE selling for $2600. He enlarged each of the six images.

Agitation constricted Alex's vocal cords. "Do you see it?"

The sheriff rescanned every photo, this cycle absorbing the finest elements. "The rust on the fenders?"

"No! Look at the antenna!"

"Oh...geez Louise! How did I miss the Jack in the Box head?"

"And we've got a winner! What do we do now?"

Davis selected the icon depicting an envelope and a telephone. He wrote the contact name, "Baxter," and the number. "Can you wave your magic wand and whip up a location?"

When Hill laughed, he sounded eerily like his grandfather. "The address for Baxter Fitzroger is listed in the online white pages. He lives on 208 Ponderosa Drive in South Fork, Colorado."

Roy, accustomed to getting dumped and unaccustomed to doing the dumping, had no experience initiating a breakup. It pained his heart to say goodbye to the women he deeply cared for, yet he also felt accountable for her safety.

Maria peered at the man tethered to a German shepherd by a bejeweled leash. "Roy, we're not even going out. In your eyes, were we ever a couple?"

"You brought pizza. I spilled my guts. Don't you recall staying over?"

"Close intimacy takes more than a slice of pepperoni and a romp in the sack. Are you off the wagon?"

"No." He stretched his arms and puffed out his chest. "I feel terrific! Will you watch Pancho until I come back?"

"What? Where are you off to?"

"On a vacation. Hopefully a short one."

"Nobody hopes their vacation is short," she sputtered. "And no one in his or her right mind cuts someone loose and a minute later asks the same person to babysit their pet while they race off and—"

Roy held forth a bagful of tennis balls. "Please, Maria?"

Saturday—December 23, 2017

The sheriff, snooping in the windows of a late-model Nissan Altima, heard a husky voice. "Lookin' for something?"

A thin as a rail old-timer walked a chubby puppy up the shoveled driveway.

Roy kneeled in the snow to pat the wriggling beagle's shoulders. "Is this your place, sir?"

"Ayuh," the homeowner said in a crisp New England accent. "Sadie's so friendly she'll get herself into hot water someday."

"Did you own a 1999 Toyota Camry?"

"Who's askin'? You a statie?"

In normal circumstances, the law officer elicited a reaction (positive or negative) using the implied power of his official uniform, plus an authoritative downturn of his prickly eyebrows if required. A half-day drive from Cochise County, Davis stood on this gentleman's property feeling like a trespasser. "Arizona sheriff here in Colorado on unofficial business."

"Are you after your woman?" Baxter Fitzroger inquired. "Has your sweetie run off and left you high and dry?"

Roy had to chuckle. "No. Not my wife or girlfriend. Still, you're right. I am here about a woman."

"Didn't think she's yours. Wasn't the type of filly even a man of your caliber could tame. What'd that she-devil do? Draw and quarter the head of the Roman Catholic Church?"

"Sir, I'd rather not say."

"'The wicked are estranged from the womb! They go astray as soon as they be born, speaking lies!'" Fitzroger expectorated chewing tobacco juice. "Book of Psalms, chapter fifty-eight, verse three."

"Praise be. Are you able to describe the female who bought your Camry?"

"Wore a big visor and dark sunglasses. A real humdingah—though not the kind who'd let you sleep without keepin' one of your peepers open." Baxter spit the wad of chaw onto a snowbank. "Brings to mind a bald eagle I saw at an aviary. That majestic bird of prey lets you step up to the cage to snap a photygraph, but, if you wanna keep your sniffer attached to your kisser, you better keep your distance. Catch my drift?"

"What gave you the sense she's treacherous?"

"Heard any stories about the Worcester State Hospital?"

"Uh-uh. Where's that?"

"Massachusetts." Baxter packed his gum with fresh Red Man. "Formally known as the Worcester Lunatic Asylum. Built in the 1870s. Demolished now—*thank the man Jesus.* I worked as a social worker in that loony bin for forty-some years. Seen my quota of crazy—learned all the warning signs."

Roy, having lived by the motto "to protect and serve," nodded in commiseration. He passed over the image from the Naco Border Crossing and a photocopy of Owen Collins' sketch. "This the buyer?"

The Northerner took a long look. "Ayuh. I asked her if she wanted to take the car for a test drive. No, suh! The lady counted out the cash, and I handed her the pink slip. Not givin' me so much as a 'thank ya, mighty nice to meet ya,' she hopped in ol' Betsy and put the pedal to the metal."

"Which way?"

The man rocked back on his heels and twisted his white beard with a brown-spotted hand. "South Fork is the proverbial fork in the road. From here, you've got yourself two choices: northwest and southwest. If it were me, I'd bang a uey and head down to a warmer clime. You must have folks at home waitin' on you."

"Can't do that, sir."

Fitzroger's index finger wavered, then aimed northwest. "With an engine running on a quarter tank, the woman you're bird-dogging couldn't get too far without ol' Betsy gettin' a drink. The next gas station is twenty miles away, in Creede."

"Thanks for your cooperation." The sheriff grasped the Yankee's palm. "For your own well-being, and mine, I advise you to keep our little talk under wraps."

Baxter picked up Sadie and stroked between her ears. "I moved from Leicester to find some peace and quiet. The closest neighbor is far enough he can't hear my night screams. I ain't sayin' nuthin' to nooo-body. Good luck officer. You'll need it."

In the small town of Creede, the sheriff motored along the main drag. Minus the rocky heights, the former mining town reminded him of Bisbee. He stopped at a gas station, went inside the mini-mart, and, after standing in line wasting valuable time, showed his prints to the clueless clerk. At a crowded café, a waitress glanced at the photograph, shook her head, and scooted off to take another order. Roy ambled down Main Street, entering every shop (except for the local Sheriff's Office). No one remembered the individual in the images.

At a veterinary office on a side road, Davis had good fortune. Dr. Nguyen put on her bifocals and tapped Owen's portrait with a chipped fingernail. "This woman came in three weeks ago. Her Siamese was due for a booster shot."

"May I have her name and address?"

The vet looked at him closely. "Who are you again?"

"A friend."

"I can't give out any protected health information."

"Doctor, no HIPAA statutes exist for animals."

"Sorry, I'm unable to be of assistance." She turned away.

The sheriff touched the sleeve of her white lab coat, and pleaded, "Please! It's important."

Tuong-Vi, seeing desperation written across Roy's wide face, opened the file cabinet and placed a purple folder on the counter. Faintly reproving her decision, she left him unattended.

The Google Maps Street View of Silver Drive rendered a roofless house with no windows or doors. The sheriff gave the border crossing photo to the receptionist. The chirpy girl confided, "Peak season, only three hundred people live in our community." She pushed the picture over the desk. "Don't quote me, but I think I saw her on Cliff Street."

On an unpaved roadway beneath a rugged escarpment, a man sprinkling rock salt on his front steps took a gander at the woman's likeness and pointed at a log cabin. Davis slapped a Pest Control Pros cap on his head, clinched a clipboard, dropped a pocket-sized revolver in his jacket, and approached the woodsy domicile. The only footprints disturbing the light dusting of snow covering the wraparound porch were his own. He rang the bell and rapped on the rustic front door. Nobody answered, so Roy circled the ground floor, climbing on snowdrifts to peep in each window. *Empty, no furniture. The eagle flew the coop.*

The sheriff returned to his rental car, carrying back a pry bar to jimmy the rear door. Inside the scrubbed and vacuumed house, he found cat litter granules on the laundry room floor and a long strand of black hair stuck in the master bedroom's shower drain. Davis put away his latent print kit. Everything down to the toilet bowl levers had been wiped clean of fingerprints.

In the two-car garage, Roy used a tree branch to snag a flattened carton from underneath the workbench. The small, square, red and white Autolite box once held a "1 PIECE FL-1 C1AZ-6731-A 6000 MILE OIL FILTER." He dialed an Atlanta area code, relieved to hear the buoyant voice.

"Send me pictures," Alex requested. "Is anything else written on the container?"

"A date is printed on the bottom. 1970."

"As in fifty years ago?"

"Yup. When the Beatles broke up, Baby Leroy was still in diapers."

"Yuck! Does the cardboard appear to have been lying there for that long?"

"Negatory. The paper hasn't yellowed. An oil smudge is all."

"I'll phone you right back." Hill hung up.

Clarke answered her cell phone. "Howdy, boss. How's your vacation?"

Davis sighed. "Every once in a while, it's nice to breathe in some clean air and frolic in the wonders of nature." In the cabin's master bedroom, he sat cross-legged on the plush carpeting with his shoulders against a rough-hewn log wall. Within the gloom, the sheriff tried to cast a light upon any harbingers lingering after the previous occupant's departure.

"That'll be the day, when Roy Davis frolics anywhere. I talked to your ex-girlfriend. God, you're such a prick."

"Nora, I thought I spelled it out for you. I am a prick *and* an asshole. Did Maria talk about my mother? Did Pancho ask how I am?"

"Your mom is well. Your dog put on five pounds eating treats. Maria is concerned about you."

"And I about her. How are things at the office?"

"It's weird not seeing your effervescent smile and hearing your constant words of wisdom."

"I miss you too, Chief Deputy. Has anybody given you any guff since I left you in charge?"

"No. In fact, employee morale has improved tenfold."

"Excellent! Is the social media lynch mob building me tall enough gallows?"

"The tweets died down to a trickle. Freddie Morales will most assuredly amp up the rhetoric as the election draws nearer."

"Let the pompous ass knock himself out," Davis muttered. "Please help me with something?"

"Sure, boss. Anything legal or, up to a certain point, semilegal."

"Could you swing by Maria's place every so often to check on her?"

"Why? Are you afraid she'll move on?" Nora pressed the receiver to her ear. "Or did you put her in harm's way?"

"Yes to the first, maybe to the second." Roy's Samsung vibrated. "I must take another call. Talk to you later."

The sheriff terminated the connection and accepted the incoming. "Alex, what have you got for me?"

"That oil filter fits a short list of 1964 to 1974 Ford and Mercury models." Hill yawned. "I looked up the part number under sold items on eBay. These babies are almost as rare as a crystal of painite. One, still in the box, recently sold for $295."

"Three hundred clams for an old oil filter?"

"Auto collectors go all out to keep their classic cars original. They'll pay a fortune to color their friends green with envy. The ad's title stated the part fits a Boss 429 Mustang. Ford produced this high performance model in 1969 and 1970."

Roy whistled through his teeth. "Those vintage muscle cars sell for a quarter of a million."

"Substantially higher at auction if the engine has low miles and everything down to the butts in the ashtray is authentic. Last week, the seller sold an OEM hood scoop to the same customer."

"Here in Creede?"

"Classic Mustang Parts sent the oil filter to the house you're at. They shipped the scoop to an address in San Diego, California."

"What's the name?"

The college student, bearing in mind the ramifications of his research, said softly, "She goes by Katherine Knight. 292 Bayard Street in Pacific Beach."

Davis chewed the nuggets of consonants and vowels, forcing their sharp edges down his maw. "How did you talk the seller into divulging the purchaser's personal information?"

"Bribery. I had to break my piggy bank. Sheriff, you owe me two hundred smackeroos."

"You'll get repaid every copper cent if that address pans out."

"I need to be there when you catch her. I want to—"

"Thanks for your support." Roy disconnected before Alex could finalize his sentiments. Sapped from his travels, the sheriff lay flat on the shampooed carpet and blanketed himself with an area rug to stop shivering. He dozed off listening to the wind slipping through chinks in the walls.

Roy dreamed in Technicolor. Helen, full of life, danced gaily around the rooms of their childhood home on Laundry Hill Road. Outdoors, alone in the woods, the vibrant saturations achromatized to a monotone. An eyeless skeleton attired in a tattered tuxedo—*Dad?*—escorted the boy to the site of his sister's murder. As Helen's putrefying corpse surfaced from the murky depths of her watery grave (her worm-filled mouth yawning open to welcome him), Roy awoke to the noise of ringing.

Sunday–Christmas Eve—December 24, 2017

Alex asked Roy, "Did you leave Creede yet?"

Davis rubbed his eyes and mumbled into his cell phone, "Huh?" *It's four a.m.* He gazed about the unfamiliar bedroom. *Where am I?*

"Sheriff, are you all right? You sound out of it."

Roy pussyfooted to the window. Outside, a van in need of a muffler delivered Sunday newspapers to the few still in want of the printed word. "Alex, you woke me up."

"My bad! After we hung up, I checked the San Diego crime blotters."

"Don't you ever sleep?"

"The sandman only comes for those born without ambition. In your field of work, did you ever stumble across a defenestration?"

"Once."

"Seriously?"

"I witnessed a self-defenestration." Roy pulled on the tip of his nose. "One fine evening, I finished off a thirty-pack of Bud and went to close the window in my mobile home. I tripped, crashed right through the bug screen. Came to the next morning in a flower bed covered with fire ants. Smeared a tube of hydrocortisone cream on the bites and drove my itchy ass in to work."

"Whoa! You can drink thirty beers in one sitting?"

"That ain't nothing. Andre the Giant reportedly chugalugged a hundred and nineteen 12-ouncers in six hours. Fill me in on this defenestration."

"A janitor saw a female push a male from a bank building's window. The man fell twenty-two floors and hit one of those rickshaw tricycles—the type where you sit in the back and someone with calves the size of tree trunks pedals you about town if you're too lazy to walk or too hammered to drive."

"Was anyone in the pedicab hurt? Were other people helping her?"

"The driver is in critical condition. The pusher seemed to be solo. Are you presuming she did it?"

"Who?" Roy sank to the carpet. "Katherine Knight, the owner of the quarter-million-dollar Mustang? Or are you referring to Natalie Bailey, the cross-dresser who honeycombed the barmaid in Anchorage?"

"Sheriff, we'll find out together. Let's book flights to San Diego today."

"Alex, thanks again, but now it's time for me to take it from here."

Chapter Fifteen

Monday–Christmas—December 25, 2017

Roy exited San Diego International Airport. He drove the gas-sipping white Kia Niro along Harbor Drive wondering why the traffic was so light. Ships floated in and out of the bay, the same as they had a month earlier when Rachel Martin boarded the jet for Alaska. By the docks, a homeless person foraged for recyclable soda cans and half-eaten sandwiches in a garbage receptacle. A Mexican serape hid his or her age.

Then it hit him: *Today is Christmas!*

The sheriff reflected upon family holidays of yore and the brother he hadn't seen in *over twenty years?* Five years ago—*or is it now ten?*—in this very city, the police charged Timothy with vagrancy. Roy should have taken time off from the job to haul his younger sibling out of the gutter. Instead of setting Tim back on his two feet, Roy had created a plethora of excuses to ignore the issue. By the time he adjusted the rearview mirror, the rubbish picker had dropped from sight. *That wasn't my brother.*

Roy had reserved an overpriced room in a downtown hotel, and, after spending the night lying on the log cabin's hard floor, he desired a soft pillow to rest his cheek on. Ten o'clock in the morning was too early to check-in. Anyhow, the sheriff had a more imperative mission. The Australian female imprisoned inside the rental car's navigation system directed the driver to take a right and steer north. He crossed above a waterway veering past the slew of cars queuing into SeaWorld. Over a bridge, across an island, and over a final bridge, Roy entered the small seaside town of Pacific Beach. With the windows down, he caught a whiff of salt and sunscreen—way too long since the desert dweller had laid his eyes on so much water and so much bare flesh.

The sheriff hung a left onto Garnet Avenue and cruised by a thousand hole-in-the-wall restaurants, bars, and tattoo parlors. A block from the ocean, he made the last turn onto Bayard, the street Katherine Knight had her Mustang hood scoop sent to. A succession of nondescript two-story apartment structures evolved into cute one-story vacation homes. At the cement roadway's tree-lined end, Roy saw her address: a well-kept yellow cottage trimmed in white with a ship's steering wheel and two rowboat oars bolted above the garage. Davis lowered the brim of his exterminator's cap and sailed by gazing straight ahead.

On a side street, the sheriff halted the automobile and weighed the few options for surveillance. He had planned to locate his vehicle within eyeshot of Knight's house. The red-painted curbs limited parking. Roy thought about William Hill as he downloaded the Airbnb application to his cell phone and studied the map. Dozens of properties in the area were available for rent during the rainy season and were far less expensive than the ritzy downtown lodgings. He booked a room with a view of the suspect's abode and notified the hotel to cancel his reservation.

Roy let himself into the neighboring building using the lockbox key. The studio apartment—a mishmash of exotic plants hanging from macramé knots, perforated metal Moroccan lanterns, and handmade Turkish area rugs—stunk of potpourri. A welcome basket included a bag of tortilla chips, a jar of salsa, and bottled water.

Davis ducked beneath the pink canopy and unpacked his suitcase on the tie-dyed bedspread. He unlocked the handgun case and loaded the untraceable Smith & Wesson Bodyguard with ammunition. On patrol in the unforgiving Sonoran Desert, Roy had discovered the Model 38 beside a man lying under a crucifixion thorn tree. The drug scout's leg was swollen from a rattlesnake bite. Black ichor leaked out of a thumb-sized hole in his temple.

The sheriff grabbed the field glasses, sat in a rattan peacock chair, and trained the magnifying lenses on the adjacent house. A cat sprawled in the front window. The one-eyed Siamese heard the garage door raise and hopped down.

Roy observed the female driver swing a green Honda Accord into the garage. *That worthless clunker ain't no priceless muscle car.* The sectional door closed before the taillights shut off, but not until he recognized the vehicle hiding in the shadows. "Shit, oh shit, that's her!"

The wild man trapped inside the lawman thirsted to sprint across the road with guns a-blazing. Nevertheless, he settled into the wickerwork seat and braced his heels on the windowsill. While the sheriff lay in wait for the killer to make her next move, he munched on tasteless fried corn wedges dipped in jarred salsa and pondered where Maria was, what she was doing, and who she was with. Roy wished he was spending Christmas with her. Dispirited, he gorged on the chips and went to sleep.

Tuesday—December 26, 2017

Late in the afternoon on the day after Christmas, the garage door on the far side of the street raised again. Katherine Knight backed the Honda into the street and headed north.

The sheriff snapped up the dead man's gun and jogged out to his rented Kia. He made an illegal U-turn into traffic, flooring the gas pedal to keep her in sight. The driver appeared to be in no rush, staying to the speed limit and braking at every stop sign. Davis followed the Accord up a steep hill. In a cul-de-sac, Knight parked at a house with a "FOR SALE BY OWNER" sign posted in the front yard. He stopped in an empty driveway to watch the tall, lean woman open a gate and enter the residence's backyard.

As the sun dropped below the horizon, Roy snuck to the grassy expanse behind the next-door dwelling. He crouched underneath a manzanita shrub, getting his first real peek at the person who bagged Park Jin-ho. *She looks like a supermodel on the cover of Vogue.* Davis set the Galaxy to camera mode, turned off the flash, and fired off a series of Knight peering over the precipice. *What is she staring at?* He accessed Google Maps, switched to satellite view, and zoomed in on the solitary object of interest: a sizable mansion with a large swimming pool. *I'm watching her watch someone else.* The sheriff skulked between flowering spikes of purple fountain grass to the perimeter of the terrace. He saw a well-toned female in a red bikini climb from a lighted whirlpool bath, dry herself with a beach towel, and go indoors.

Roy hustled to the cul-de-sac, slapped a magnetic real-time GPS tracking device under the Honda's rear fender, squeezed into his Niro, and rolled downhill.

Olivia Stewart strode back to her car, got in, and checked the hour. *Six p.m. on the dot.*

Each afternoon, Rachel Martin adhered to the same rigid schedule after driving away from her swanky La Jolla medical office. At home, poolside, she began her intense exercise routine by riding a stationary bike for precisely thirty minutes. Twenty-five freestyle laps and a half hour lifting free weights came next. Finally, following a fifteen-minute soak in the custom spillover hot tub, the psychiatrist went inside to dress for the evening.

Olivia ripped open a foil package of Pop-Tarts. *She'll be leaving soon.*

At a taco stand, Roy ordered a carnitas burrito and—Dos Equis XX Special Lagers packed in a bucket of ice chanted his name—a Diet Pepsi. He sat at a table with a million-dollar vista of the moon floating above the Pacific Ocean and started the tracking application on his smartphone. The blue-colored dot representing Knight's Accord remained at a standstill at the Havenhurst Point cul-de-sac. Then, just as his teeth sank into the juicy flour tortilla, an alert beeped. The blue spot moved eastward. Davis took one more healthy bite and threw the lion's share in the trash.

From a safe distance, Stewart let Martin lead her down the winding roads. On Interstate 5, the sluggish Honda had to weave through traffic to keep pace with the 600-horsepower Mercedes-Benz. Both cars left one of the nicest areas in San Diego, the "Jewel by the Sea," to go to a place the naysayers had christened the "Homeless Ghetto."

At a stoplight in midtown San Diego, Olivia watched Rachel park her boxy SUV at a closed smog test station and open the rear door. She dropped a bottle in a large shoulder bag. *That hellion is up to trouble tonight.*

Even with no solid proof, the Handler believed her Patron had extirpated her predecessor, Howard Grossman. Olivia had vacated her cozy log cabin in mountainous Colorado to set up an observation post in the vast wastelands of Southern California. *Keep your friends close,* she thought, *and your enemies closer. Tell me, Olivia, what friends do you have?*

After Stewart heard news of a recent defenestration, she became suspicious Martin had broken the tenet her organization had engraved in granite: *Don't kill outside of 57, no matter how much you may want to.*

To revitalize the popular Gaslamp Quarter, city politicians had pushed the homeless-serving nonprofits into the East Village. Rachel didn't need to walk far along the dusky streets to find what she searched for.

The placidity the doctor retained upon returning from her successful hunt in Anchorage had swiftly evaporated, leaving her anxious and depressed. She hadn't intended to clobber her Handler with his own Bible. *Shit happens.*

Howard Grossman had mistakenly revealed his nearby home address. When Martin arrived uninvited on his doorstep, the porcine man's holier-than-thou attitude and misogynistic belittling drove her into a rage. She seized the first thing she saw on a bookshelf, a thirty-pound, leather-bound, four-hundredth-anniversary edition of the King James Bible, and bashed his brachycephalic skullcap to a pulp. For the voracious cross-trainer, digging the desert grave turned out to be a super upper-body workout.

Howie's death, rather than tranquilizing Rachel, had electrified her. She constructed her own 57 Varieties list, crossing off Asphyxiation – Drowning; Other Weapons – Microwave Oven; Narcotics – Methamphetamine; Transfixion – Pins and Needles; Blunt Instruments – Book; and, not long ago, another entry under Other Weapons: Defenestration. The psychiatrist couldn't wait to check off number seven: Immolation.

Roy knew from the motionless blue dot on his phone the latitude and longitude of Katherine Knight's parked Accord; still, he had no sense of which direction her toes now pointed. The Arizonan sheriff, acclimated to open spaces, felt hemmed in by the East Village's many residential and office buildings. Eager to find the female he pursued, Davis rotated on the balls of his feet unable to peer over the tall walls of steel, concrete, and tinted glass. *North? South? Dammit, I should have stayed closer.*

A tremulous palm touched Roy's shoulder, and a liquor-slurred voice asked, "Spare a war hero some change?"

The sheriff turned to see two hazel eyes staring from a black-bearded face. Caught off guard, he grasped at straws. "Tim? Is that you?"

The vagabond, a "Roland's Plumbing Services" patch sewn to his filthy overalls, used a shopping cart overburdened with purloined copper piping to shore up his tottery legs. "The Grim Reaps came for Brother Gravy on the Day of Thanks. Tied him on the back of a three-legged horse and galloped off to the hot place where there's nary a drop to wet your whistle. Gravy had a terble case of," the panhandler unkinked his degenerating spinal disks and mouthed the next syllables with conviction, *"hep-a-syph-a-fuckitis."*

Roy recalled the mobile hand-washing sinks stationed on each street corner and the hepatitis A advisory posters taped to every lamppost. "Was his name Timothy Davis?"

"Damned if I know. Hey pardner, gimme a ciggy-ret?"

"I quit. Are you Roland?"

The beggar clawed at the oval embroidered moniker. A saliva bubble formed by the unsealing of his lips burst as he uttered, "Dat man dead."

Roy held up Owen Collins' drawing. "Ever seen this woman?"

After Roland tucked the sheriff's Jackson into his underwear, he hooked an index finger at the Central Library's glowing dome. "The Duchess of Pain is where I come from—Camp Woe."

Rachel trotted by the library's brightly lit entrance, mindful of the security cameras mounted to the colossal cement columns. Although the doors stood wide open, at closing time, people flowed out, not in. Bookworms with a home to get to rode the elevator to the parking garage or raced to the nearest public transportation stop. Those who expressly used the book repository to stay warm and dry lounged on the steps, tramped across Park Boulevard to the squatter encampment, or, seeking the great unknown, wandered into the night.

All the rescue missions were crammed into a region bordered by Balboa Park, the Gaslamp Quarter, the Embarcadero, and Interstate 5. Thousands lived here on the streets. Martin only needed to pick one—*the person who properly answers my question.* She had canvassed the county's various homeless hot spots—Escondido, Chula Vista, National City, and Oceanside—always querying the identical five words. "Will you be my sacrifice?"

Each vagrant's naked terror, or worse, his or her catatonic stare, made Rachel irate. *I must finish this tonight. Should I lower my standards?*

Martin approached a long string of tents and lean-tos packed against a fence surrounding a new construction site. A handful of men and women sat outside on coolers or lawn chairs, guarding their shopping carts and bicycles. She shook the rainfly of a 2-person pop-up tent. "Pardon me! Anyone in there?"

A voice croaked from the portable shelter's interior, "Who's asking?"

"A friend. I've got something for you."

"What?"

"A present."

The unzipping nylon door vented a blast of fetid air. A gray-topped head poked between the flaps and looked up. "Let me see."

Martin initially thought the round face belonged to a man. Her eyes penetrated the deep folds of flesh. *It's an old hag in a sleeping bag.* "If you answer my question correctly, or at least come close, you shall receive this lovely," the doctor extracted a plastic bottle of cheap rum from a brown pouch, "gift."

The woman's toothless gums glistened. "That's all I have to do?" She popped in a set of yellowed dentures. "Then, fire away. Try to stump me. I used to be an English lit teacher."

Rachel shook the quart liquor container filled with gasoline. "Tell me your name, dear."

"Isabella. Isabella Hayes. Everybody calls me Izzy, except for my students. They called me Ms. Hayes." Isabella's palsied fingers snatched at her prize.

Martin unscrewed the cap. She reached into her pocket for a strike-anywhere match, then hesitated. A candle stuck in a wine bottle flickered inside the tent. "Izzy, will you be my sacrifice?"

Isabella's wrinkles gave birth to more wrinkles. "Say again?"

"Will you sacrifice yourself for me?"

"You mean, kill myself?"

"No, dear. Suicide is a mortal sin. I'll do the work for you. Just give me your permission."

"Lady, are you off your rocker?" As the ex-schoolteacher cupped her hands to scream, the psychiatrist squeezed the flexible flask. High-octane fuel squirted into Isabella's mouth and onto her green polyester sleep sack. The wine bottle wobbled as she kicked her legs to break free from the insulated body bag.

Spittle shot out of Rachel's lips. "Say yes, Izzy! Say you'll die for me!"

A stone's throw from the library, at a small city park now serving as a makeshift camp for the destitute, Olivia Stewart's silenced Walther P22 spit muffled pops as she marched out from under the date palms and into the intersection. The Handler's inherited client had gone rogue, and she resolved to end the mayhem posthaste and without hesitation.

Over the week Olivia followed Rachel around the County of San Diego, she had spotted the doctor talking to scads of street people—never near enough to distinguish the individual words. Tonight, the Handler picked up each blared phonetic unit loud and clear. Olivia, a fugitive who had lived among the outcasts of society, did not relish seeing her fellow sistren and brethren being taken advantage of.

Stewart aimed the laser sight higher than Martin's head in a calculated effort to scare, not exterminate. When the Patron flung the open bottle of gasoline inside the tent and disappeared into the campground, the Handler regretted her resolution to avoid collateral damage. As Olivia rammed a fresh magazine into the pistol, somebody carrying the essence of slow-roasted pork knocked her into a plot of Spanish daisies. The Walther flew out of her hand and skittered across the pavement. A metal grate prevented the firearm from flying down a storm drain.

One of Olivia's foster "dads" had been obsessed with televised professional wrestling. She didn't use Wild Bill Longson's neck-breaking piledriver or Killer Karl Kox's stupefying brainbuster to inflict maximum devastation. Stewart used a collegiate wrestling fundamental, the reversal, to rock and walk her hips out from underneath *him*, and a Krav Maga self-defense technique to twist his gun down, wrench the grip from his injured hand, and stick the barrel in his. . . . *You've got to be kidding me.*

The luminous, resourceful eyes Owen Collins had penciled in his messy bedroom merged into the golden-brown eyes staring down the sight of Roy's own Smith & Wesson Bodyguard. *If she wants to murder me, why hasn't she?* The sheriff, pinned to the bark chips by her muscular thighs, contemplated his situation. All of Davis' ideas for escape concluded with him making an express trip to the Pearly Gates, Saint Peter pulling a skull-capped lever, and an iron trapdoor dropping his unworthy ass into the ninth circle of hell.

Katherine Knight bounced to her feet and demanded, "Get up!"

Roy examined his bent digit and winced. "You broke my trigger finger." The man doubted he had the strength to achieve a leg scissor takedown. *I should have spent more time pumping iron at the gym and less time sitting behind a desk lifting mugs of Irish coffee.*

"Don't be a baby." Knight kicked Davis in the rump. "Stand up! We must find her!"

The sheriff sat upright. "Find who?" A bright flare, followed by a wave of radiant heat, singed the side of his face. He swiveled to home in on the origin of the shrills.

A green caterpillar inched from an open tent, stood to shed its burning cocoon, and, now an orange and black butterfly, fluttered toward them.

Knight raised Davis' revolver and shot the flaming woman twice in the chest. Momentum carried Isabella Hayes four additional steps before she collapsed in a smoldering bundle of rags.

"We need to catch the monster who turned this poor woman into a living funeral pyre. Sheriff, you may liken me to Lizzie

Borden, but there are people—your friends and neighbors—who make me look like Mother Teresa." Knight extended the still-smoking gun, butt first. "Shoot me or come with me. Either way, hurry up and choose. The doctor is getting away."

Roy, deciding his survival lay in acquiescence, repossessed his .38 and dashed after her.

Maria had just filled a glass with Merlot and was watching her favorite television show when she heard a double knock. Pancho, snoozing next to her chair, leapt to his paws and padded to the front door.

Perturbed by the intrusion, Flores tossed the remote on the hassock and pressed her eye to the peephole. A thickset male and taller female stood on the brick stoop. "Who is it?" She switched on the porch light and placed her fingers on the deadbolt. The utility workers wore matching tan work boots, brown pants, gray shirts, and red caps.

The woman moved frontward, and said, "Southwestern Gas! We're investigating a leak!"

Maria sniffed the air, not identifying the malodor of rotten eggs. "I don't use natural gas. Merrellgas is my propane supplier." She removed her hand from the lock.

The female gestured to the male who, standing back a foot, delivered a kick to the door's lock rail. His steel-shanked heel drove the fiberglass door inward, smashing the homeowner's forehead and sending her into a glass side table. The imposters stamped into the living room.

"Where's the sheriff?" the redheaded woman shouted above the dog's barking. She withdrew a caping knife from a leather sheath.

Maria inhaled, and yelled, "Stellen!"

The snarling German shepherd had taken a defensive position in front of his newest master. Triggered, Pancho coiled his powerful hind legs, sprang, and clamped his teeth onto the wrist holding the knife. The blade devised to flay the skin from a trophy animal's face clattered to the hardwood floor.

Enraged, the bald aggressor clasped a lamp and beat the dog on the back. The lampshade crumpled and the lightbulb shattered. Pancho still refused to let go.

Flores folded her fingers around the caping knife's handle and swung the curved blade in a long arc. The flat spine grazed the man's meaty calf on the backswing; however, the honed edge cleaved his flexed ankle on the forward swing. Sentinel Lucas Ross (known to his backup partners as Jack or Sonny) keeled over clutching his severed Achilles tendon.

Maria used the couch arm to right herself and charged the female punching Pancho in the nose with her unrestrained hand. Sentinel Abigail Powell (Jill or Cher when teamed with Lucas), seeing her own weapon pointed in her direction, booted Flores in the solar plexus. Winded, Maria slipped on the broken glass, lost control of the knife, and landed on Ross' chest. The enforcer rolled on top of the nurse, wrapped his stubby fingers around her thin windpipe, and grunted, "Where the fuck is your boyfriend?"

As Maria's world turned a final shade of gray, her attacker's eyeballs bulged, his neck convulsed, and hot liquid poured down her cheek and into her ear. She smelled dead fish. *Dog breath! Pancho!* Ross' choking hands slackened. As his head flopped downward, Flores stared into Powell's orange-speckled irises.

"Christ, Jack," Abigail criticized, towing Lucas' limp body to the side. "Must I to do everything myself?" She held the cutting tool to Maria's throat. "Darling, I'd love to get my associate a rabies shot before he bleeds out, but my boss will tan my hide if I don't ask you again. Where is Sheriff Davis?"

Maria Flores wasn't born a violent person. If a spider crawled into the bathtub, she shepherded the wayward arachnid onto a piece of newspaper and set it free outside. When she glimpsed Roy's dog lying in a bloody heap, she saw red. Flores twined her calves around her assailant's buttocks to draw her in close, and hissed, *"Tu madre es una puta fea. Vete al infierno!"* She leveraged the split second her opponent wasted translating her swear words to anchor eight fingers behind the intruder's ears. Maria jammed both of her thumbs into the woman's eye sockets and twisted. Powell shrieked and dropped the blade.

Maria slid the caping knife between Abigail's ribs and, after a few exploratory jabs here and there, stopped the cardiac organ from pumping. She shoved the deadweight off her chest and stood up.

A trail of gore led the nurse out the door, down the steps, and into the front yard. She yanked the dying man's chin up, put a palm over his lips and pinched his nostrils with her thumb and forefinger. It didn't take long for Lucas Ross, or Jack or Sonny or whoever he was, to cease to exist.

Flores hunched on the doorstep cradling her throbbing head in her hands. She heard a noise and spun. Pancho rose from the dead—she hadn't detected a pulse—and sneezed crimson snot onto the wall. "You're alive," Maria cried. "So am I." She lay next to him cheek by jowl. The woman's aching fingers combed the dog's matted fur for wounds. In turn, Pancho licked Lucas and Abigail's blood from her face.

Chapter Sixteen

Wednesday—December 27, 2017

Olivia zigzagged through the first clusters of tents. She peered backward, and chided, "Keep up!"

Roy, his calcified heart pounding and his potbelly churning with spicy burrito juices, paused to catch his breath. "Are you after the woman you were watching in the swimming pool?"

Stewart whirled and aimed the Walther at his face. Her countenance vacillated between very beautiful and very terrible. "I'm screwed." She dropped her arm in frustration. "If they discover that I'm with you, they'll kill me. And you, my friend? Sheriff, you're already dead. You just haven't realized it yet."

Davis perceived the weight of the loaded Bodyguard. *She'll put a slug in me before I get the fucking thing from my pocket.* "You've had two chances to put me out of my misery. Why not? What's your problem?"

Olivia pictured Tom lying across the silk sheets. She stunned herself by saying, "Maybe, I'm losing my edge."

Maria, instead of calling 911, punched in the number for Nora Clarke. Maria and Nora had become lunch buddies. Some days, the women talked about themselves, their families, and their jobs. Much of the time, the ladies compared notes on the individual they had an affinity for—Roy Davis. Clarke wanted to carp about her boss. Flores needed to learn more of the man she cared for.

At one a.m., Chief Deputy Clarke exited her vehicle and walked up Maria's gravel driveway. Amid her new gal pal's telephoned sobs, Nora had caught the phrase "home invaders" and the names "Pancho" and "Roy." She was unprepared to find a prostrate male on the lawn, his esophagus shredded to pieces. Clarke followed a blood trail up the steps, through the splintered door, and into the remains of the living room. A female lay on her back in front of a television playing a rerun of *Keeping Up with the Kardashians*. Besides the knife embedded in her sternum, the corpse lacked eyes.

The chief deputy, intending to radio for backup, heard water running in the rear of the house. She tore her service weapon from the holster, and yelled, "Cochise County Sheriff's Office! Come out with your hands up!"

A woman hollered, "Back here!"

Nora sidled down the hall to the only lighted room.

In the bathroom, Maria Flores sprayed a German shepherd dog with a handheld showerhead. Red fluid and clumps of black hair swirled into the drain. She glanced up. "Pancho tracked blood onto the carpet, so I'm bathing him. Other than a nasty bump on his head, he appears to be fine."

Nora, confident the rug was unsalvageable, shut off the faucet. "Maria, are *you* feeling all right? Who are those people?"

"They were looking for Roy." The nurse stroked the red welts on her throat. "Hurts to talk. Thought I knew where he is. Tried to strangle it out of me."

"Do you know?"

"No. His phone just rings and rings. I think Roy is in some kind of trouble."

"So do I," the chief deputy concurred. "The sheriff contacted me four days ago. Said he was having a ball on his vacation and wanted to hear how it was going at the office. My boss never takes time off. *Not ever.* Then came the real reason he called. Roy wanted me to drive by your house to see if you're.... Oh no, I let them get to you!"

"Nora, you couldn't be guarding me 24/7." Maria snatched a clean towel. The white terry cloth rapidly turned pink.

"I'll call this in and send for a doctor. It's going to become a madhouse around here. You need to get your story straight. Explain to me exactly what happened."

Step by step, Flores told Clarke what took place, skipping over the method she used to return Lucas Ross to his Maker.

As the squawking police and fire sirens faded with distance, Olivia stopped running.

Next to a green Honda, Roy asked, "Isn't this your car?"

Stewart pressed the unlock button on the key fob. "I doubt the doc went home. Still, I need to check. Coming?"

Davis, unsure of her motives, or his, dropped into the passenger seat and snapped on the seatbelt. The Accord's interior reeked of fresh cannabis and stale junk food. When she turned the engine over, he inquired, "Do you often drive the Boss 429?"

Olivia turned the front wheels north. "Is the Mustang how you found me?"

"You left an oil filter carton in your garage." Roy hung on to the chicken handle as she simultaneously steered clear of a braking flatbed truck and slipped a purple vaporizer out of the center console. "And, after moving to Pacific Beach, you bought a hood scoop from the same dealer."

"Stupid of me. How did you locate my house in Creede?" Olivia inhaled from the heated tube and blew a chemical fog out of the rolled-down window. "Want some?"

Roy was dying for a double-hit of laughing grass. "No thanks. I'm trying to get my red sobriety chip." He huffed the secondhand vapor. "Mr. Jack I. Box gave you away."

"Jacky, who?"

The sheriff clarified. "The video shows a Jack in the Box ornament mounted to your Camry's antenna. My advice? Don't purchase high-performance parts on eBay or buy your junkers on Craigslist. Way too easy to trace."

"I never noticed a clown head on my antenna." The Handler brooded over her blunder. "Shoulda taken that little YouTuber for a joyride out to Death Valley. Didn't see that snake in the grass either."

"So, you murder kids?"

"Minors are off-limits."

"But you do kill adults?"

"Are you taping this conversation?"

Davis, taking out his Galaxy to prove he wasn't doing anything underhanded, noticed the screen was fractured. "Look, my phone is dead. Must've fallen on it when I tackled you."

"You're old and slow, yet you managed to sneak up on me." Stewart lowered his window. "Chuck the battery and chip. If you have any more recording devices, tell me now."

"Pull over."

She pumped on the brakes. "Why?"

"I put a tracker in your fender."

Olivia jammed the GPS apparatus under the Honda's rear tire. "Show me your boo-boo."

Roy, hoping for a soft touch, yelped as the woman clutched his wrist with her left hand, and, on the premature count of "two," yanked the crooked digit with her right.

"There we go. Your finger was just dislocated. How's the joint feel now?"

"Much better." The sheriff sucked the swollen knuckle and smiled in relief. "Thanks."

At daybreak, Maria watched a pair of men with the reflective letters "PIMA COUNTY MEDICAL EXAMINER" written on their black jackets load two white body bags into a van. She asked Nora, "How come they didn't arrest me?"

"Because you're not accused of any wrongdoing. It's obvious that man and woman broke into your house and assaulted you. The door is breached, and you have strangulation marks on your neck. Defending yourself isn't a crime."

Flores tugged the yellow "CRIME SCENE – DO NOT CROSS" tape extended across her front yard. "When will they let me back in?"

"In double homicide investigations, the CSI team takes weeks to collect all the forensic evidence." The chief deputy stretched for the small satchel the victim had been permitted to pack. "Come on. You're staying with me."

Maria clung to the bag's shoulder strap. "I must contact Roy."

"You require sleep," Nora advised. "Let's discuss it in the morning."

"This is the morning! I can't go to your house. It's not safe for me, *or you*."

"Maria, I'm a sheriff armed to the teeth. No one would dare to step foot on my property. If I'm at work, my fiancé shall be with you. Aron's taller than I am *and* a better shot." She bent to pat the damp German shepherd. "And don't forget we've got Pancho the Superdog."

"Can you pull up Roy's credit card records and track his cell phone?"

"The real world of law enforcement is not the tripe you see in a movie or on TV. There's no nerdy analyst who, in the blink of an eye, hacks into the Kremlin or the Great Hall of the People. Communications and bank networks do not interconnect. Agencies don't collaborate. We're not the NSA. In any case, you'd need court orders from a judge."

Flores' mind evoked the faces of the two human beings she had just killed. She shuddered foreseeing a future jam-packed with nightmares and night sweats. "Who were those thugs, and what did they want with Roy?"

Clarke shrugged. "Our department will run their fingerprints and search for mug shots. Roy acted oddly after Bill Hill's funeral. He sounded befuddled when I questioned him about a specific investigation—mentioned quitting. Roy urged me to go against Morales in the election."

Maria's eyes and mouth opened wide. "Huh? That damn job is his whole life!"

"Don't I know it."

"Nora, what can we do?"

"We'll get you set up at my place," the chief deputy said. "Then, I'll go to work and check his office."

"One of the rooms in his trailer is wallpapered with crime photos of his sister."

"The sheriff gave me a key to his house. I'll search there too."

Maria handed her overnight bag to Nora. "A kid at the funeral service passed something to Roy on the sly."

"Bill's grandson?"

"Not sure. We weren't introduced."

"He handed the sheriff a piece of paper," Nora said. "I made a joke."

The nurse recalled the punch line. "You asked Roy if he received a coupon for his funeral."

"Not so funny now." The chief deputy stuffed her bloodstained booties and gloves into a biohazard trash bag. "Get me William Hill's contact information."

In the first class of the day, Alex's chin slid from his fingers and fell to his chest. His twitching eyelids revealed the whites of his eyeballs. Despite how hard the college student tried, and how much this class figured into his overall grade average, he seldom stayed awake in Humanities 101. For the umpteenth time, Hill opened his eyes, reset his elbow, straightened his arm, and propped his jaw in his palm.

Alex listened to the familiar thrum of Professor Whitlow's modulation. "The Greeks believed the gods had human emotions. Poseidon, the sea god who fathered the winged horse Pega...."

The value of paying attention isn't what sucked the undergraduate from the hot, salted, soft pretzel daydream and into the fluorescent light of a packed auditorium. What roused him was the sudden absence of sound, replaced by: "ALEX HILL! ARE YOU HERE?"

A kid sitting behind him kicked his seat. "Dude!"

Alex sat up and raised his hand. "That's me, Professor Whitlow. I'm here."

The teacher waved for him to come to the podium where a man in blue waited. At the bottom of the steps, Whitlow instructed, "Please go with this gentleman."

Alex, apprehensive something had happened to his parents, followed the armed Georgia Tech security guard through a door and down a labyrinth of hallways. *Mom's been complaining about Dad's cholesterol.* Then, fearing for his own welfare, the hacker listed the agencies he had broken into. *The ASPCA, the Sheriff's Office, Interpol...oh fuck, the FBI is on to me.*

In the College Admissions office, the guard gestured at a telephone on a desk. "A call for you, Mr. Hill."

He pressed the handset to his earlobe. "Hello?"

"Alex?"

"Yes?"

"This is Chief Deputy Nora Clarke of the Cochise County Sheriff's Office. I have Maria Flores on the line with me. You may remember us from your grandfather's funeral?"

"Lots of—"

A different female, powerless to conceal her angst, interrupted. "Are you able to tell us where Roy Davis is, or how we can get ahold of him?"

"Why?"

The same tense voice answered. "Last night, a man and a woman battered down my door and asked me—"

Hill slammed the receiver onto the base and fled from the building.

Olivia stopped the Honda downwind from the six-thousand-square-foot house on Waverly Avenue. She double-checked her Walther and reached for the door handle.

Roy latched upon her shirtsleeve. "Katherine, who are we going after, and why?"

"Sheriff, we have no time for small talk. Rachel Martin is a psychopath posing as a child psychologist. Rachel is a great white shark circling your tiny rubber boat. You're the helpless hen, and she's the cunning fox. She's the rabid dog tearing off half of your face. We must put this bitch down before we wake up and find her standing over our beds swinging a gas chainsaw. *Capisce?*"

"Yes. I saw what she did to that woman. Are you really Katherine Knight?"

"No, Leroy. Katherine Knight is the name written on a gravestone in Oklahoma. However, to build trust between you and me, I will provide you with my actual name."

When her full lips thinned, he prompted, "Go on."

"If you look at my wanted poster, please keep in mind there are two angles to every story." Tentative, she put out her right hand. "I am Olivia Stewart."

Roy—not seeing the elephant-sized albatross lifting from the woman's shoulders and winging out to sea—clenched her palm. "Only my mother calls me Leroy. Roy catches my ear. Well then, Olivia, why are we still sitting here?" He stepped out of the Accord and cocked his Bodyguard.

Alex—three degrees from a mental meltdown—left the campus grounds. Watching his six, he trudged Atlanta's backstreets passing a progression of seamier and seamier bars and package stores. The underage nineteen-year-old compensated a willing pensioner double for two big bottles of Colt 45.

Lost in thought, Alex found himself in Piedmont Park at Lake Clara Meer. Beneath a thicket of sweetbay magnolia, he unscrewed the first forty-ouncer, regretting he hadn't also grabbed a box of Cheez-Its. The malt liquor certified to "Frick you up every time!" smelled of corn, apples, and burned biscuits. To the computer science major, the amber elixir cascading down his esophagus tasted of the ingredient he paid little for—oblivion.

Chapter Seventeen

Wednesday—December 27, 2017

Surveillance cameras stared down from every corner of the custom-built architectural masterpiece. Besides the redheaded parrots screeching high in the date palms, the neighborhood appeared deserted.

Roy said under his breath, "She's watching us."

Olivia nodded. "Probably from miles away on her phone. I wager Rachel grabbed her bug out bag and headed for the hills. You go out back. I'll take the front." Stewart bared her fangs—a woman in her prime. "Shoot her, not me. Deal?"

Davis—likewise feeling hyper-alive with a loaded gun in hand—gave his *partner?* a little salute. *What will she do once I finish assisting her?* He pushed the gate and descended a concrete stairway to the pool. Roy proceeded past a Peloton stationary bike and a metal rack stacked with free weights to the rear entrance, a thirty-foot-wide length of sliding glass panels. For him to get indoors without throwing a boulder through the double-panes, he needed to know the keypad code. Footsteps bounced off the building's curvilinear walls.

Stewart curled a five-pound dumbbell when she identified the obstacle Davis scowled at. "I cut the telephone line for the alarm. Stand aside, please." Olivia used the weight to knock the plastic keypad off the wall. She twisted red and black wires together. A motor whirred as the glass sections rolled apart. "Didn't your instructors teach you breaking and entering at the police academy?" Her Blackberry hummed. The Curator's urgent message asked: *Why are you with the sheriff?*

Atop Mount Soledad, ground squirrels played hide-and-seek below a thirty-foot white cross. Rachel had a panoramic view of the Pacific Ocean and her home. She accessed the video surveillance application on her smartphone and checked the motion alerts. The doctor selected the "Swimming Pool" high-definition camera and tapped the "LIVE" symbol. The woman who had shot at her and her male companion were outside her house. *That must be my Handler, Lorelei.*

In the home automation app, Martin pressed a round power icon labeled "Rear Sliding Door." A hilltop cell tower relayed the command to the local internet provider. The wireless router in her home office sent an encrypted signal to the electronic gadget plugged into a wall outlet in the room facing the pool. A switch clicked inside the small, rectangular box releasing current down two wires and into a blasting cap stuck in a package of Composition C-4.

Three miles of distance muffled the explosion, and a grove of eucalyptus trees masked the flash, but Rachel observed puffs of gray smoke drifting inland. After she refreshed the camera's live feed, the viewing window displayed the reassuring status: "DEVICE IS OFFLINE."

Thank God for the Internet of Things, Martin thought. She revved up the AMG G65 and, bursting into a Bee Gees song, drove down the hill.

For the second time in a month, the sheriff gained consciousness believing he had passed beyond the veil. Far above, an undulating white orb beckoned for him to draw nigh. As Roy's lips parted to catechize the grand question, a long string of bubbles rose to the—*surface.*

He kicked past sinking chunks of stucco and metal scraps breaking through the liquid-air interface into the land of the living. Roy floated among spruce studs, wads of insulation, and charred Barbie dolls watching the house burn. *Olivia.* In a panic, he paddled around the rectangular pool. In the deep end, a foot poked out from beneath bobbing patio furniture.

Davis swatted away the chair and hooked his arms under Stewart's armpits. He towed her unresponsive body to the shallow end of the pool and dragged her up the submerged stairs. The sheriff, trained in CPR, discerned no pulse beating on her neck or respiration blowing from her nose.

Roy gave Olivia alternating mouth-to-mouth resuscitations and chest compressions. She coughed up a puddle of chlorinated water and fluttered her eyelashes. Olivia saw concern etched on her savior's face; an emotion rarely directed her way. "What happened? The last thing I remember is—"

"Your doctor must have rigged a bomb. The percussion blew us into the pool. I came to at the bottom. You? Not as lucky. I performed...never mind all that. Let's bring you to the hospital."

"Was I out for long? Do I have brain damage?"

"How would someone who has brain damage know if somebody else has brain damage? What's today's date?"

Olivia blinked. "Wednesday, December. . .twenty-seventh, 2017. The president is—" She struggled to her feet and plucked a glass shard from her forearm. "Let's go before the cops get here!"

Alex felt something long and wet slither across his cheek. In disgust, he cried, "Gaaagh!" and sat up. The blue-eyed horse licked Hill on the mouth and, for good measure, lifted its hind leg to mark the arm of his jacket.

A girl called from afar, "Brutus! Get back here!" The black-and-white Great Dane made a spectacle of covering his pee and loped off.

Alex disentangled himself from the pricker bushes, stood up, and swept the dead leaves off his jeans. At a week since the winter solstice, the days died early, and the northern wind chilled him to the bone. Hill, instead of stuffing the stinky jacket in the trash can, rinsed and wrung the offensive sleeve in the lake's freezing water.

The college student slouched on a park bench watching an elderly gent fling bagel bits to a raft of mallards. His head and stomach ached. Mung carpeted his tongue. Alex wished the sheriff had allowed him to go to San Diego. When he dialed Davis, Android Andy intoned, "This voicemail box is not activated. Goodbye."

Should I have spoken to those women on the phone? Why did I run away? Alex stroked his temples and moaned. *Because I didn't know who they were, and somebody could be listening. The lady who claimed to be a chief deputy—Nora Clarke—said she attended my grandfather's funeral. She must work for Sheriff Davis. Maria Flores? Who is she? And who broke into her house?* Streetlamps flickered to life along the walkway. *I've got to talk to them.*

In the public library's computer lab, Hill sat next to a well-dressed executive viewing images of diapered men sucking supersized baby pacifiers. He entered "Chief Deputy Nora Clark" in the search field. Google found a Nora Clarke on the Cochise County Sheriff's Office website. A blond woman positioned in front of an American flag stared into the camera lens. *She seems okay,* he thought, rating her integrity by the sincerity of her smile. Clarke's bio declared the former Marine led search and rescue teams and was the first female SWAT officer in Arizona.

Maria Flores' Facebook profile picture portrayed an attractive Hispanic woman. The "About" established she worked as a caretaker at the Arbors Memory Care Center. Alex scrolled down her timeline to the latest posting on Christmas Day. He looked closely at the selfie of Flores and a German shepherd at a park. The subject stated: "Pancho misses his daddy. Roy Davis, come home!"

That's the sheriff's dog. He never mentioned a girlfriend. Alex typed "Maria Flores" in Google News and found today's headline in the *Herald Review*.

Woman and Dog Kill Two Home Invaders

> SIERRA VISTA, Dec. 27 – The investigation into a suspected home invasion continues. Maria Flores, 41, and her retired police dog fought back when a man and woman forced their way inside her Mission Hills house last night. When Flores answered a knock at 8:45 p.m., the intruders kicked the door open and assaulted her. Pancho, K-9-trained, bit the male attacker in the throat. Flores gained control of the female aggressor's knife and stabbed her in the chest. Both assailants perished at the scene. The unidentified bodies were conveyed to the Pima County Medical Examiner's Office. No additional details have been issued.

Alex inhaled and exhaled to steady his nerves. He strode up and down the stacks of books. *How can I safely contact Nora and Maria?* In the Transportation section, Hill saw the *Beginner's Guide to Ridesharing*.

Chief Deputy Clarke, swamped with paperwork and worried about her incommunicado boss, responded to faint rapping on the doorframe. "Marge?"

The lead dispatcher entered the room. "Your car has arrived."

"What car?"

"Uber or Lyft. Not sure which."

"It doesn't matter." Nora signed another work order. "I didn't order one."

"I will inform her it's a mistake." Connors turned to go.

"Wait. I'll talk to the driver."

In the lobby, a young, malnourished female, heavily tattooed and lightly pierced, browsed a recruitment brochure for the Sheriff's Office.

Clarke walked up to her. "I did not request a ride."

"Uh, yeah, you did," the Lyft driver insisted, motioning for her to follow. Outside, she handed the chief deputy a note. "He asked me to show you this."

"Who?" Nora unfolded the gum wrapper containing the single word "Pancho," and gasped. "Where are we going?"

The girl held the door to an old but spotless maroon Buick LeSabre. "Two stops. First, we must get someone. I'm guessing you know who? Then, we head over to the city of Douglas."

"And you are?"

"Spirit."

"Like in Spirit Warrior?"

"Nah, I don't think so. My mother and father were hippies. I hate the name."

"Spirit, I live in Warren on Tener Avenue. We'll pick up a woman and a dog."

With Maria and Pancho stowed away in the Buick's big back seat, Spirit cruised twenty-seven miles east on AZ-80. On North

Sulphur Springs Street, she stopped at a used tire dealer. A "CLOSED-CERRADO" sign hung in the window.

Nora questioned, "Now what?"

"This is the correct address." Spirit updated the Lyft app to indicate their arrival. "Shall I wait?"

The chief deputy nodded. "Leave the meter running."

Someplace on the acreage, a phone rang.

Pancho's ear pivoted and locked.

Maria gestured excitedly. "Over there! Around the building!"

Behind the warehouse, an artifact from the days before cell phones stood against the galvanized wall. Flores opened the folding door and entered the aluminum and glass box. She raised the payphone's old-fashioned handset. "Hello?"

"Where is he?" a youthful male voice asked. "Do not say anything specific, especially names."

"We hoped *you* knew. He isn't answering his cell phone. Why did you hang up when we spoke earlier?"

Alex stood on the steps of the town library. "I got rattled after you told me somebody bashed in your door." He held the Nokia to his mouth. "I read the news article. You're extremely lucky."

Maria agreed. "I had four-legged help."

"What'd they want?"

"The same thing we need to find out. Where is he now?"

"Our acquaintance bought airline tickets and rented a car." Alex wiped the moisture from his nose. "Their hackers will use this information to track him."

Clarke crowded inside the telephone booth and leaned in to the receiver. "What hackers? Who are these people?"

"All I know," Hill said, "is their organization is big, really bad, and they have a finger stuck in every pie."

"How did you learn of this?"

"Someone in my family carried out a great amount of research."

"Your grandfather?" Maria asked.

"Yes. Our colleague hit the road to find the person responsible for my grandpa not celebrating his next birthday—and something else."

The chief deputy inquired, "What else?"

"The event blowing up on social media."

"You must mean the unpleasant incident with the South Korean. Is the shooting linked to the bike riders?"

"Yup." Alex zipped his jacket up to his chin. "The driver swerved. Both times."

"On purpose? Why?"

"For shits and giggles. Pure entertainment."

"Oh, boy."

"You can say that again."

Maria looked over her shoulder. "And for us to communicate, this level of secrecy is necessary?"

"Even though I'm holding a bagful of burner phones and you're at one of the last remaining public phone booths, we're not invulnerable. How do you think your two visitors discovered your association with our friend?"

Maria sighed. "Was it the Facebook posting of me at the park with his dog?"

"Social media is a huge no-no," Alex admonished. "The last time I talked to our man, I provided him with a woman's address. Couldn't tell you the location he is staying at or even if he's still in the area."

Maria asked, "Where does she live?"

"You only get that information if I go along with you."

"Fine! Is it closer for me to come to you, or should you come to me?"

"I'll fly to Tucson." Alex started walking back to the college campus. "We'll rent a car."

"Tomorrow," Flores said, "book the earliest flight. Meet me at two p.m. under the *Spirit of Southern Arizona* sculpture."

"Are you guys all right?" Spirit called from atop a pyramid of bald truck tires. A tire iron swung from her right hand. "This is a rough neighborhood."

"We're done here." Maria set the handset in the cradle and banged the phone booth door shut. "Let's drop Chief Deputy Clarke and Pancho at the Sheriff's Office. Then, please bring me to the airport."

At the LeSabre, Nora handed their driver a business card. "Spirit, you look like you can handle yourself. Contact me if you're interested in a career in law enforcement. I'll help you fill out the background questionnaire and give you a good recommendation."

Olivia tossed Roy the Honda's keys. "You drive. My head is killing me...and you might have cracked one of my ribs." She sat in the passenger seat and pulled the recline lever.

He sealed the AC vents (the exterior air stank of smoke). "I'm taking you to the ER."

Stewart grinned, grimaced, and groaned. "What cockamamie tale will you tell the triage nurse?"

"I'd say you—"

"Take me home now! It's in—"

"Pacific Beach?"

"Oh, I remember. That damn hood scoop led you right to my front door." Before Olivia closed her eyelids, she added, "That fruitcake better not be hiding in my bougainvillea."

"You think Rachel Martin has the gall to chase after us? How do you know so much about her?"

"When her last Handler went missing, I took over as her manager. Martin's a honey badger—small, won't quit till you're dead or pray to God you were."

Roy felt peculiar being her chauffeur, yet he had to confess, following months of stagnation, today had been exhilarating—like the morning his military boots initially touched Iraqi dirt. *Ready to kick some terrorist ass. But, here and now, whose ass shall be underneath my boot?* The sheriff appraised the drowsy woman. *Hers?* He ran into his Airbnb rental, packed his belongings, then drove across the roadway into her driveway. "Wake up. You're home."

Olivia, her eyes widening in muddlement, recognized Roy, and relaxed. She flipped down the visor and pressed the garage remote.

Davis rolled alongside the Mustang, shut off the ignition, and got out. He slid between the cars and opened the passenger door.

Inside the house, Stewart let go of his arm, and shut the garage door. "Make yourself at home. I'm taking a couple of Tylenols and lying down for a bit."

Roy, uncertain if concussion victims ought to sleep, heard Olivia ascending the steps to the upper level. He explored the kitchen, living room, and dining room, finding nothing out of the ordinary. She lived as sparingly as he did: no bowl of fruit still-life painting, no framed photograph of mom and dad at a Fourth of July picnic, no dusty Statue of Liberty brought back from a New York trip. At an oil-stained workbench in the garage, Davis handled shiny tools and paged through dog-eared repair manuals. A pulled chain bathed the candy apple red Mustang in warm incandescence. He smiled in admiration. *Here is the only place where she can be herself.*

At the kitchen counter, something brushed Roy's leg. A cat with one blue eye leapt up on the center island and meowed. He squinted at the engraved tag hanging from the Siamese's collar. "Kasha, are you as hungry as I am?" The feline strutted along the countertop and rubbed its jaw on a cabinet knob. Davis found a bag of cat food in the cupboard. He shook the dried pellets into a metal bowl.

To quiet his own stomach, the sheriff microwaved a frozen block of cheese ravioli. He ogled the stocked wine refrigerator, wondering if Maria had forgotten him. Roy threw the emptied plastic tray in the garbage bin, washed off the fork, and went upstairs.

In the largest bedroom, Olivia lay on a queen-sized bed. After Roy checked her pulse and felt her forehead, he closed the shutters and covered her with a blanket. Marijuana and a pipe rested on the nightstand.

The sheriff changed into dry shorts and a clean shirt. On the living room couch, he watched Kasha give himself a lick-bath, all the while resisting the gravitational forces of the wine in the kitchen and the weed in the bedroom. When the horizon turned from tangerine to plum, Roy stretched out on the cushions. As he dropped off, his mind sifted through a mixed bag of scenarios—each action having a problematic reaction.

At the foot of Bayard Street, the twelve pistons in an obsidian black Mercedes-Benz AMG G65 idled. The individual in the driver's seat clinched the steering wheel. Rachel was shocked the blast hadn't vaporized her nitwit Handler and her male sidekick. She also couldn't savvy how the lamebrains didn't see her tailing them.

Should I take care of these cretins tonight, or is it more practical for me to complete my project and return tomorrow? The doctor aimed a semiautomatic handgun, a hefty Desert Eagle, at the house the man had driven Lorelei into. *I botched the explosion. If I'm going to do this at all, I'm going to do it right.* She took her toes off the brake and sped to her self-storage unit.

Chapter Eighteen

Thursday—December 28, 2017

ROY AWOKE AND CHECKED ON OLIVIA. She grumbled into the pillow and towed the covers over her head. Later in the day, his patient came downstairs for lunch. Roy heated a can of chicken noodle soup and made Olivia swallow the last drop. On the living room sofa, the two watched the talking heads on cable news laud the left and rant about the right. Kasha leapt from lap to lap, garnering unlimited affection. After the evening meal (frozen dinners), they sat on the back patio sipping ice tea. The man and the woman laid bare their childhoods, each discovering he or she had more in accordance with the other than not.

As the three bright stars of the Orion constellation appeared above the horizon, Olivia offered Roy a space on her mattress. He politely demurred and curled up on the couch. She retired to her bedroom. His eyes shut midway through an episode of *Keeping Up with the Kardashians*. Roy dreamed of Maria dancing in a lightning storm.

Rachel was proud of her do-it-yourself project. She waited in her car for the darkness outside to match the pitch-darkness permeating her soul. When the streetlights shone brighter than the sky, the Patron approached her Handler's house.

Octagonal signs warned of a security alarm, and blinking video cameras hung from under the roof eaves. Stewart made a beeline to a garage window and held still. She tucked the Desert Eagle into her belt, and used a pocketknife to pry out and tug off the rubber beading around the window frame. The doctor tilted out the glass and set it to the side. Since no Klaxon clamored, Rachel clung to the windowsill, jumped up, and slid her waist over the lip. In the garage, she maneuvered between the two automobiles and eased the interior door open.

On the wall, the LCD on an alarm pad flashed "DISARMED." *Am I walking into a trap?* As Martin's eyes adjusted to the kitchen appliances' dim digital glow, her retina's rod cells detected the reflective tapetum lucidum behind a vertical pupil. The feline lowered its head to nibble kibble.

Rachel heard women bickering. She moved on hands and knees past the dining room table toward the source. In the front room, a television illuminated a male figure lying on a sofa. *Where is Lorelei? Upstairs?*

As Stewart had surmised, Martin carried a bug out bag of sorts. The backpack accommodated energy bars, water bottles, a rope, a flashlight, a poncho, a Mylar sleeping bag, extra .357 Magnum ammunition, counterfeit IDs, five thousand dollars in cash, and what she needed now: a military gas mask and an FEP container filled with homemade chloroform.

Rachel returned from the kitchen with a dish drying rack and a hand towel. She flipped the plastic frame upside down, delicately resting the thicker part on the couch's armrest and the thinner end on the snoring man's chest. The psychiatrist covered the rack with the towel and pulled the rubber gas mask over her face. She opened the plastic bottle and drizzled the sweet-smelling anesthetic onto the improvised head tent.

Martin ticked off five minutes, then prodded the sleeper in the schnoz with her gun. *He'll be zonked out for a while.* After Rachel tied his wrists and ankles, she soaked the cloth with additional trichloromethane.

In the upper story master bedroom, Martin used a more efficient—*and more fulfilling*—procedure to subdue her Handler. She smacked the woman she knew as Lorelei over the nape of the neck with the butt of the Magnum, bound her limbs to the bed, and stuffed lace panties in her mouth.

Alex let the rented Jeep Cherokee glide down the west slope of the Cuyamaca Mountains. The high beams brightened the increasing greenery clinging to Interstate 8's broad shoulders. Imperial Valley had been dry as a camel bone. He had never seen that much sand or been so far below sea level.

Maria passed him a sugary bear claw and put his Cherry Coke in the cup holder. She tapped an icon on the navigation system and reported, "Fifty miles to go. Unless we get a flat, hit a deer, or you drive us off a cliff, we should be there in forty-five minutes."

"Great." Hill prayed they were not too late. The two strangers, united for a common cause, had chatted intermittently during the six-hour journey. Maria told Alex about her nursing job at the Arbors. Alex told Maria of his computer classes at Georgia Tech. They both shared their fondness for William Hill. Neither discussed what might happen once their destination was reached. "So, how long have you and the sheriff been together?"

Flores, her mouth overloaded with pastry, washed the almond paste down her gullet with black coffee. "Hmm. We're not together."

"Why not?"

"A month ago, Roy took me out to dinner. A few weeks later, I stayed over at his place. Then, he booted me to the curb and left town. I'm such a dummy for being taken in by one more loser."

"You're no dummy, and he's no loser," Alex consoled. "The sheriff only tried to keep you safe."

"And how did that work out? Phony utility workers broke into my house looking for him. I took two human lives! Now, I'm a basket case. Tell me who we are facing!"

Hill summarized the knowledge he had unearthed, and by what means. The butterflies crawling the walls of Maria's stomach took wing upon learning an international organization arranged "homicidal holidays" for the 1%.

As the car crossed the bridge into Pacific Beach—blocks away from the woman liable for multiple deaths—Alex wanted an explanation. "Maria, may I ask you a personal question? Why are you putting yourself in jeopardy? Do you love Roy?"

The nurse depressed the passenger window button and inhaled a cool blast of courage. "What I can tell you for sure is I'd kill for him again."

The hacker stared at her. "That doesn't answer my question."

Maria bit off a hunk of the bear claw and licked her lips. "Uh-huh, Alex. It most certainly does."

When Roy's eyelids finally functioned, his vision was blurred, his equilibrium was off, and his sinuses felt as if they were packed with wet cement. *Why am I so exhausted? Did I drink those bottles of wine? I need some aspirin.*

The sheriff attempted to sit up. Unable to locomote his arms or legs, he flopped back onto the couch. *Olivia hog-tied me. Knew that murderer couldn't be trusted.* Davis, filling his lungs to call for help, held his breath as the doorknob turned. A female pushed the front door open with her posterior. She dragged a canvas sack across the threshold. *Olivia?*

Roy strained to free himself from the nylon manacles and fetters. "Let me go!"

The woman—*not Olivia...the doctor?*—dropped the bag on the floor. She poured a clear solution out of a bottle onto a dishrag and pressed the fabric over his nostrils. "Sweet dreams, dear boy. When you wake up, you'll see what I have planned for you."

Alex parked the blue Jeep a block from an unostentatious two-level home at the intersection of Bayard and Loring. He read the address. "That's it!"

Maria pointed. "The house with the small patch of grass and the black SUV in the driveway?"

"Yup." Hill frowned. "Not what I envisioned."

"What did you imagine you'd find?"

He scratched his cheek. "Machine gun turrets on the roof instead of solar panels? That house is no different from every other one on this street."

"Whoever's living there wants to remain under the radar." Flores pulled the car door handle. "Just because the outside looks benign, don't trust a bear trap isn't chained to the welcome mat."

As they walked along the sidewalk, Alex asked, "*Are* we ringing the doorbell?"

"No. To quote Sun Tzu, we will 'Emerge to their surprise.'"

"You read *The Art of War*?"

"Once, in a book discussion club. The second time was for myself. The general's ideas are still relevant."

When Maria cut across an adjoining yard, he glommed on to her arm. "Someone's coming out."

They crouched behind a power transformer watching a slim female in a black jumpsuit take a cardboard-wrapped rectangular object out of the Mercedes-Benz's back seat. She closed the car door with her hip and carried the bulky item into the house.

After the front door had shut, Hill whispered, "That woman does not resemble the woman in the photograph—Katherine Knight."

Flores gestured for him to accompany her.

What Alex saw between bent slats in the front window blinds compelled him to inhale sharply and choke on his own saliva.

Maria clamped her hand over his lips. "Don't you dare make a peep. Hurry! We haven't much time."

The twosome moved clockwise around the structure, trying the lower windows and the rear patio door. On the garage side of the beach house, a pane of glass lay beside an open window.

"Give me a leg up!" she ordered.

He created a stirrup with his fingers. "Wait. I've got an idea."

"Quick! What is it?"

"After you get inside, I'll press the ringer and say I'm selling magazines for school. That should distract her long enough so you can—"

"Kid, you're too smart for your own britches."

"Doesn't that mean I'm a conceited asshole?"

"Does it? Okay, do that thing again with your hands."

"Alley-oop!" He boosted her over the windowsill.

Maria peered down at him and tapped her wrist. "Push the doorbell in four minutes."

Alex stuck up his thumb and dashed out to the road, his heart hammering twice as fast as his brain could count.

Roy kept his eyes closed and his respiration in check. He listened to metal clanging against metal, the clicking of a ratchet wrench, and the occasional muttered obscenity. A flat, padded surface supported his spine. *She's building something.* Davis flexed both wrists to assess the strength of his bonds. *Did she have to use zip ties?* He compressed his fingers and pulled against the restraints. *If I can—*

The sting from the stiff-armed slap across his cheek was sudden, intense, and ended the sheriff's futile game of playing possum.

The woman Roy had seen swimming in the same pool he had nearly drowned in removed a pair of safety goggles. "How was your nap? Oh, my apologies." She twisted the sock out of his mouth and used the wet end to mop his perspiring brow. "I've been working on this for months. What's your initial impression?"

The trussed man's drugged mind switched from simple curiosity to abject horror as he comprehended the tall apparatus' ultimate purpose.

"Tongue-tied? That's understandable. *La Machine du Silence* is quite a work of art. During the glory days of the French Revolution, executioners used similar devices to liquidate thirty thousand lawful citizens."

Roy shook off the mental cobwebs. "I know about you. You're that crazy shrink, Rachel Martin."

"No need for name-calling, Leroy Davis." She waved his Arizona driver's license. "Oh yes, I know who you are too. Sheriff, you never should have left your Podunk town."

He raised his chin to the bindings' limit, and said as calmly as his trembling lips allowed, "I am going to kill you."

"In every action film, the hero screams that worn-out cliché. Sylvester Stallone and Bruce Willis hire talented screenwriters to type them out of any jam. Here, I am penning the script and directing the action."

"If I don't get to you, somebody else will."

Rachel rapped an upright wooden beam with her knuckle. "Sturdy. Last night, I finished *La Machine du Silence*. Didn't have a chance to stain the frame, nor did I thoroughly test the mechanism. Nevertheless, I believe she'll operate as designed. The history of the guillotine is fascinating. First, skilled carpenters built a scaffold at the designated execution site. With no room for a stage, we'll make do with this plastic tarp."

She deliberately circled the contraption. "You are lying on a *bascule*, the French word for balance or seesaw. Without time to build an authentic tilting bench, I took advantage of this adjustable weight bench. These braces support the guillotine's perpendicular frame. In the olden days, workers used small trees for the vertical posts. I purchased these ten-foot cedar 4x4s at The Home Depot. The nice man even used a table saw equipped with a special blade to cut these dadoes."

Martin ran a forefinger along the eight-foot-long grooves. "Smooth as a baby's bottom. I sanded these channels myself and used tallow for grease. The upper and lower crosspieces provide rigidity and separate the rails to the proper distance."

Roy asked what he understood might be his final question this side of heaven or hell. "Who murdered my sister?"

"Why would I know?"

"You work for the organization that kills people."

"Fine detective work! But I'm a client, not an employee. Well, used to be. I got sick and tired of all their preposterous restrictions." The psychiatrist stooped close enough for her warm breath to curl his eyebrows. "What's your sister's name?"

"Helen Davis. She attended Bisbee High School."

"Did Helen die expeditiously? Or was her death slow and. . .painful?"

"Someone bludgeoned her with a golf club during the spring of 1982."

"Such a coincidence! She died the year of my birth. The vacation database lists 'Golf Club' under 'Blunt Instruments.' I can't tell you which member received credit for murdering your sister."

"What database? Are you able to look up who did it?"

"No. The website administrator revoked my access. Anyway, only upper management has elevated network permissions." On her feet, Rachel grasped a cotton rope connected to a pulley. "Let's get back to it. Lastly, the most important components of our guillotine: the blade and the *mouton*."

Roy had to arch his throat and roll his eyes back to see a two-foot-wide sheet of metal.

Martin pulled on the cord. "I knew a blacksmith in Tijuana who performed odd jobs for the drug cartel." The alloy steel knife slowly ascended between the lubricated timbers. "Mr. Martinez forged this angled blade to slice cleanly through the thickness of an average neck. The sixty-six-pound iron *mouton* bolted to the top of the fifteen-pound cutting edge will—" She paused to secure her grip. "Later, you'll be glad Mr. Martinez made the thing so damn heavy."

At the highest reaches of the cathedral ceiling, the blade clacked over a rocker arm and locked in place. The doctor released the rope, stood back, and grinned in satisfaction. "Now, we can upgrade your seat." She rushed to Roy's feet and wheeled the weight bench frontward until the rear of his skull bumped over a curved board and his upturned throat aligned with the sharp tool. Rachel extracted a peg, and the upper half of a moon-shaped board slid down. Although the *lunette* immobilized the sheriff's neck, his view of his impending death had undeniably improved.

Martin adjusted the laundry basket beneath Davis' head. "If I yank that trigger, the *déclic*—whish-wham—it's all over in a millisecond. *Fini!*"

A bladder spasm darkened the front of his boxer shorts. "Maria!"

"Maria is Lorelei's real name? Would you like your girlfriend to have a front seat in the audience?" After Roy didn't articulate matching enthusiasm, Rachel crammed the sock in his mouth. She climbed the stairs to the master bedroom.

The muted conversation stopped and, moments later, footfalls echoed from the upper hallway. Maria took a boning knife out of the butcher block and crept to the living room. When she withdrew the hosiery from Roy's lips, his clenched eyelids flew open in bewilderment. "Hold still, honey. I'm cutting you free." She sawed at the cable tie holding his right hand.

The sheriff craned his neck toward the dining area. "My revolver is on the table. Thumb back the hammer, turn off the safety, and shoot her in the fucking—"

Above, a door slammed, a wall shuddered, and a female moaned in discomfort.

"The doctor has a gun," Davis mouthed. "Get mine." As Flores scurried into the other room, he realized she forgot to reinsert the sock.

Rachel strong-armed Olivia along the balcony. The Handler's mouth was gagged, her hands were fastened behind her back, and clothesline hobbled her ankles. Stewart's eyes popped out of their sockets when she saw who was strapped to a guillotine.

Alex had no way of seeing what dangers waited on the opposite side of the front door. He depressed the lighted doorbell button and put on his winningest smile.

Chapter Nineteen

Thursday—December 28, 2017

Rachel and Olivia were halfway down the stairway when the doorbell chimed.

Martin drew her .357, pulled back the slide, and hissed at Stewart, "Who is that?"

The silenced captive grunted, resisting the suicidal impulse to shoulder her captor down the stairs.

Rachel sat Olivia on a step. "Don't move." She slinked to the front door peephole. "It's a kid selling candy bars or some other useless crap." When the doctor retreated from the irritant, the bell rang thrice, followed by a round of loud knocking. She opened the door a crack, and growled, "Shoo. Go bother somebody else."

Alex pushed his face into the gap. "Good evening, ma'am! I'm an honors student at Mission Bay High. My biology class is selling magazines to fund our expedition to Costa Rica. Loggers are decimating the rainforests and—"

As Martin pulled the door wide enough to yell, "Get lost!" Hill seized her hair and walloped her forehead against the doorframe.

In the confines of that small room, several actions transpired concurrently or in instantaneous succession.

Maria cocked the sheriff's Smith & Wesson Bodyguard and thumbed off the safety. She aimed the gun sight at Rachel's back but, terrified of hitting Alex by mistake, did not squeeze the trigger.

Roy tore the cable tie Maria had sawed in half and waved for her with his right hand to remove the remaining. She ignored his plea, aiming the revolver at the enemy.

Martin ripped out a chunk of her own scalp disengaging herself from Hill's strong clutch. Sensing greater danger behind her, she pirouetted and raised her Desert Eagle, confounded to face down a duo of equally ferocious she-tigers.

Olivia, hopping down the staircase to oppose the rogue Patron, tripped over a long socket wrench. She landed in front of Rachel.

Alex exploded through the door, grappling for Rachel's gun.

Flores, with Hill again in the line of fire, faltered.

As Martin lowered her weapon to blow away Stewart's face, Hill jammed his thumb between the Desert Eagle's firing pin and hammer. Olivia headbutted Rachel in the lady parts.

Although the psychiatrist dropped her pistol, she wasn't done yet. Rachel hurled herself at the decapitating device and yanked the brass *déclic*. The lock fulcrum, yoked to the trigger by a rod, pivoted, and the *mouton* released. Maria shrieked as the guillotine's razor-sharp blade thundered downward.

Flores pummeled Martin's nose with the Bodyguard. She rammed the barrel underneath the doctor's bloody chin. *"La muerte es una perra!"*

"Don't shoot her! The neighbors will hear the shots and call the cops."

"Fuck the police," Maria said. "She's dead."

"You're right," Alex agreed. "Let's kill them both!"

"Maria! Alex! Stop!"

Flores whirled, astonished to behold the bloodless guillotine. The round laundry basket stood empty except for a dirty sock. Roy's head remained connected to his neck. The blade hovered a few inches above his throat.

Davis bucked his hips against the bindings. "Get me out of here!"

Maria clouted Rachel extra hard in the jaw and fetched the boning knife. She sliced the zip ties and hoisted the *lunette* high enough for Roy to withdraw his brow from beneath the filed edge. The overjoyed woman hugged the relieved man tight enough to inflict bruises. "Why didn't the guillotine work? Is the blade stuck?"

"After you freed my right arm, I snagged this ratchet wrench and held it—" He pointed to a greased slot in the post, then stroked his throat. "That woulda been a mighty close shave."

Maria cried, "Thank God!" and kicked Rachel in the ovaries.

Alex, on the ground beside Olivia, dragged her by the ponytail. Martin's Magnum looked huge in his quivering fingers.

Davis, seeing murder in the Hill's darting eyes, commanded, "Let her go!"

Alex hesitated, unsure which section of her cranium made the best point of entry. "She poisoned my grandpa!"

The sheriff went to the vengeful young man and laid a callused palm on his shoulder. "Son, I need her still breathing. Hand over the gun."

When Hill withheld the Desert Eagle, Davis squatted next to him on the blue tarpaulin. "If you fire that cannon, SWAT will be outside before the muzzle cools. The team commander shall gather they are mixed up in a hostage crisis and give the sharpshooter the green light to put a hollow-point in the center of your brainpan. After the coroner zips you into a body bag, and the mayor awards the sniper a medal, they'll all go out for Grand Slams at Denny's."

"I don't care. As your girlfriend says, 'Fuck the police.'"

"We'll be arrested. Is that what you want?"

"Then leave." The student waved an arrogant goodbye. "I'll shoot them both and turn myself in to the cops."

"Alex, I was so scared to die I pissed myself. My DNA is sprinkled all over this place."

"Not my problem."

Roy patted the tarp. "Concrete subfloor. The bullet might ricochet and strike someone outside. Are you up for a kid getting hurt?"

Hill loosened his handhold on Stewart's hair. "That's one chance in a—*I still don't care.*"

"It's a gamble you do not want to take." The sheriff's eyes glistened with contrition. "In Iraq, eradicating insurgents was our prime military objective. The men close enough to see their eyes? I knew I hit them. Most targets were distant. A movement in a window? A shadow behind a tree? I'll never be sure how many I killed, wounded, or missed entirely. Or that I didn't hurt innocent civilians. Children. I've got to live with what I've done. Inner demons can drive a man batty. It's the main reason I became an alcoholic. Alex, don't throw your life away."

"Why do you need her?"

"She may be able to track down whoever is responsible for my sister's death. Over the last few days, I've gotten to trust her. Olivia's not all bad. I have faith she can be rehabilitated."

Hill ungagged the person he despised, and asked her, "Tell the truth. Can you help him?"

"I'll try." Stewart bowed her head. "Sorry about your grandfather. It wasn't personal."

Alex pressed the tip of the Desert Eagle to her temple. "You poisoned him with saxitoxin!"

Roy held up his hands. "Her boss didn't leave her much of a choice. Olivia feels remorse for her actions. I believe her."

Hill exhaled and swung the barrel to Martin. "What should we do with this wacko? Give her to the police?"

Olivia verbalized her thoughts to Roy. "The doctor must vanish without a trace."

Maria bellowed, "Sheriff Davis, now!" and stomped off.

He followed her into the kitchen.

Flores switched on the overhead light. "Who is this woman? And what have you been up to?" She paced between the sink and stove. "I traveled all the way to San Diego to save your ass and find you shacked up in her little love nest."

Roy embraced Maria and kissed away her tears. "Olivia belongs to an organization culpable for—"

"Murdering innocent people. Alex explained everything on the drive. He claimed you ended our relationship to keep me from harm."

"Were we in a relationship? You said it was just a romp in the sack."

Maria pounded his chest with both fists. "Stop fooling around."

"Sorry, I'm new at this." He grasped her hands and pulled her close. "This is no joke." His voice cracked with emotion. "I love you."

Agog, she stepped back. "Love me? Since when?"

"From the moment I realized I spent more time thinking about you and me sharing a life than I did lusting for a carton of Lucky Strikes or a case of Bud. I only need *you*!"

Maria giggled and smooched him on the lips. "Roy, you are a born romantic, but before I move into Château Davis, we need to work on your decorating techniques."

By the time the harmonious couple returned to the front room, Rachel was gagged and secured to the makeshift *bascule*.

Roy applauded Alex and Olivia. "Good to see you two working in unison!"

The college student lowered the *lunette* to the exposed throat. "Aren't the doomed supposed to lie facedown so they can't see death coming?"

The sheriff took ahold of the cotton rope. "Dr. Demento didn't do me any favors."

Maria snatched the long cord from Roy. "Let me do it!" After the giant blade was secured at the upper crossbar, she addressed the group encompassing the guillotine. "Does anybody want to say anything?"

"Ask the condemned," Olivia advised.

"Terrific idea." Flores uncorked Martin's mouth. "Have you any final words? I recommend you ask your God for forgiveness."

As Rachel inhaled to utter her final insult, Maria jerked the brass *déclic*. Eighty-one pounds of gleaming metal slid down the machine's slick grooves severing the psychologist's head with the ka-chunk of a butcher hacking through a pig's hind leg.

Alex, getting an eyeful of the blood splattering the guillotine, furniture, and their legs, bent over and vomited bear claw and Cherry Coke onto the groundsheet. Maria, about to scrub her red palms on her white pants, wiped them on Rachel's black jumpsuit instead.

Olivia withdrew the sock from the plastic wash basket. "What happened to her—?"

Roy hunkered down and pointed. "There! Under the coffee table!"

Hill's face squinched in revulsion. "Can the beheaded speak? My history teacher said King Charles of England bawled out the names of all nine of his children."

Stewart guffawed. "She's not a chicken." The Handler gripped her Patron's head by the hair and slapped the waxen face. Rachel's cheeks blushed—the downturned lips opening and snapping shut. "Just an involuntary muscular reflex. Neurons giving one last hurrah before," she tossed the dripping head in the laundry basket, "her soul drops down the garbage chute to hell."

Alex stabbed a fingertip at Olivia. "Where do you reckon your soul is going?"

"Same place as yours, bud—*Gehenna.* You helped me strap her to the guillotine."

Davis restrained Hill. "Compose yourself. We're all edgy."

Flores sped to the bathroom, reappearing with an armful of towels to sop up the fluids. "What should we do now? How do we get rid of the body?"

Olivia unlocked her Blackberry. "I'll bring in a cleanup crew ASAP." She saw two messages from the Curator. The previous day's text seemed hazily familiar: *Why are you with the sheriff?*

Alex stuck his thumb in his ear and pressed his little finger to his mouth. "Wow, you can call somebody? Like the Wolf in *Pulp Fiction*?"

"Harvey Keitel?" Olivia reread the vexing words. *How could Morrigan know the man with me at Rachel's house was a sheriff?* The second communication from an hour ago generated even greater concern. She transferred the phone to Roy.

The sheriff knit his brows. "What's 'ZZZ and verify'?"

"My supervisor wants me to neutralize you, then send a photo of your dead body for proof."

"And?"

"If I decline, there's no going back. They'll scour the four corners of the earth. When my boss lays her hands on me, she'll cremate me—*while I'm still alive.*"

Maria elevated the Bodyguard. "Then, we're in a real pickle, aren't we?" She scowled at the guillotine. "I vote to fire up this sucker one final time. Afterward, we burn this house to the ground."

Roy felt his headache making a comeback. "No, that's not happening."

Alex's palm shot up. "You're outvoted, Sheriff. We can't trust her for a second. I already lost my grandfather."

"With my vote, it's a tie." Olivia looked at the ceiling. "My laptop is upstairs. Before you lop off my head, let me find out who killed his sister."

Hill ran up the stairs. He returned and set the computer on the dining table. "I'll be watching your every keystroke."

Stewart signed in to the 57 portal and typed "Helen Davis" in the advanced search box. The record displayed her name followed by an asterisk.

Roy rapped the screen. "What's the star for? And why are the fields blank?"

"Your sister's murder occurred prior to the age of the internet," Olivia said. "Reams of older documents weren't digitized. The 'P' in the footnote stands for paper."

"Where are Helen's paper files located?"

"All of my clients are recent enrollees. I've never used the archives."

"She's covering for someone!" Alex reached out. "Pass me the laptop!"

Stewart pushed the computer across the tabletop. "Have at it, champ. Even I don't get to see everything."

This new wrinkle tested Roy's patience. "Who would?"

"My manager, the Curator. She goes by Morrigan."

"Mulligan?" Maria scoffed. "That's catchy."

"No M-o-r-r-i-g-a-n. Morrigan means the 'Queen of Demons.' My boss is nobody to play mumblety-peg with. If she knew you three were in my house, we'd be ashes blowing in the wind."

Flores crossed her arms. "You sickos are so twisted. Who started your dumb organization?"

"According to lore, eight Terry's Texas Rangers."

A vein bulged in Hill's forehead. "Those rednecks fought for the Confederacy."

"Yes. The majority of Rangers took up the cause after Texas seceded from the Union. Following the Civil War, during Reconstruction, the federal government disbanded the Texas Rangers for three years. These rebellious, rootless men had no families or jobs to return to. Soldiers from the North and the South missed the action. Those who yearned for further bloodshed had no safe way to express their dark desires. Here is when the Circle of Eight comes into the picture."

"Is that the name of your secret gang?" Davis inquired. "The Circle of Eight?"

"There is no official title. Internally, we call it 57. Over the decades, men and women of all levels of government and society have joined. When the Curator recruited me, she alleged a United States president and a Supreme Court justice were former members."

Alex lifted his fingers off the keyboard. "Tricky Dick?"

"Morrigan didn't elaborate. The founder of the Circle of Eight, a seasoned battlefield medic, treated infantrymen for both physical and spiritual injuries. In the late 1800s, the military termed what is now known to be posttraumatic stress disorder as 'soldier's heart.' Dr. Hart Henderson kept extensive medical journals. He observed many men revealing signs of acute mania after witnessing the inhumanity of war. Others, the 'less excitable,' craved more blood and guts. These abnormal individuals, coined by the medical world as the 'unscrupulous,' violated humankind's ethical or legal expectations without batting an eye."

Hill jabbed a forefinger at Stewart. "Psychos. You should know as you're a perfect example."

"Because I feel extreme guilt for poisoning your grandfather and wish to atone for my transgressions, I don't categorize myself as a true psychopath. William Hill is the only blameless life I took. That being said, I appreciate why you see me as villainous and morally flawed."

"Is this your interpretation of an apology?"

"No, Alex. I haven't begun to make reparations. When I do, you'll be first on my list."

He clucked his tongue and resumed striking keys.

Maria thumped her chest. "The doctor deduced that wickedness lurks in the hearts of men. Big whoop! Abel arrived at that identical conclusion right before Cain caved in his head with a stone."

Olivia nodded. "Psychopathy isn't a new concept in this day and age. At the turn of the last century, the notion of behavioral genetics was groundbreaking. Whereas many adolescents and adults turned to crime, violence, or sexual assault as a by-product of their upbringing and environment, a small percentage of the population exhibited all these traits at birth. Dr. Henderson shared his findings with like-minded scientists. Seven experts agreed with him that for modern civilizations to thrive, those suffering from this chronic mental disorder were a necessary evil. The Circle of Eight formed a charter to safeguard both the sheep and the wolves. Henderson maintained that offering one or two of the weakest lambs each year to an alpha wolf protected the whole flock."

"What the Sweet Jesus are you talking about?" Maria screamed. "This isn't some Old Testament blood sacrament. These are human beings under the knife, not sheep!"

Roy stretched for Maria's hand. "Numerous studies indicate one percent of the U.S. population scores high on the Hare Psychopathy Checklist. These people are out there and need to be contained and controlled. If those with antisocial personality disorders were permitted to run rampant, don't you think bodies would be stacking up in the streets like cordwood? 57

has substantial cons, but its pros, however controversial, make a certain amount of sense. Moreover, the members must adhere to strict guidelines or face drastic consequences." He swung his arm at the headless torso in the living room. "Case in point."

Maria faced down Roy. "And you're okay with your sister being one of these sacrificial lambs?"

He looked down and bit his lip.

She glowered at Stewart. "And what's your daytime job, besides snuffing out old men?"

"As a 'Handler,' I select new prospects. Once 57 recruits a 'Patron,' I ensure his or her weeklong vacations are enjoyable and risk-free. I direct the two-person backup teams. These 'Sentinels' jump in to assist if required. They also certify the outcomes."

"What outcomes?"

Olivia sliced a palm across her throat. "A Pawn is dead."

Davis went to the kitchen, rejoining them with glasses of milk and a box of frosted strawberry Pop-Tarts. "How do you single out likely customers?"

Hill chipped in. "Do you hang around insane asylums?"

Stewart smirked. "Not since the 1980s. Now, we use the latest technology to track almost every transaction on the internet. Public news aggregations and social network services are a big help. And of course, the forums on the dark web." Olivia, visualizing Tom Hayden presenting her with the bouquet of gorgeous wildflowers, smiled faintly. "Lately, advanced facial expression emotion analysis software has been the most productive means of finding candidates."

The mention of a computer program caught Alex's attention. "You hack into webcams and spy on people?"

"Laptops, tablets, and phones work the best. . .ATMs too, yet we've had promising results finding future members using baby monitors."

Maria sneered. "Then what? You buy them a cup of coffee and declare you're enrolling psychopaths in your murder club? 'Sir, for the month of January, we have specials on stabbings in the South and knifings in the North. Are you interested in signing up?'"

"Essentially, yes." Olivia stifled a yawn. "Sometimes, a little encouragement goes a long way to close the deal. We cannot let anyone tattle to the police or the press. Everybody we meet with has to join or. . .I knew I had no options."

Alex twiddled his fingers as the SQL search query took forever to complete. "You say these maniacs are clients. Do they pay dues?"

"Nothing worth doing is without a cost. An 'Accountant' handles the finances. It's not cheap."

"What if the people you have diagnosed as psychotic can't pay the membership fee?"

"There is a special fund to help those whom we deem valuable to society. The less desirable are," Olivia broke off a piece of toaster pastry, "painlessly relieved from their suffering."

"What's with all the bizarre methods of killing?" Roy questioned. "In 2015, Park Jin-ho flew to Russia to poison a widow with strychnine. The same year, he tortured a woman in Mexico City with a car battery. In 2016, he did some sick shit with a framing nailer in Egypt. Park traveled to India to drown an old yoga instructor in the Ganges. Then, that pond scum came to my town to run over bicyclists. What gives?"

"New and challenging adventures keep life stimulating for those with a never-ending taste for carnage." Stewart tapped her eyebrow. "I've seen—"

"Found it!" Hill shouted. "The archived documents are in Washington, D.C." He rotated the laptop screen to unveil an image of a block-long Romanesque revival building topped with a tall clock tower. "The files are locked in a basement vault."

Roy swiveled to Olivia. "Are armed men guarding the door or just an old spinster requesting to see your library card? Will the person in charge let us in?"

The Handler shrugged. "It depends on the thoughts going through Morrigan's head. I haven't replied to her messages. By now, she might conclude I *am* trouble and not *in* trouble."

Alex stood, and said with fervor, "We must get in and out of the vault before your boss raises the alarm. Off your asses! What are we waiting for?"

The sheriff walked to the living room. "For starters, we have to clean up this ungodly mess. Olivia, do you stock bleach and trash bags?"

"A half-bottle of Clorox is in the laundry room. Not enough to do the job right. I do have a big box of Glad bags from Costco."

"Torch it."

Roy spun. "What did you say, Maria?"

"As I suggested, this house needs to burn, but not till your friend responds to her boss' text messages. Something short and sweet, such as, 'The sheriff forced me to bring him to Rachel Martin. Leroy Davis is ZZZ.'"

"If Morrigan wants a photo of me dead," Roy rubbed his hands, "let's give her one!"

Olivia came forward. "How?"

"Hand me that knife." Roy wedged the boning knife in a guillotine joint and bent the thin blade back and forth until the handle snapped off at the bolster. He kneeled beside Rachel. "We've got gallons of blood. All we need is a bucket."

The photograph Stewart shot on her Blackberry came out better than everyone hoped for. Davis, a knife handle protruding from a slit in his shirt, lay in a pool of Martin's coagulating blood. Olivia sent her manager the fake picture along with Maria's succinct justification for being with the sheriff.

After they showered and put on fresh clothes, Alex hauled gas cans in from the garage. Roy unbolted the cutting blade and *mouton* from the guillotine. Maria did her darnedest to reattach Rachel's head to her neck. Olivia put Kasha in a cat carrier and packed a bag.

Hill questioned Davis as they splashed racing fuel throughout the lower level, "How long before the cops make an ID?"

"Burned body? Without dental records, it'll be tough. Hopefully, the detectives won't tie this arson to the blown-up house in La Jolla."

Olivia held out a set of keys and a pink slip of paper to Alex.

His eyelids crinkled in suspicion. "What's this?"

She jingled the keys. "The Mustang is yours now. I'm pleased someone shall get the opportunity to let her run wild, and that you'll be the driver behind the wheel."

Alex threw up his hands. "I can't take this. My parents will flip out if they see me pull up in a ride this expensive. They'll ask me things I cannot answer."

"Park Scarlett in a storage unit until you land your Silicon Valley dream job. Squirt engine oil in the cylinders and keep the fuel tank topped off to prevent corrosion."

"Who's Scarlett?"

"I named the car after my mother."

Roy looked startled. "You told me you never knew your mom."

Olivia's eyes became misty. "That was no lie."

Hill grudgingly accepted the key fob and certificate of title. "Do you think giving me this car makes up for what you did? Nothing ever can."

"I'm not pretending it does." Stewart disconnected the power cord from the stove to disable the spark igniters. She cranked the gas knobs to "HIGH" and lit a tall candle.

Alex circumvented the main roads driving north in his new Mustang. Maria tagged along in the rented Jeep. They dumped the guillotine parts in a brackish water lagoon. The fugitives watched the sun rise over the Pacific Ocean from a motel window near the Santa Monica Pier.

Roy steered Rachel's SUV southward. Olivia trailed close behind in her sedan. Near the Mexican border crossing, they ditched the unlocked Mercedes-Benz and Honda leaving the keys on the dashboards. After a trolley ride north, the sheriff returned his rental car at the San Diego International Airport and hired a private pilot to fly them to the capital of the United States.

Chapter Twenty

Friday—December 29, 2017

IN A SECLUDED CORNER of the international hotel's lofty atrium, Roy held the maintenance door for Olivia. They descended four flights of stairs. After the roar of the Gulfstream's jet engines and the hubbub of Ronald Reagan Washington National Airport, the dank bowels of the old building's lowest basement seemed deadly quiet.

The "vault" housing the 57 archives turned out to be a forgotten storage room at the dim end of a lengthy tunnel. No trigger-happy sentries or bespectacled librarians guarded the entrance—merely a steel door to repel the inquisitive.

Stewart dispensed latex gloves, and elbowed past Davis. "Make room for a professional." She inserted a needle tip in a battery-operated lock pick. Olivia pressed the electric gun to the brass cylinder and clinched the trigger. The key pins jiggled the driver pins allowing her to retract the bolt and open the rusty door.

Inside the square storeroom, caged lightbulbs hanging from the low ceiling emitted circles of brilliance onto a long table surrounded by reading chairs. A dozen aged oak file cabinets lined the left wall, followed by twice that number of taller metal repositories across the rear. Cardboard file boxes hid the right wall. A dusty '70s-era Xerox machine and a pre-millennium flatbed scanner flanked the doorway.

The sheriff, aware he had entered a charnel house built for the interment of paper souls, dropped his voice in reverence. "How many homicides are we looking at?"

"In addition to the entries in the online database?" The 57 Handler rubbed her thumb repeatedly over the tips of her index and middle fingers—the money sign. "Enough to keep every undertaker on the planet filthy rich until the Last Judgment."

"And detectives drowning in cold cases. Help me find my sister."

Olivia went straight to a cardboard carton stamped "PAWNS – May-June 1982." She lay the thin manila folder labeled "Helen C. Davis" in front of Roy. "Should I leave you alone? I can wait outside."

The sheriff tugged out a seat and sat down with a heavy heart. "Thanks." Ten minutes later, after reading his sister's brief profile and a summary of the Sheriff's Office's investigation, Davis let Stewart back inside the vault. He passed her a document. "Who is Nancy White, and where is her contact information?"

Olivia leafed through the pages. "In those days, hyperlinks did not exist. As a 57 member, her file will be stored in a separate carton." When the container marked "PATRONS – W-Z" proved unfruitful, the Handler had a thought. She placed a box entitled "HANDLERS/CURATORS – S-Z" on the tabletop.

Roy read Nancy White's human resources file aloud. "Born June fourteenth, 1953, in Pittsburgh, Pennsylvania. At sixteen, her mother died in a car collision. The father, a steelworker, remarried. It says an overhead crane crushed him in a work-related mishap. No siblings listed. She earned a bachelor's of science degree in chemical engineering at the University of Tennessee. Worked in the power industry until she received an offer from the Environmental Protection Agency. White married a hotshot Virginian lawyer named Richard Campbell when she turned thirty-six." He flipped the page. "As a site assessment manager, the EPA sent her cross-country to proposed Superfund sites. Chemtronics in North Carolina. In upper New York, she worked at the Love Canal and Griffiss Air Force Base. A couple of mines in New Mexico and...."

Stewart saw that Davis' mouth had quit moving. "What?"

"This other site is in northeastern Arizona."

"Where?"

"In 1982, Nancy White, now Nancy Campbell, spent three months in the Navajo Nation studying wastewater discharges from closed mines."

"Bisbee was a mining town."

Roy turned the page. "A year later, your organization hired her for a Handler position at a salary of one hundred thirty-five thousand, plus benefits. About the same time, Virginia state legislators elected Richard as an appellate judge and the EPA promoted Nancy to director level."

Olivia remarked, "They're climbing right up the social and economic ladders."

"How much are they paying you?"

"I'll show you mine if you show me yours."

"A hundred K. Plus the car." He uplifted his eyebrows. "Double that?"

She chuckled. "Five times, plus bonuses. My manager is in the seven figures."

"Guess I'm in the wrong line of work."

"At least you sleep well at night."

"Oh, you're a laugh riot." Davis read on. "1992 was a big year. The United States Senate confirmed Richard Campbell as a representative of the Washington, D.C., Superior Court. Nancy Campbell became the EPA's Deputy Chief of Staff, and 57 promoted her to Curator. Then. . .aw shit. . .the last page is blank."

"Simmer down. Now, we've learned her name, the husband's name, and where they worked. Won't be too hard to figure out the rest." Stewart checked her Blackberry. "No signal below ground level."

Roy took photos of Helen's and Nancy's files. He returned the boxes and pushed the chairs under the table. "Ready?"

"More than." Outside the hotel, Olivia used her phone to seek out Nancy Campbell. "She's currently the EPA Chief of Operations. A general telephone number is listed, a mail code, and this biography." Stewart held the thumbnail photograph up for Davis' review. *Is she the foster mother I had in Akron, Ohio?* Her jaw tensed. *No that's. . . .* "Fuck me!"

Roy grabbed the Blackberry and enlarged the image on the screen. The sixtyish woman with high cheekbones could pass for the lead actress in the movie *Fatal Attraction*. "Who is this? Do you know her?"

"That's Morrigan, the Curator."

"Your boss murdered my sister?"

Olivia sighed. "Should have known all along. That's the logic for Morrigan wanting you dead."

"I've been hunting Helen's killer for thirty years. Why didn't she do away with me earlier?"

"57's rules must never be broken. Minors are verboten, as well as members of the same family. Seeing that you're so close to solving the mystery, the Curator is sticking her neck out."

"And now *her* head is on the chopping block. Look up the husband."

Stewart showed Davis a portrait of a stern, silver-haired, politician type. "Holy cow! Richard Campbell is the Attorney General to the District of Columbia."

"Where do they live?"

"The government web pages list official office addresses. We'll follow them home from work." His outstretched palm caused her to back away.

"Olivia, it's time for you and me to go our separate ways."

"I want to see you through this!"

"No. Create a new life far, far from here. Someplace nice where you can reinvent yourself."

"Roy!"

"Confronting Morrigan is my cross to bear. I'll be fine. What will you do?"

Olivia's cheeks turned a pretty shade of red. "There is someone I've developed feelings for."

Roy smiled. "Who?"

"A Patron I manage. Maybe I can sweet-talk him into running off with me to some tropical paradise."

"The guy would be cuckoo not to. I pray you find happiness in this fucked-up world."

Olivia drew him near and kissed his cheek. "Sheriff, you're a good man. Whatever you're planning, don't let it destroy you."

Davis watched Stewart run across Twelfth Street and melt into the crowds streaming into the Federal Triangle Metro Station. He doubted he'd ever lay eyes on her again.

Roy touched base with Alex. "How're things? Great. Be sure to stay indoors. You found four jars of gold coins in the Mustang's trunk? Yes, Olivia left those for you. They'll pay for your college and a down payment on a house. Yeah, I'm fine. Busy. Hang in there. Soon, this shall be over, and we'll all go home. I'd like to speak to Maria too, but first, please wield your magic wand one last time and get me a street address."

Northwest of Washington, D.C., in the upscale community of Wesley Heights, Roy leaned on an outdoor balcony overlooking a blue pool, a green guesthouse, and the gray, defoliated trees of

Battery Kemble Park. Six miles away, red aircraft lights blinked atop the Washington Monument.

Davis had explored the twenty-million-dollar mansion, finding the item he searched for in the downstairs fitness room. A clock chimed eleven times. He went indoors to the darkened trophy room. The taxidermized heads of elk, moose, buffalo, wildebeest, bear, and a menagerie of other mounted wild game covered the oiled wood paneling. An entire stuffed black rhino dominated the rectangular space.

A yellow golf club bag rested against an ebony Steinway grand piano. The sheriff placed the Walther P22 on the enameled piano lid (he had traded guns with Olivia), and slid the 5-iron out of the leather bag. Roy stroked the steel head, wondering if the Curator had used this same club to kill Helen. He overlapped his gloved fingers around the rubber grip. Although the adult had never completed a full round of golf, the inner child recollected how to hold the club from Saturdays playing putt-putt with his sister at Pirate's Cove in Sierra Vista. He spread his boots on the handmade Persian carpet. The iron sliced air on the downswing nearly hitting the hanging crystal chandelier on the follow-through.

Roy sat in a wing chair angled toward the front bay window. He laid the golf club on the windowsill and screwed the noise suppressor onto the pistol. As Davis watched for the homeowners to pull in the driveway, he counted the years it had taken for him to reach the conclusion of his lonely crusade, a seven-thousand-square-foot house at the end of a long and winding lane. Glass-eyed animals listened as Roy spoke to his dead and buried sister. "Helen, I feel bad for suspecting Luke Bell. God knows your life ended horribly, but what of the toll your murder has taken on us, the living? How different my life might have been if on that day you had just—"

Out on Chain Bridge Road, a black sedan signaled to turn. The driver steered the Bentley into the circular driveway. Below the floorboards, machinery groaned as one of the four garage doors raised and lowered. Davis chambered a round, lifted the 5-iron, and stood by the piano. Much as the vigilante hoped Nancy Campbell would resolve his questions before he meted out his long-awaited punishment, hard-earned experience had taught the sheriff to be flexible.

A door whammed shut, high heels clacked along a corridor, and, after a click, cold light radiated into the adjacent rooms.

"Are you with me, Helen?" Roy whispered. "Give me the strength to make it through another day." He distinctly heard his sister reply, "I am always with you." Davis walked under the arch into the bright kitchen. He aimed the gun. "Drop the bag."

Unfazed, Nancy set the sequined evening clutch on the quartzite countertop and faced him. The woman wore a black cocktail dress as if she had come from a party. "Sheriff Davis, you're either one or the other: a phantom of my imagination or a barefaced lie from the traitor who works for me. Which is it?"

"Neither. Olivia is dead. She attacked me. I shot her."

The Celtic goddess of fate, war, and death cast aside his obvious falsehood. "May I likewise assume Dr. Martin will no longer be practicing child psychiatry?"

Roy confiscated Nancy's Blackberry and used the Walther to distance her from the knife block. "Where is your husband?"

"Rick is at the office working late or out picking up bimbos at Duffy's. Our marriage is open. He could be anywhere and arrive home at any hour."

"Of all people, why did you choose my sister? Answer honestly and perhaps we can come to a truce."

"You want to bury the hatchet? Or as the Lamb of God preached, 'And forgive us our debts, as we also have forgiven our debtors'?"

Roy eyeballed the Grey Goose, Seagram's, and Bacardi stocked in a glass cabinet behind the Curator. He wanted to take a swig from each bottle.

"Care for a libation, Sheriff? We stock our bar with top-shelf liquor, not that rotgut you're used to guzzling."

Sweat formed on Davis' brow and in his armpits. "Why were you in Bisbee in 1982?"

"My director sent me to Arizona to record the ecological conditions of uranium, radium, and vanadium ore mines. The owners used caustic chemicals to leach the ore from the waste rock. The cyanide and sulfuric acid polluted the groundwater."

"For the Environmental Protection Agency?"

"Correct. We instituted the initial Superfund sites to subsidize the cleanup of hazardous material. Present-day, this country has over thirteen hundred. We've done a lot of good work. How did you determine I am employed by the EPA?"

"I found the paper files."

Nancy's thumb dimpled her chin. "I thought they shredded the archives years ago."

The sheriff clasped the 5-iron tight enough to turn his knuckles white. "Tell me how my sister wound up afloat in a drainage ditch."

"After a week collecting water samples in the hot sun, I needed to unwind. There's a golf course near the Mexican border. I cannot name the town or the course, but I do recall the proprietors bragging they built one of the longest holes in the world."

"The Rattler at Turquoise Valley?"

Nancy smiled at the memory. "Yes, the fairway resembles a long snake, the two bunkers being the eyes."

"This was on the twelfth of May?"

"If you say so. I might have left that page blank in my diary."

"And then?"

"Roy, I could tell you what your frayed heartstrings long to hear. Swear on a stack of Bibles that I accidentally ran over Helen on the way back to the hotel. Claim that after the school bus let her off in downtown Bisbee, as she climbed the steep hill to your house, a dog darted in front of my vehicle. Those alleys are barely wide enough to shoehorn a golf cart through. And the roads lacking guardrails? Puh! I swerved to avoid sending somebody's pet to the doggy heaven and. . .oops. . .I hit your beloved sister instead. Unhinged with guilt and the fear of losing my job, I acted irrationally and irresponsibly. I hid her body in the first place I came to—a trench. Yet, that's not fair to you, is it? You hunger to devour every gory detail, and I am willing to throw you a meaty bone."

"How did you trick Helen into getting inside your car?"

"Simple. Teenagers believe everything they hear. 'Hi, I'm Mrs. Jones from up the street. Your brother broke his leg riding his skateboard. Your mother asked me to bring you to the emergency room.' The little lamb climbed right in beside me."

"You knew who I was?"

Nancy shook her head. "Eighty percent of Americans have at least one sibling. If Helen said she was brotherless, I'd drive until I came across someone else."

"Where did you kill her?"

"Not far from the ditch. A ghost town by an open-pit mine."

"You took Helen to Lowell?"

"I parked at an abandoned gas station on Erie Street. The old-time pumps advertised a price of only twenty-two cents a gallon. Those were the carefree days of sinful excess, weren't they?"

Roy hefted the 5-iron. "Is this the club you used?"

As the Curator's ruby red lips parted to reply, the kitchen floor vibrated.

The sheriff pushed Nancy into a corner and cautioned her to be silent. He pointed the pistol down the hall.

"Don't hurt him," she pleaded. "Rick knows nothing of my side job."

When the door to the garage never opened, he clenched her shoulder. "Where's your husband? What's taking him so long to come upstairs?"

Nancy grinned as a stiff object nudged the middle of Roy's spine. He hypothesized from its width that an elephant gun was the bearer's weapon of choice.

The Curator confiscated his P22 and released the magazine. "Sheriff, you disabled the security cameras and the primary alarm, however, you missed our secondary systems. Let me introduce you to Richard Campbell. My husband is the head of the organization you find so intriguing." She stripped the bullets from the clip and slid the slide to eject the final round from the chamber. "On the night I clubbed your sister to death—a completely random act—Rick appeared out of nowhere. He helped me load Helen into the trunk and dump her in the gutter. On the ride home, Rick filled me in about 57—the whole ball of wax. My better half sought me out for my predilection for violence. Dear, please hold Sheriff Davis steady while I change into something more practical."

Although Mr. Campbell had not one word to say, his respiration increased. Warm garlic-breath puffed against Davis' throat.

The woman unzipped the designer dress and let it fall to the floor. In bra and panties, she slipped into a disposable plastic apron and tied the drawstrings behind her back. Nancy snatched the iron from Roy's hand and waved the grooved head in his face. "Sheriff, is golf your sport?"

"Is miniature golf considered to be a sport?"

"Fun for the entire family!" The Curator planted her feet, clutched the shaft, and wriggled her hips as though to make a decisive putt. "Remember the pride you felt scoring a hole in one through the clown's open mouth?"

Roy watched Nancy's stance widen as she prepared to execute a power swing. "I wasn't any good."

"Me neither. I had to practice like mad to keep my golf balls out of the rough or from sinking to the bottom of a pond."

"Morrigan, you should be institutionalized in a maximum security prison for all of your remaining days."

"You know my sobriquet? That validates Ms. Stewart is still walking among us." She twirled the golf club in a cheerleading routine. "You viewed the body diagrams in the autopsy report and the crime scene photos? Those graphic images must be burned into your psyche. Helen refused to stay down or shut up. I had to hit her eighteen times to—"

Nancy's lips clamped closed as a fourteen-inch antler plunged in the nape of her husband's neck and poked out above the Windsor knot in his paisley necktie. Rick, a deer skull sticking from the back of his head, dropped facedown onto the slate tiles. Roy scrambled underneath the kitchen table to retrieve the big bore rifle. Nancy dove for the unloaded Walther on the counter. The Curator jammed a .22 Long cartridge into the handgun's breech, but when she tried to shoot the sheriff in his hind end or the newcomer between his piercing blue eyes, the trigger locked.

Olivia entered the doorway. "Morrigan, as a safety feature, my gun won't fire without a magazine inserted." She held the 5-iron and a glass vial. "Your decision, boss lady. Either I bash your brains in with this golf club, or you drink from this bottle. If you want my advice? I'd take the poison. Saxitoxin is relatively painless. You'll leave behind a nicer-looking cadaver and less of a mess for us to mop up."

Davis frowned at Stewart. "The destiny of this murderer is not for you to decide. Hand me the club."

Olivia beamed at the man who had just skewered the District of Columbia's Attorney General with a deer horn. "Roy, this is my boyfriend, Thomas Hayden. He works on Wall Street. Tom, Roy Davis is the sheriff of Cochise County."

Davis extended his palm. "Thanks for saving my bacon."

Tom grabbed Roy's hand. "My pleasure. Olivia was worried about you, so I drove down from New York. Alex directed us to this address." The stock trader gazed at the red blood thickening on the black slate and tickled his five o'clock shadow. "And ta-da, here we are."

Olivia said to Roy, "It's getting late, and we have a plane to catch. Give Tom the gun. Return to California and be with Maria."

Davis aimed the large-caliber weapon at the person next in line to run 57. "It's time to finish this. I can't let my sister down."

"Roy, as your friend, and for Helen and Maria's sakes, I am asking you not to bloody your hands." Stewart smiled conspiratorially at Hayden. "Us psychopaths differ from you vanilla folks. Not superior, not inferior. Just unique. We'll handle this situation with aplomb and integrity. . .and not give it an afterthought." She pocketed the vial of saxitoxin and tightened her grasp on the 5-iron.

Roy turned away from Nancy Campbell and surrendered the burdensome firearm to Tom. He pressed his lucky talisman into Olivia's fingers (she later hung the bullet on a necklace).

As the grandfather clock in the trophy room knelled midnight, Sheriff Leroy Davis stepped out of the big house on the end of Chain Bridge Road. At dawn, with a warm sun at his back, the man headed due west, not quitting until he found the woman he loved. Roy never learned the fate of the evildoer who killed Helen, and many happy years passed before he lifted another gun.

Under new management, the clandestine organization known to some as "57" continues to grow at a frightening rate.

No one is doing anything to stop it.

Lightning Source UK Ltd.
Milton Keynes UK
UKHW011951230622
404893UK00008B/136/J